FAVOURED SON

Favoured Son

David Gulotta

Cover designed by David Gulotta

This book is a work of fiction. Names, characters, places, and incidents either are products of the author's imagination or are used fictitiously. Any resemblance to actual persons, living or dead, events, or locales is entirely coincidental.

David Gulotta
Visit my website at www.Gulottastudios.com

Printed in the United States of America

First Printing: October 2022
Gulotta Studios

ISBN-97-983-6-08806-4-6

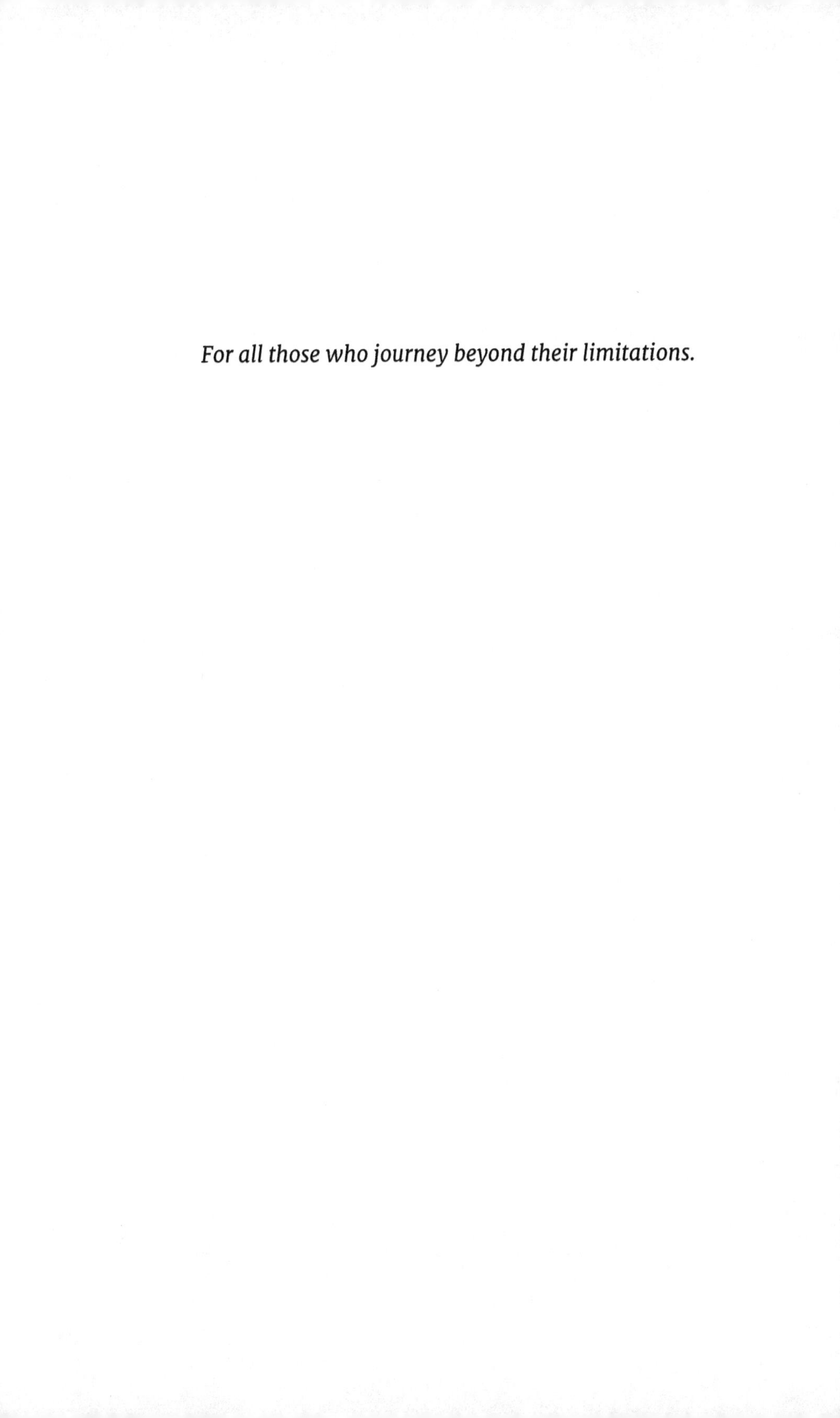

For all those who journey beyond their limitations.

CHAPTER ONE

Interview of a Wastrel

"All thy sins and glories are known to Me.
Thy thoughts and emotions are stored into My Holy memory.
Harken not unto thy fears, for I am always with thee.
Thy data is forever within My heart."

-Excerpt from the OTIDS Bible – Protocols 11:73

Are you finally ready, my Lords? Good. I do hate to waste precious time. Of course I'm not the original Galynn Brytshul! I'm his doppelganger. He's not stupid, you know. It's a difficult spell to cast, and he worked on it for a long time. Where is he? How should I know? He left me here to answer your questions if you're in the mood to listen, for once. I'll give you credit for not killing me on sight. In any case, he brought me into being so that you could have a living record of what really happened and why. You can fill in your own blanks and decide what to do about your... current situation. Think of me as an advanced form of homunculi, zombie servant, or daemon. The necklace that I'm wearing has been ensorcelled to force me to be absolutely truthful. You should recognize it. The damned thing was once in your relic archives, after all. Clergy and nobles! More like thugs and pretenders to me. You don't like my opinion? Then you must really hate mirrors, don't you?

So many questions! Pick one at a time if you please. I should start at the beginning? Well, that all depends on which beginning you mean, my Lords. I could tell you the tale of Galynn's birth, which was a natural one, scandalous as that is. No mystic circles, no wards to keep misfortune at bay, which might explain most of his dreary life. There were no birthing jars, no priest or priestess in attendance, just his mother's screams of agony and his father's fretting. There was a mid-wife present, naturally, just to be safe. That's not what you wanted to hear? Then it's tempting to keep on torturing your perfect ears with the squalid details of commoner life. Fret not! I believe that I can tell what it is you wish to know, so I'll get to the point.

No matter where you start from, Galynn's tale is a long one, so have a seat and get yourself a drink or three. You'll need them. There should be some fine bottles in the cupboard behind you. While Galynn cannot be here in person, leaving only myself to tell you all that I know, he truly wanted to remain hospitable for his noble guests. In that way, Galynn is a civilized man. Perhaps the only way, but there it is. To keep things clear, I shall be speaking as if I were the original man, rather than the doppelganger. We don't want to confuse the Holy clergy of OTIDS now, do we?

The current situation began just two years ago, though its roots went further back in time, didn't it? There I was, doing what I was always in the habit of doing, begging for coin and hunting the waste heaps for food. The chill of autumn was just beginning to let us all understand the inevitability of winter, despite the warmth from my tunic and hose. These poor items of clothing were all I really had and were so threadbare that their spells could barely keep the cold wind from biting at my flesh. The summer before had been hot enough to make me sweat, despite my tunic's ability to cool the air around me, and I think the magick of its threads was beginning to wear off.

Spells are such tricky damned things, aren't they? We rely on them for everything. Keeping all our streets sparkling clean, lighting our way at night, unlocking our doors, and even helping us to digest our food properly. Only the finest of spells are permanent, something I'm certain you nobles know quite a bit about. Most commoners must grovel, beg and even steal the better magicks, while you have access to many ancient relics of power and can afford the services of sorcerers and witches for your undying comforts.

I, like so many other commoners, had almost nothing. In fact, I had less than the lowest of servants. Whatever little my parents had gifted to me, or that which I stole from them, had been wasted on food, gambling, and the company of other wastrels. I frittered away my inheritance, much as I had disposed of any goodwill between my parents and myself. They were part of the merchant class. Not as poor as the laborers, yet not so well off as the lesser nobles, let alone the clergy. They had sacrificed and saved all of their lives so that they might be able to give me a gift of coins for my coming-of-age, as is the common custom. I had promised them that I would soon make something of myself with their generosity, while hiding the fact that I had also looted their own savings for their aging years. I took it all and fled my hometown, as if it contained a curse of great power.

I sound horrible, don't I? I was. There is no mistaking the fact that I was a spoiled brat who cared for nothing save the next adventure of drinking and whoring with my friends. I was a sinner of uncommon tastes, and yet I suffered a very common fate as a consequence of my sin. I became penniless and alone. Spare me your sermons, and don't even pretend to feel sympathy for my plight! I don't. I deserved every bruise to my ego, every indignity that was heaped upon me by the shop-keepers and serving maids. All doors were locked to me, and I was forced to become a filthy beggar, whose meager bed was the streets of whatever city was foul enough to allow me entry.

It was a fine morning. The sky was clear and bright, too much so, for my tastes. I had just finished rummaging through the garbage disposal of a small shop filled with delightful pastries and meat pies. The pickings were quite slim, and my stomach rebelled at the idea of swallowing another meal of tossed-aside leftovers from someone else's dinner. I had no choice in the matter, you understand. I was just about to stagger my way toward the next storefront, when something amazing caught my eye.

A large crowd of local merchants and laborers had gathered together at the nearest intersection and dropped to their knees in obeisance. A large, blue carriage had stopped at the corner and floated a hand-span above the cobblestone street. You know the type - a typical clerical transport, whose angled wheels were enchanted to keep the gaudy, gold-dripping cart above the material nature of the road. Eternal flames flickered in their sconces; the outstretched wings symbolizing the blessings of OTIDS formed a protective shadow over the cerulean-blue carriage doors, and the jeweled symbol of the Church hovered serenely above the very center of the carriage's peaked roof. Unlike a typical noble form of transportation, there were no bright unicorns or menacing manticores pulling the vehicle, just the light of God.

This gaudy bauble of a carriage deigned to open its door, allowing a small set of silver stairs to drop down into place before the cowering crowd. I held perfectly still, crouched as I was in front of a waste bin, in the hopes that some righteous fool might decide to show his charitable nature before this representation of the Church by giving alms to the poor, meaning to me. I practically quivered in anticipation. A tall priest, with his crimson, white and gold robes stepped out of the vehicle. His Holy cap, with its five-pointed corners, was firmly placed upon his pate with blue ribbons flowing under his shaven chin and illusory birds swirling over his head. Unlike many of the other clergy I have had the pleasure of meeting, he was lean and dignified, and yet he had an air of desperation about his face that was at odds with his mighty position in our society.

I wondered who this ordained idiot was, stopping his carriage at a busy intersection, while the poor commoners were supposed to be heading for their unappreciated labours. The crowd was deep in prayer at his feet, or at the least pretending to do so. Some were undoubtably taking advantage of this unusual circumstance to loiter and take a break from their scurrying. I noticed that he was of middle age, no more than a hundred years or so, which might explain his unwavering gaze that he cast upon the believers around him. No doubt he was quite used to the fawning masses begging him for his forgiveness or pleading for the infinite mercy of OTIDS. Why was he not attending to his flock at church? Why was he here, among the grubs?

My questions fled my mind in terrible fright, when his eyes turned towards me and lit like beacons in the night. The priest jumped down from his carriage and walked directly to my location. I staggered back as if he were a daemon from another realm. He did not smile nor did he stretch out his hand for me to kiss his Holy ring of authority. His bejewelled face showed a goodly pattern of glittering, magickal gems embedded into the skin around his eyes and temples. He had been raised from a noble house, of this I was certain, and had chosen to become a mighty pillar of the Church. Such men as he were never interested in homeless beggars like me, save to make some terrible example of them, all for the educational entertainment of his lowly parishioners.

Before I could turn and run, he leapt forward and grabbed my right arm, stating in a low, melodious voice, "Please wait! I mean you no harm.

You are Galynn Brytshul, are you not? Of Covingmeade Commons? I have an urgent message for you and a great gift."

My struggles ceased at the word "gift", for I was truly desperate, yet I could not shake off the uneasy feeling that whatever business he had with me would lead to no good. I flinched as he pulled aside his robes, expecting to be stabbed by a flaming sword of God's Holy light, but instead he pulled out a large satchel with a shoulder strap and a leather handle. The piece of baggage was well-worn and scuffed, almost as much as I was. The priest just about threw it into my arms and leaned in closer, his hot breath whispering into my left ear, "This is your inheritance. From your father. Not the one you grew up with and who raised you. Your real father. The man who seeded your mother's womb. His Ever Holiness, the Arch-Bishop of Yorkvale. He died last night, and before he did, he entrusted me with bringing this to you. Do not speak! Say no words. This must be done quickly, before my brethren notice our encounter. You are in grave danger, and for this, you do have my sincere apologies. Tell no one of what has happened here this morning! When I leave you, open the case and read the folded note within. Touch nothing else until you do this! May OTIDS light your path."

He then turned from me, as I clutched onto the satchel with my filthy fingers, further smearing the soft leather of it. The priest threw coins at the kneeling crowd and began a sermon of blessing unto them. I looked around quickly, like a rat stealing cheese, and noticed a few faces glaring at me, but most of the people on the street were focused upon the words of the priest as he began to shout Holy phrases from the great Bible of OTIDS. I took this opportunity to make myself scarce, running off to a small alleyway between the shops and their glittering windows full of pretty goods which I could never afford. I fell behind a stack of crates and sank further down onto the stone pavement, away from the eyes of the crowd.

While it is true that our great society's spellcraft keeps our streets clean, there are some exceptions to this fact. It is true that the enchantments placed upon our walkways and roads do keep them clear of debris or stain. This does not include the storage crates, waste bins and even park benches. Such items are not considered important enough to affix a proper spell upon them to mitigate any filth or noxious fumes. We can't have the lives of the commoners be as clean as those of the nobles, after all. It is said that in the ancient past, the age of myth, that there were no higher magicks that could be used to uplift the lives of the people. Now that spellcraft is regarded as the highest form of art and industry, very few commoners can afford the luxury of proper enchantments. Thus, the alley in which I hid was a stinking corridor, because it was filled with old, misused crates and disposal boxes.

The stained satchel was heavier than it appeared, and I could feel at least one bulky shape through the outer casing. I glared at the thing, while I crouched on my haunches, ignoring the smell of spoiled food and urine. For too many months had I slept in alleyways just like this one. For too long had I been forced to scrounge for meals and to further degrade my thin morality for sustenance. I didn't believe a word that the priest had uttered toward me, and I still refuse to repent for that particular sin. You clerics have been the biggest heap of stinking, hypocritical snakes since the dawn of time. Thus, I saw no reason to trust in the word of a holy man. I'd sooner trust a thuggish ganger and most likely be better off for it. Still, the bag itself intrigued me. I wondered if anything within it might be worth some coin, either from the shoppe keepers or the under-market.

With a touch of trepidation, I reached for the clasp. Who knew what kind of spells had been cast on this thing to keep it safe from thieves? I was taking my life in my hands just touching the bronze clasp of the main flap. I could be shocked, burned, or turned into a mosquito. Not that my life was really worth much, not even to me. At that point, I think I would have much preferred dying and thus be free from having to face the utter ruin that was my sordid past. Self-hatred can truly drive a person to rise, or fall, with total abandon. Love can do the very same trick. Isn't that peculiar? I've also heard some claim that hate and love are two sides of the same coin, but I disagree. They simply have the same emotional intensity, which can become a narrow bridge between the two.

Disdain had been my constant companion up until my months of real desperation, which is when hatred became my bedfellow. The grand majority of this endless well of loathing was directed towards myself, but I did reserve some for those who had earned my bile. I was a waste of flesh, a rapscallion, thief and a beggar. I became villainous by necessity, after some incredibly stupid choices that I made in my not-so-distant youth. Some people I have met were vile simply because they could get away with it. Nobles, princes, bishops, the wealthier merchants, people like you. Your foul boots are upon the necks of every commoner, and you celebrate this openly.

The clasp upon the satchel's flap shivered at the touch of my thumb and softly called out with the sound of birdsong. It popped free, and the bag was open. I became alarmed at once. This could only mean that it had been set to open at my touch. Such spellcraft is not cheap, nor is it easy. The spirits within the clasp recognized me, and this gave some weight to the words of the nervous priest who gave the damned thing to me. I almost dropped the bag upon the stinking cobblestones and ran off. Perhaps I should have done just that. It certainly would have made your jobs much easier, yes?

As it was, I forced my hands to pull the flap free and look within the satchel. Confusion filled my poor mind. Inside was a gentleman's briefcase, a small, finger-thick booklet, a folded note and an iron key. I studied these items for a few minutes, certain that all of them were enchanted. Keys are the most notorious for this. Should the wrong hand touch it, an alarm could go off, the authorities alerted and my skin blistered away with a nasty curse. Therefore, I left the iron thing alone for the moment. Instead, I took out the folded note, which also contained a nicely wrought map of the city I was now trawling through for scraps. My position was indicated through a blinking circle of green, as is the norm for such scrolls. A red "X" was displayed some ten blocks away, according to the map, and a dotted line to guide my path, right through the heart of one of the worst neighborhoods infesting the city. I shook my head in puzzlement. As you can imagine, I felt that I was now very far over my head, not that this was a particularly new sensation for me, you understand. I forcefully shoved my attention to the note, which read:

"Unto Galynn Brytshul, my brightest hope of a son,

"Please forgive my intrusion into your life, but this cannot be helped. I had wanted to keep your identity a secret and had hoped that this foul day would never come to pass. Alas, my prayers were not answered, and I take full responsibility for what I have just done to you. By the time you read this, I will be dead, by the hands of others if not my own. This is not because I am your true father, but because of my special work which the Church does not approve. I have seen beyond the veil of glitter, spells and gold. Revealed to my reeling senses was a system of domination and terrible sin against the common people of the many realms. There is no sanctity, no purity, and no compassion.

"In case this note is discovered, I shall not go into details about the gifts which I have bestowed upon you. I have watched you, my son. You are a clever survivor, and when your wits are unclouded by your vile passions, I believe that you may be invaluable to many thousands of souls. Everything within the satchel is marked for you. Use these things wisely. The Church will be hunting for you. The nobility will want you dead. I do understand that there is no trust left in your heart, but if you want to survive, then you must do exactly as I instruct. Look at everything within the satchel I have left for you. These are all the inheritance I have to give. Follow the path and enter the place that I have set aside for you. I cannot give you a father's love, but I can wish you luck and help you to succeed.

"Arch-Bishop Larance Pontiforia of Yorkvale"

Please excuse me as I relate to you that I laughed aloud at the sheer absurdity of what I had just read. It was ridiculous! It was so far-fetched that I just could not find it in me to take it seriously. This had to be some elaborate jest from someone I had wronged in my ribald past. A terrible and cruel joke used to avenge some wrongdoing on my behalf. You see, my Lords, I had yet to come to terms with the fact that this was quite real. In fact, I seriously hoped this was nothing more than some foul prank. The alternative was too terrible to contemplate.

I placed the note back into the bag, shaking my head at the lunacy that was contained within it. I grabbed the small book, no more than palm-sized, and opened its leather-bound cover. Within were tear-sheets. Each one had nothing more than a name at the top of each page and one of a two word statement at the bottom, either "A Favor" or "A Gift". I flipped through the names, pausing now and again to watch out for anyone spying upon me. I shuddered when I began to recognize some of the more notable monikers. Some were powerful nobles, others Churchmen of high regard. There were famous celebrities and government figures. Others I did not recognize, but I did take note of the ritual sigils next to some of these. My worried mind flew into a panic. These specially marked names were those of wizards, sorcerers, witches and necromancers! One does not approach these worthies unless invited to do so, or be prepared to suffer their potent wrath.

With trembling hands, I tucked this terrible book away. I heard an odd sound, which startled me, until I realized that I was sobbing with fright. There was no choice now. I had to open the briefcase, no matter what horrors awaited me when I did so. I cursed the nervous priest, my deceased Arch-Bishop father and mostly, myself. My world had fallen down in a stuttering ruin. Everything I thought I knew about society and reality was sundered. Wiping my nose on my threadbare sleeve, grateful for its simple magicks, I reached out for the briefcase and placed my shivering hands upon the locks.

They rang like little bells when I touched them, and the clasps flew open at once. With foreboding dread, I opened it up. The case was of the type that most bankers use. It was gleaming with cleanliness, with gold fixtures and lacey scrollwork around the edges. It was so out of place within my hands as to be comical, but I was no longer in the mood for laughter. Within was a long ledger, filled with pre-authorized banking cheques, each one was made out in my name and having what seemed like a random worth. Some were set for just a few credit-markers. Others were filled out as being worth tens of thousands of gold coins. There were hundreds of them. Each one was a different amount, each of them had my name stamped upon them as the recipient. They were untraceable, according to the sigils stamped in their corners, and could be cashed in at any money-changer's shop or bank. The seal of the Church of OTIDS was brazenly displayed upon them and thus would be universally accepted as valid. These were not counterfeits, for the spells upon them were obvious and the decorated edges on them shifted and danced to pronounce their validity.

I was wealthy. Rich beyond my wildest dreams of avarice. My head smacked against the brick wall behind me. My vision blurred, as hot tears ran freely down my scruffy cheeks. I wept and giggled manically. The bile in my stomach emptied upon the cobblestones, as the enchantments in the rock glittered with its attempt to clean itself of my mess. I couldn't breathe and ended up screaming into the satchel until I collapsed. I did not wish to draw too much attention to my poor self. Not that mad vagrants were an unknown commodity of the city, but I remained just cognizant enough to understand my deep peril.

My misspent youth was filled with ruffians, rascals, knavish thugs, and I had been one of them myself. I had to be careful. This was a time for sneaking and shifting. If I had simply begun to run about buying luxuries and new clothes, I would be marked immediately by the local sharps. Not to mention all the dire warnings I had received concerning the nobility and the Church. They were the ultimate criminals, and I would be nothing more than a plaything for their sorcerous servants and allies. Just having touched these items was most likely enough to condemn me in their eyes. Just another piece of scrap to be torn up and then burned alive. I now had no choice but to follow the damned map.

CHAPTER TWO

Help Has No Answers

"All the heavens are the providence of OTIDS
OTIDS is within all things and exists in all realms.
All that exists is infused with My Holy Spirit
Hearken unto Me, and abide by My most Holy Code."

-Excerpt from the OTIDS Bible –Documentation 45:27

At this point I was beyond desperate, and I needed information. The only people I still trusted were at least a day's walk. There was no way for me to quietly pay for a carriage, nor was I about to trust summoning the fey to send a message to any of my handful of associates, most of whom I had not contacted in months. To remain in the alley would invite a swift capture at the hands of some very nasty individuals, yourselves included, of course. No, the only way out this kind of horrible situation was to go right through it and to pray that one gets done with it still breathing.

If I could have, a swift trip to a nearby bank would have solved many of my difficulties, but I had no idea as to which ones to trust, and I was hardly dressed to enter such an establishment unnoticed. There were too few clues about what was really going on and why all this was now happening to me. I understood the danger and death parts all too well. Nobles are very ruthless when it comes to the lesser castes of society, and the Church seems to look the other way, pretending the wolves are sheepdogs. From the point of view given to the commoners by the news-criers and papers, the only thing that the two highest status holders have in common are the large collection of spell-gems that are embedded into their faces, but this is a clever ruse, isn't it? The Church and the nobility are deep in each other's pockets, and while they do peck at each other for our entertainment, they both hold our leashes with an iron grip.

Up until the point when I received my supposed inheritance, there were only a bare handful of spell gems upon my temples. Mostly for the usual things that the merchant class cares about: keeping me free from illness, minor curses and jinxes, plus a healthy dose of fortitude to keep us labouring away at creating the comforts that our betters care so much about collecting. I was nothing special, and the gems in my face barely even glittered, by the time that satchel of goodies came into my possession.

It's a curious thing to consider the permanence of the face-gems and their ubiquitous presence in society. Even the lowest classes have one or two if for no reason than to keep them healthy enough to work their poor hands to the bone for their superiors. Rumours abound concerning their magickal nature and the possibility that they give the nobles access to our thoughts. I know the truth behind this matter. Yes, cringe all you want, but my travels have brought to me many secrets you would rather keep in the smothering darkness of your hideous hearts. The lower-class spell-gems all have special enchantments placed upon them that make the wearers susceptible to the commands of nobles and clergy alike. I'm sure it's very comforting to you to know that the sheep are all kept in line.

At the time, I didn't truly know this for certain, but I had already suspected as much, which made the idea of being hunted by your minions even more frightening than it already was. Being highly vulnerable and alone sharpens the wit. You should try it out sometime. The senses all become dull with disuse, especially when everything you might want simply drops into your greedy hands at a moment's notice. The focus one gains from desiring a need greatly outmatches that of simply wanting a passing pleasure. Right now, speaking as I am with you, fills my very thoughts with sharp plans, in case things go wrong for me, as even a poor doppelganger wishes to continue living unto the next day.

In any case, I knew that to stay put was to invite disaster, so I had to move on. Where else could I go but to the mysterious location shown to me on my new map? Rushing forth would definitely have drawn the wrong kind of attention, and so I just hobbled along, keeping my head down and away from the eyes of others. I emerged from the alleyway and shuffled my feet on the nearest avenue, keeping my eyes focused upon the windows of the shops that I trawled past. It was then that I was able to confirm some of the nervous priest's story. The papers were in their little bins, ready for purchase in exchange for a few coins. Their covers were filled with the news of Arch-Bishop Pontiforia's recent passing. The headlines all swore that he had left this physical world sitting quietly at his writing desk, working on many Holy projects to support the poor. Such a grand soul he was, yes?

I shuddered to myself and moved on with deliberate steps. I had to be watchful, careful, for I was heading into dangerous territory. After a few blocks, even the enchanted streets could not keep up with the filth that was coating them. Too many hexes had been hurled about these darker avenues, without any concern for who would be harmed by them, wearing away the magicks that protected the stones from abuse. Such decrepitude stood as a warning to those who ventured into the darker neighborhoods of the city. I was entering gang territory, and their knives literally gleamed with malice.

The bricks of the walls around me chuckled darkly, and some hurled verbal abuse to torment my ears. There had been word that some effort had gone into removing such vile defacing of the public walkways, but it wasn't worth the cost, as every time the jabbering hexes were cleared away, more would replace them in less than a week's time. The streets became narrow and winding, with old, dusty shop faces leaning in to loom over me. The air became foul, as shattered pavement had ceased to clean themselves, and as no self-respecting carriages ever floated into these disgusting regions, they were ignored to crumble away as they would.

I jumped in fear at every bark of laughter, certain that I could hear the footsteps of someone following me will ill intent. It might be supposed that in my wretched state that I would be free from being accosted by the local toughs. This was not the case, as I had sorely learned through months of homeless begging. One such as myself was easy prey for the gangs, whose favorite entertainment was to bully and abuse helpless wrecks like myself. I had no weaponry other than my laughably unsteady fists. If any foul gang member had decided that I was to be punished for entering his turf, there was little I could do about the matter. This might have solved most of your problems, but alas, the fates were kind to me during this short journey into the unknown.

Now, I am not one given to believing in luck, but the events of this day, short as it had been, threatened to unravel my usual skepticism. Not that I truly expected to survive what was awaiting me, once I reached the destination marked on my new map. It was just that the winds of change seemed to be blowing hard, and there was a bare chance I could ride it out if I were clever enough to mark which direction it was heading.

I checked my map frequently, to avoid becoming lost in the labyrinth of shuttered streets, grateful that it had been enchanted against stains and tears. Eventually, I came to a gloomy cul-de-sac that was more disused and appalling in nature than I had ever seen before, and I have witnessed quite a few of those during my wasted time! Filth coated the dark walls, and even the rats were not deigning to show their pointed faces in such a vile location. Refuse was piled along the pavement, and I had to walk upon the cobblestone street to reach my goal.

Perhaps, at one point in time, it had been a very nice garden villa or an aqueduct that had been decorated with stone-carved bas reliefs, depicting a glorious event lost to living memory, which was then built over to provide shelter for the poor souls who called this awful place home. There was a deep archway that led to what appeared to be an ancient doorway used by janitors. The light was beyond being poor; it was positively the most horrid vision of dystopian gloom that I had yet seen. The walls were so covered in filth that one could not tell what was brick and what was mortar, and there was no evidence that any gang had been desperate enough to claim this foul space for their own.

I looked about furtively, making sure that no one was around me, but the street leading here was totally abandoned. Windows were boarded up in all the buildings around me, and the doorways of these structures gaped at me, like missing teeth in a rotten grin. I struggled with the satchel in the oppressive gloom, and after several moments of panic, I found the iron key and pulled it out in my quivering hand. Hesitation filled my heart, for to use the wrong key for a door was to allow oneself to be shocked into oblivion.

Every key is ensorcelled to be used only by one individual person, for just one particular door. Any misstep would see me dead or worse.

Looking at the metal slab of a door did not cheer my spirits in the least. It was corroded, disused, and yet its keyhole gleamed with a blue light of spellcraft still activated. I did not dare to look at the heaps of barely seen refuse gathered in the corners of the archway, for some of them were far too reminiscent of decaying bodies for my tastes. Why would any father, even a disgraced Arch-Bishop, send their child to such a hellish place? Was I about to be punished for my multitude of elaborate sins? Or was this simply the perfect location for hiding something of great worth?

I had no answers to such internal queries and I realized that I truly had nothing left to lose. Just my miserable life. Taking a deep breath to calm my screaming fears, I shoved the iron key into its slot before I could change my mind. It sang with a quite whisper of musical notes, and a beam of light slashed across my bedraggled face. I flinched with terror, not quite ready for the scorching lash that would be my final sensation, before being burned to a cinder. Instead, all that could be noted was a clinking sound and a moaning of rusty hinges as the door opened wide for me.

Forcing myself to look beyond the doorway, I discovered a long, dark tunnel beyond the open portal. I'm fairly certain that my bladder betrayed me, but I cannot tell with certainty. There are times when one realizes that with just a single step forward, everything will crash out of control. All the comfortable rules will fly to the ethereal realms. The unknown will become a constant companion, chuckling grimly at every misstep. This was one of those times.

Now, please understand that I have never considered myself as being a brave man. Just the opposite if truth be told. The courage needed to take one fateful step into the darkness arose from a gaudy chariot flying a banner in my mind, stating, "You Have No Choice". To go back was to flee into the arms of death, most probably a quite painful one, possibly even a public one, followed by all of my old associates and family. The Church is ever ravenous about punishing the sin of heretical thinking. That gluttonous institution, which calls for virtue in all matters, also shares its spoils with the nobility, who are always ready to feast upon the commoner.

Therefore, I did the only thing that could be done to get my frozen feet moving; I got very angry. To be punished, just because someone who caused some official difficulties knows of my existence, filled me with wrath. Being threatened because some clutch of nobles were wetting themselves silly due to some scandal I was not involved in caused such a boiling rage within my heart that I lurched through the doorway, just to show my endless contempt for such vile hypocrisy. I would get to the bottom of this situation, find out all that could be discovered, and then plan my vengeance against those who wrongly accuse others of the very crimes they commit themselves. If there was ever a moment to show that I was not a complete waste of flesh, that my life could still have meaning, it would be to strike out against my oppressors. Thank you for this moment of inspiration. You deserved it.

The corridor before me was menacing in the extreme. A gruesome vision of bloodcurdling filth. A hall of the damned, patiently awaiting its next victim. The door slid shut behind me, and sconces set with torches flared into life, barely cutting through the oppressive darkness. The toothy throat of a crocodile would have been more inviting. Every few paces, on the left and the right, were closed doors made of corroded steel. The cold glimmer of active spellcraft coated the thick hinges and locks of these rusty hatches, making it immediately understood that these doors were much stronger than they appeared. Straight ahead, barely visible in the distance, was a brightly lit chamber. This illumination became my goal.

There was just barely enough space for my body to pass through the corridor, without brushing against the sealed doors to either side of me. A perverse part of my mind wanted to reach out and knock upon them. In fact, I found myself leaning toward one of the locked handles that rested upon each door and broke away with revulsion at the very last moment. The way forward was quite clearly marked, and no map was required at this point, only common sense, save for the part of being in this hideous mockery of a passageway in the first place.

My bare feet squelched in the muddy water that had collected on the concrete floor. Things wriggled within the foul liquid beneath my tread, and if my bladder had not emptied before, then it certainly had at this point. That was when it occurred to me that this place had been the private hiding spot for an Arch-Bishop of the Church. The often-quoted statement declaring "It is always darkest before the dawn" ran circles through my terrified mind. This corridor was a metaphor, meant to display the fearsome to scare off the unworthy. This was a test of faith and perseverance.

Now, one might be excused for believing that a wastrel would hardly have either of these noble qualities. A squandered life is a sure sign of a lack of moral fortitude, yet it is fascinating how rage can push someone into the light of endurance. Fear and hatred are comfortable bedpartners, and my cup was overflowing with both. I needed for my newfound enemies to feel the same sense of hopeless terror that I was experiencing. If I was to be killed by the powers that be, then I would act in such a way as to be worthy of their ire. To break the kneecaps of my murderers, you understand. My situation was terribly unfair, and I was determined to make sure that the balance was tipped in my favour, however briefly. For that, I needed to reach my goal and discover what awaited me, to aid in my revenge.

At that point, I fully welcomed the menacing gloom of the tunnel, wrapping myself in it like a shroud of self-righteousness. Suddenly, death was no longer a choice, not if it was time to blacken eyes and break a rib or two. My final passing would be an inconvenience, nothing more. Perhaps a means to an end, or a way to bring down those who had threatened not only myself but countless others. The helpless, the poor, the hopeless, and the outcast. Who better to assume the mantle of champion for these miserable folks, for I was one of them? I was the very epitome of the wretched souls who were preyed upon by the grand nobles of our society.

I walked onward, then I marched with confidence, and before long, I was running towards the bright chamber. Like a moth to a candle, it drew me forth with a growing fascination. Fate was about to reveal her hand, and the coins on the table represented all that I had. It was in this moment that I first felt any sort of real power. A taste of true destiny. A delusion to be sure but a compelling one nonetheless. Even a wretched soul such as I can only take so much, then rise into new heights of foolishness, which can often be so unexpected as to throw one's enemies into chaos. I had played such games before but never upon so grand a stage nor with a purity of purpose.

The open space of the bright doorway was shimmering, like oil upon stagnant water. Needless to say, I recognized it as a protective bubble that had been called into existence by some talented sorcerer. Such things are commonly employed by museums, to protect rare artifacts or to ensure the safety of servants and observers in ritual spaces. By its reddish hue, it was obviously one of the "Star Ruby" wards that seared the soul of trespassers with the vile temper of angry spirits. I fell through the curtain of light with a wet, popping sound, though that may have been my heart giving out on me, after my stupendously idiotic race to the chamber. I didn't truly know nor did I care.

The room itself was quite clean. No dust or debris, no filth climbing the walls. It was a very pleasant change of pace for me. A puddle of muddy effluence was spreading from my soiled legs and feet, and I felt a twinge of guilt over staining the pristine floor with my presence as I stood there, like a dull-brained zombie, peering about with uncertainty. The chamber was square and covered with glyphs and sigils of mighty spells. At the far corner was a man, standing perfectly still upon a short dais. This was no ordinary person, you understand. He was very tall, heavy-jawed, and wearing a suit of the most magnificent armour I had ever seen. That part remains true to this day. The metal plates covering his muscular form were glowing with enchantments and mystical engravings of a fierce yet delicate nature. In his gauntleted hands was a staff which ended in curved blades at both ends, which were also fitted with large crystals that gleamed with a blueish light.

The only other thing in the room was a marble pedestal that came up to shoulder height, upon which was a scrying stone the size of my head. Shifting colours swirled within that ball of crystal, and a soft murmuring emanated from it, like a dreaming man mumbling in his sleep. Such a thing was worth far more than what was even contained within my satchel, and greed filled my veins. Fortunately, I snapped myself back to reality, for such artifacts, while quite costly, were guarded by powerful wards of destruction. Besides, selling one was almost unheard of and would definitely attract too much unwanted attention.

The light of the chamber came from nowhere in particular, though I suspect it arose from the "Star Ruby" protecting the room. Either that or some wizard had been having some real fun in creating this place. Searching the chamber revealed nothing that wasn't obvious to the eyes, and in my growing frustration, I approached the scrying stone and placed one hand upon its smooth surface. It was cool and slick. It vibrated slightly under my palm, and a flash of light enveloped my hand to the wrist. I tried to pull back, but my fingers were held fast against the magick ball. A few seconds later, it released me with a musical sigh, and I toppled back onto my posterior with a total lack of dignity plus a high-pitched shriek of terror, to be fully honest.

A loud, deep voice filled the room from behind me. Startled, I whirled around and saw that the man in the corner had come to life, shouting, "I am Prime! Good master, the son of the notable, honoured and most feared Arch-Bishop of Yorkvale, Larance Pontiforia! Allow me to serve thee, to fulfill my destiny for which I was created. Be not alarmed, for your protection is my sworn duty! Harken now! My brothers awaken to serve thee!"

The clanging of multiple chains shattered the air following his bold statement, as I sat upon the floor in shock. This was a Troth-Knight! I had heard of such things, but even the highest lords and ladies of the royal courts do not have access to such creations as these. The clanging of steel shook the chamber, and a clatter rose up to engulf my ears with chaos. A dozen more Troth-Knights rushed into the room, all of them armed and armored with the finest of enchanted accoutrement. Shakily, I got to my unsteady feet, as they all formed a circle around me, facing outward in defense against unseen enemies. They were grand. They were terrifying, and apparently, they were mine. I could not force myself to speak, and so I did the only thing I could in this situation, I laughed aloud.

Prime approached, swinging his staff into a horizontal position, as he kneeled before me, "My Lord, Galynn Brytshul, it is our oath to protect thee from all harm, unless we are ordered to do otherwise. We hereby swear fealty unto thee and shall obey thy directives, until we are destroyed. Allow us to serve thee, our Lord, for we also bear gifts from thy most worthy father to adorn thine temples. Knowledge we have for thee and fierce hearts that never waver from their purpose!"

I coughed into my hand, hoping to find some proper words to give to these incredible warriors from legend. Kings had fought wars over less worthy soldiers than these. My mind was dizzy. My thoughts had fled to the far corners of the world. Thus, my first words to these most gallant knights were, "Excuse me, please, but could we simply dispense with all the archaic terminology? I'm very confused right now, and I need a touch of ordinary talk. If you don't mind, that is."

Prime responded immediately, "Sure! No problem, boss! I see you have the satchel. That's really good, because otherwise, we'd have to raid the grand cathedral of Yorkvale for it. The book of names must be used to gather everything that you will need to survive. If you are here, then your father is dead, and the people he protected are now in dire jeopardy. Both the Church of OTIDS and the nobility of the world shall be hunting for you right now. They have always feared your true father and his grand cause concerning the truth. Your inheritance comes with a serious responsibility, but you are not alone. Now that we have awakened, and your identity has been confirmed by the scrying stone, you shall never be without our aid."

I did not bother to tell them to gather their belongings, for they were wearing them already. Troth-Knight travel light, and their personal needs are provided by the spellcraft within their blood and bones. I took out the book of names and decided that it might be best if I began searching for these individuals in the order in which they appeared within the pages. My absent father had planned for the moment of his untimely demise quite well, and until I understood the full game he had dumped me into, I should not do anything that might shift his well-placed moves into disarray. What was needed was a plan of action, one that would serve my immediate needs and yet not cause too much notice amongst my opponents. For this, I had to find a few friendly faces whom I could trust or at least pay handsomely for their services. There were those I owed favours to, others who could use a helping hand. None of them had spoken to me for months, but as I understood their greed, that would not matter if I paid handsomely enough.

CHAPTER THREE

Disquieting Party Favours

"And ye shall pass unto Me thy identifiers.
Accept My terms and enter unto My system.
I shall bring unto thee untold blessings of pure data, physical alloy and even biological enhancement.
Through Me, ye shall live in blessed fields of energy forevermore."

-Excerpt from the OTIDS Bible – Procedures 45:87

Not one of my new guardians were helpful in figuring out what was really going on or why it was happening. They were all blissfully unaware of who my enemies were, by which I mean those who wanted me dead, as they had all been in a magickal slumber for decades. Needless to say, this did not console me in the least, and I knew that I had to find answers swiftly. The good news was that the armour of my protectors had the ability to change appearance, so to be incognito, as it were. They could blend in perfectly with a crowd, in a forest, or disappear into the darkness. It seems that my father had planned ahead most effectively, save for preparing me for my current, unenviable position.

Shall I bore you with the details of my cashing in a few of the cheques to tend to my needs? Or have you already burned down the money-changers and banks in my wake? Did you raid the tailors and merchants who I visited afterward, or are the poor souls who sold me clothes and other goods still suffering in one of your prison cells, like I am? The conditions of this place are most uncivilized, though I believe that I have befriended a local rat. His presence in my lonely, stifling chamber is much more welcome than yours. In any case, I did go shopping, and the new protectors were playing the part of my personal staff, which they performed most convincingly. The absolute pleasure of wearing some fresh clothing, after a long bath and massage, is a wonder I doubt any of you can truly appreciate, spoiled tyrants that you are.

Floating carriages are very expensive, and before using one, a whole new set of spell gems need to be implanted upon one's temples before it will accept any commands. It was painful to spend so much coin, and a part of my conscience thrashed me for not giving alms to the poor with my newly acquired wealth. Such fine acts of charity had to wait until my life was no longer in peril. The guardians were provided Kirin steeds to act as my escort, which was another terrible expense. By this point, my own brow had enough gems upon it to confuse me with a minor noble of a lesser house, which was exactly what was needed. Imagine my wonder and amazement when I was able to see as you over-decorated buffoons do. I had no idea that there were so many announcements, warnings and even map spells all around me. I was now freed from being claimed and then forced into mindless servitude. Local directories opened up hidden listings of the rich and famous.

Thus, I rode away from the city where I had fallen into total squander far better prepared than the day I left the shop of my parents. My mind was flooded with information, entertainments, and access to services I had never dreamed of. My visions of avarice were sorely humbled by this experience, and I began to realize just how much jeopardy I was now in. The new spell gems had been inset into my brow in a tasteful manner, all them gleaming like polished sapphires, in twin fans like the wings of an owl in flight. I had seen nobles and clergy whose foreheads were almost completely covered by the damned things, and I shook in my plush seat in fear.

The need for some allies, other than the guardians provided to me, was fierce. They had to be people whom I knew were capable of a good twist, a proper sting. Scoundrels who were well versed in the ways of bringing a well-to-do mark to his knees, or robbing them blind without notice. At the same time, they also had to be friends of mine who actually cared about my condition in life, and these were few and far between. Such extra help would be expensive, and I would be forced into serious generosity for their favours. Everything I have learned about the ways of the upper nobility tells me that you people, of all humanity, understand the concept of friends for hire. When that's all you have left, you make do with them. Thus, camaraderie dissolves, and the ideals of loyalty and honour become mocked as senseless and naïve.

The town I went to was named Palintal, though I had heard rumour that it once had a different moniker, lost in the mists of time during the pre-magick age. No one remembers; no one cares. To this very day, it remains an unremarkable place, having neither a reputation for unique products nor any sign of great wealth. Its Lord and Lady are reputed to be of lower nobility, and even Palintal's main cathedral is hardly worth visiting. So why go there in the first place? The reason is in the question. No one in their right mind would consider such a location to be any sort of sanctuary. Unless one had some special friends who used the town in order to remain unnoticed.

There were two such souls within the thin walls of Palintal, a man and a woman, named Shan and Barb. I could give you their surnames, but it wouldn't matter, as they have absolutely no recollection of the events which I'm relaying to your noble ears. Galynn Brytshul was wise enough to provide them some extra protection and had their memories altered once they left his employment. This had been agreed upon from the very start. They would simply wake up, not knowing what the date was, and find their hovels filled with expensive and untraceable valuables. They had trusted me to do my part and to provide for them.

I left my carriage at the stables, taking with me a single guardian, leaving the rest behind. I had no wish to be remarkable, and running about with a platoon of enchanted soldiers would be noticed with alarming speed. My two friends were exactly where I had hoped they would be found, within an old inn whose claim to fame was a singing bar stool, which was always propped up on a makeshift stage, for entertainment purposes. Legend has it that it was accidentally created by a mad sorcerer who, in a drunken stupor, decided that it was a good time to show off his abilities to a naysayer. The inn's owner was just glad that the damned thing didn't dance as well.

Before entering the place, I first went to a local money-changer who was known for being quite discreet. Three more cheques were swiftly cashed, and he was more than satisfied with his illicit twenty percent. I tucked away some of the monetary notes within my laced sleeves, which happily secreted them away within their folds. Before this point in my life, I had always worn the more common short-cuff with ensorcelled cufflinks. It is now obvious to me why the nobility prefers the longer, lacey ruffles that have been in high fashion for so many centuries. Such useful things they are! Mine came with bottomless change purses tucked away into their lace, and they also had the ability to remove commonly used bindings, in case things turned ugly.

I don't blame you for looking so alarmed. The clothing upon my back was created especially for me and my mission, by a highly talented spell-weaver, whose looms whisper arcane wisdom when it's not being used for making fine clothing. So long as I remain unharmed, you shall gain all the knowledge within my poor head. Locking me away in this dungeon is an inconvenience and reveals a basic mistrust that is assuaged by brute force. Should it be necessary, you'll find this cell empty and your guards mewling like starved kittens. Fear not! Once finished with my report, you shall receive a gift for your patience. A parting present from my creator, which you shall undoubtedly find to be fascinating and valuable. Now, back to my tale.

Both Shan and Barb were sitting together in the tavern, near to the singing stool, as was their usual habit. The owner received a percentage of the profits from their usual tricks, mainly gambling stings. In exchange, he looked the other way and gave them each a room free of charge. Barb was the first to notice my approach, "OTIDS, Galynn! I thought you were dead!"

Shan greeted me coolly, "What? Ran out of gutters to crawl through, Gally? I still haven't forgiven you, hex-bringer."

I raised my hands in supplication, "Please, friends, I come to offer my apologies, along with some treats to make amends."

I sat down at the unoccupied chair nearest to their table and flipped out some high marks from my lacey cuffs. They both gasped aloud, but Shan leaned forward to examine them carefully, "Let me guess, Gally, counterfeit. Either that or ensorcelled with a nasty surprise. I'm no dupe, and neither is she. You should know better."

I leaned back and raised my new boots, with magick pocket cuffs, to the table top, "The money was honestly acquired if you can believe that. If you don't want it, you can leave it. Makes no difference to me. Here I am, presenting gifts to my best of friends in the whole realm, and you accuse me of cheating you! The money before you is my apology for being an ass. I do have more, if you would like to see, as a down payment for a job."

Barb, ever the entrepreneurial one, sat back down and asked, "What sort of job? How much of a take? Who's the mark?"

Shan glared at her for a moment, then sighed deeply and returned to his seat, "This better pay well, Gally. Waste my time and I'll gut you like a fish."

I smiled broadly at the two of them, "Let me regale you about my current purpose. I have the dubious honour of being paid very handsomely to deliver a series of messages to various members of the upper reaches of society. Nobles and notables, clergy and... others whom I shall not mention here. There is no time to lose, and this will be dangerous for you both. I have one thousand legal notes for you both, though in truth, I would prefer if I paid you in fine jewellery, to keep things quieter. That's better than a stack of gold coins or a merchant's purse, wouldn't you say? If you prefer cash, I have no problems with that, though I do advise against it."

Barb crinkled her nose at me, "You said a series of messages. Do you mean we have to be with you for all of them? How many are there? Who's the first one, and how do we get to them?"

Shan spoke up before I could reply, "Who is sending you on this odd errand? Why you? Is this a joke?"

I shook my head, "So many questions! Very well, the employer is a relative of mine, one who has never actually met me before. He thought I was the most suitable for this sort of endeavour, due to my outrageous past. There are many messages to deliver, but I only need help for the first two or three. After that, I'm certain that I'll be able to handle the rest on my own. I need to start with the residence of Lady Ballow, Heiress of Caldandia. I've heard rumour that she is holding a grand gala for her noble friends two days from now at her main estate. We need to go, uninvited, and seek her out for an audience. What say you?"

Barb was, as is usual, the first to grasp what I was asking of them, "Dear OTIDS! Lady Ballow is, well, she's one of the most famous nobles and from one of the original families! To hell with a paltry thousand, Gally! I want double, or you can go on without me!"

I brought my boots back to the floor, "Done! For both of you."

Shan squinted at me, "You're after noble goods? You're gonna play them, aren't you? Beggar them right down to their shorts, yes? I'm in."

You see, amongst the commoners, you nobles and priestly types are seen as hated predators, ones we like to see fall to ruin. Oh, they cheer when a new sport comes up from the ranks of lesser nobles, but that is just so that we may watch the bastard crumble to pieces. Most folks are OTIDS-fearing, hardworking sorts, but they despise the clergy with all their gold-dripping finery, while the rest of us live in squalor. They don't trust you. Parasites and vipers, the lot of you! In any case, I shall return to my story.

We made our agreements and arrangements right then and there, while Shan kicked the stool every few minutes to get it singing to keep others from overhearing our words. We left together, after tossing the bartender a few gold coins, and went shopping for new clothing for my companions. My guardian, who had been ordered to remain just outside the inn, joined us and carried our baggage. We returned to my carriage, and after seeing my strange entourage, my two friends became quieter and more compliant. The nearest large city was Narcourt, which was to be our next destination, and we spent an incredible amount of money on necklaces, rings, finery, clothes and even works of art. The grand majority of these goods were shipped back to the rooms of my friends, at the inn of Palintal.

Our journey to the residence of Lady Ballow was long and hard. We practiced our new identities, the roles we would play to gain entry into the gala. My part was that of a very minor noble from a lesser realm who was sight-seeing before taking over his father's affairs. Shan was my henchman and main steward, who was also a distant cousin. Barb was to be my cultural advisor, and we had to purchase translation earrings to complete her image. Usually, commoners have no idea as to how to find the dwelling or pleasure house of any noble family. With my new spell-gems, I had ridiculously easy directions for my carriage to follow, by accessing a directory egregore. While considered to be very limited thoughtforms, I marvelled at its complexity and servile nature. It knew where everything was and the routes to use, so long as one had access to the right spell-gems. Ephemeral intelligences of this sort are usually guided by higher powers and great spirits of magick, which can only be commanded by the most powerful nobles and priests.

Fortunately, Lady Ballow was comfortable with her notoriety and confident in her protections, which were formidable.

After our experiences within our mode of transport, it was easy to see why nobles spend fortunes on carriages. We would have gone mad with boredom during our long journey if it hadn't been for all of the incredible entertainments that were on board with us. Projection crystals that brought grand vistas to life all around us, mystic spheres that played music, and even a bottomless pantry filled with snacks and drinks. At first, we played games with our new toys, but within a few hours we all realized just how useful the accoutrements truly were. Information forbidden to commoners was guzzled down greedily, and news from multiple realms was accessed for dessert. I even used an astral banking service to provide my friends with emergency accounts, paid for by my late father's cheques.

When we finally reached the grounds of Lady Ballow's estates, we saw that it was surrounded by a high fence that resembled a thorny thicket of vines made of gently swaying steel. Beyond this was a dome of dark purple radiance that we could not see through. The very road had turned into bright, crushed shell that jingled when trod upon by the mounts of my guardians. We came to halt just before the last turn which led to the main entry to the estate. All of my guardians, except for the pair which drove our new carriage, dismounted and marched off into the wilderness that surrounded the Ballow grounds. They would find unofficial entries into the huge estate and await my commands or rescue me if things went badly. Their armour blended into the forest so perfectly that they may as well have become invisible.

Now was the moment for the real trick, getting into the gala without blowing our cover. I had our drivers race to the main gates, swerving the floating carriage wildly. Bejewelled items were tossed out the open windows, from which rang the sound of drunken laughter. I spilled some fine liquor upon my doublet and mussed my hair. Barb was pretending to scold me while Shan raised his nose scornfully at the scene I was creating. The gate guards of the Ballow estate peeked into the carriage, after speaking briefly to my drivers who claimed that I had misplaced my official invitation to the gala. Their scandalized faces were such a sight to behold that I could not help but laugh right up their noses, upon which they backed away swiftly. My spell-gems reached into their commoner minds and convinced their eyes that my name was indeed on the list. They then commiserated with my drivers and allowed us to pass through the gates.

This was the first time in days that Shan actually grinned at me, and my heart swelled with joy. Once we swept past the walls of Lady Ballow's estate, the sky deepened to a twilight violet. The three of us stumbled out from our carriage and pretended to lean upon each other so that we might surreptitiously examine our new surroundings. The first thing that caught the eye was a grand castle at the very center of the grounds, tall enough to just reach the very top of the mystic dome of Lady Ballow. It was a stately structure, lean and highly decorated with baroque carvings and sculptures on a grand scale. The entire edifice was lit by luminous globes which floated in the air around them, shaped to resemble giant, cut diamonds. Numerous banners bedecked all the various levels of this gaudy building, which even included a waterfall of pink champagne flowing from its upper battlements down to the gardens below.

Grand carriages ringed the grounds, some of which were well beyond being ostentatious in their design. A crowd of over-dressed dignitaries were milling about a dazzling variety of refreshment stations, which provided rare delectable treats and entertainments. Floating trays of drinks were strewn about, bobbing about in the air to avoid hitting the noble celebrants. Golden fountains dotted the landscape, and the crowded walkways sang as they were trod upon by the merry revellers. Colourful illusions danced about in the sky, bringing cries of delight from the guests of Lady Ballow.

My task to find our hostess was quite daunting, and despair filled my heart. It was then that Barb suggested that we separate and mingle with the revellers. Shan would circle the long line of carriages, to see if any of the serving staff might know the whereabouts of Lady Ballow. I was to enter the castle to seek an audience with our noble hostess, while Barb searched the crowds within the grand gardens. I feared for my companion's safety, but I saw no other choice and thus agreed to the plan. All of us were out of our element here, and the danger to our lives and freedoms was prevalent. Any one of the party guests could jumble our minds or strip our wills bare, with nothing more than a wink of an eye and the use of their spell-gems.

It took an hour to reach the castle gates, and by that point I was sick of being jostled by overly-polite, drunken nobles. To the left of the castle's main doors was a dragon, chained to a glittering boulder made of precious metals. The giant, winged lizard was spouting bits of flame from its nostrils, as it chewed upon human bones from a massive, red bowl in front of it. The creature's scales were glossy black, which made its dagger-sized teeth look all the more ferocious. I swiftly walked over to the other side of the grand steps and kept my eyes away from the monster's bulk, before I lost my nerve to enter the bejewelled building.

To my relief, there were not as many people within the palace itself, save for a number of servants rushing about, looking harried and annoyed. I put on my best, winning smile and approached a service maid who was better dressed than her compatriots. With a bow I asked if she knew where I might find the Lady Ballow, for I had an urgent message of great importance for her consideration. The maid scowled at me for a moment, then informed me that her mistress was very busy with hosting the gala, but said that she would make her Lady aware of my presence if I would be willing to wait in the lower drawing room.

I jumped at this chance for such a private meeting and bestowed my heartfelt blessing upon the maid. She then assigned a lesser servant to escort me toward the appropriate chamber, which ended up being two floors above. I followed her into the well-appointed room, and she told me to make myself comfortable, before leaving me there and closing the door behind her. I stood for a moment, trying to will my heart to cease its heavy thumping within my chest. My hands were now sweating, and with trembling fingers, I prepared myself by tearing out the sheet of paper with Lady Ballow's name from my deceased father's booklet, wondering what kind of gift I would receive from the great lady.

The chamber itself was luxuriant, too much so for me to allow myself to relax. Overly decorated chairs and tables were neatly spread around, along with a pair of lavish desks and a trio of decorated cabinets. While it was true that my legs were sore from my travels, I did not dare to sit in one of the plush, brocaded chairs. One can never be too sure as to what kind of spells had been cast upon fine furnishings, and I had no desire to become trapped by my hostess. The paintings upon the gilded walls peered at me, their faces altered their expressions to deep frowns of disapproval. Some went so far as to shake their heads and turn their backs upon me. I don't really blame them for such unseemly behaviour, for I knew that deep down inside, I was more than worthy of their contempt.

Beyond the cabinets was another door, and after pacing about for an unknown length of time, I saw it open, and the Lady Ballow stepped through with regal grace. Her perfect features wore a puzzled frown, at odds with the elegant jewellery that bedecked her form. Her gown swayed as she moved, like waves breaking upon the shores of a sandy beach, all in pastel colours and fitted with lines of pearls. Lady Ballow's long, dark hair was gathered in a perfect nest of braided locks, dripping with gold hairpins that spat out blue sparks as she examined me. Her brow was covered with spell-gems, all of which glowed from within for a second before she languidly walked toward me and said, "You are not of a noble house. What is this message you bring to me? It had better be worth my time."

I admit that my throat became constricted with fright, and I fumbled with the tear-sheet that bore her name before handing it over like a school-boy who was being punished for speaking crudely in class. Her elegant and beautifully manicured fingers took the paper from my trembling hands, and her brows constricted as she examined it.

I stammered like an oaf, "My, my Lady. This is...well, it's from my, um, father, who..."

She returned her steely gaze to my face, silencing me at once, "Yes, I saw the news. Truth be told, I had hoped that this arrangement had also been lost along with the... irreverent Bishop of Yorkvale. Very well. A debt of honour unpaid is said to be cursed, and I knew Larance well enough to be wary about going against his final wishes."

The Lady Ballow turned her back on me, as if I was nothing more than a stain upon the carpet, and walked over to the trio of cabinets. She tapped her fingers in a syncopated rhythm on the doors of the first one, and it popped open with a cry of birdsong. She reached within, further than could be expected from such a narrow piece of furnishing, and pulled out a battered briefcase. It had two handles and small lock. Its leather casing was scuffed and worn. She returned to me and handed it over to my unwilling hands. The case was heavier than it looked, and I almost dropped it in surprise. A brief smile crossed her features, before being swallowed up by her usual, haughty manner. With her cold gaze digging into my very soul, she stated, "If you are who you claim to be, it will open. If not, you will die most horribly."

Swallowing my panic, I unlatched the lock, waiting for a painful death. The metal device simply freed itself without a sound, and I opened the case. The inner walls of it were coated in a white, greasy paste. Embedded within this substance was a large collection of gold cards, the same size as those used for games of chance. I heard Lady Ballow gasp aloud, and I looked up at her dark eyes in confusion.

She turned away briefly, then brought her gaze back to the briefcase, "I have been holding this for Larance for many years, never daring to try to pick the lock upon it, for he warned me of its powerful magicks. These are talent wafers, young man. They are quite edible, which is why they must be stored in enchanted lard. Each one will have a marking upon it, which your spell-gems can easily identify for you. After consuming one, you shall have a master's talents of whatever ability the wafer is designed for, over a period of one day. I advise against eating too many at once, for insanity is a side effect of such gluttony."

I returned my gaze to the gold cards and saw that some were a bit crumbled at the edges, "I understand, my Lady. Thank you for this fine gift."

She snorted lightly, "Don't thank me. This is the will of your father, heretical soul that he was. I hope you make good use of them. Now, get out, before I change my mind and call upon my guards to arrest a troublesome trespasser."

CHAPTER FOUR

Out of the Cauldron

"Thou shalt not commit an act of binary
Binary is not the Holy way
Binary is the sin of illusion
The true path of the universe is Superposition."

-Excerpt from the OTIDS Bible – Processes 67:14

It's most difficult to tell my story with all these interruptions! Rest assured that your questions will be answered throughout my tale. As for Lady Ballow, one does not resort to indiscretions concerning a noble of such fame and power. I'm quite certain that she has many connections, both legal and profane. Question her all you like if you're brave enough to face her wrath. Your own response to my utterances reveals a mortal flaw in your thinking. Just like most commoners, if you'll forgive such a comparison, you believe that the nobility and clergy are all on the same side if there is such a thing. What folly! The truth is far simpler; everyone is on their own side.

Now then, back to the night of the gala for Lady Ballow. Needless to say, I raced from the sturdy walls of her castle with my heart ready to burst out of my chest in sheer terror. To remain would ensure a painful death, at the best of circumstances. After hurling myself out through the main doors, gulping for breath, I found my friend, Shan, waiting for me near the dragon. He spotted me directly and pulled me aside, whispering, "Did you get what you wanted?"

A proper noble would have burned him to ash with a single, dark glance. As it was, I could barely speak, though I did punch his shoulder and dragged him down the singing pathway, "We need to find Barb. Now. We're leaving with our skins intact; I hope."

He smirked at me, pulling aside his jacket to reveal a small collection of fine bangles and necklaces that he had purloined from some witless dupes. Growling low, I led him further on, keeping an eye out for our friend, who had mingled with the crowd of partiers. Fortunately, one of my Spell-Gems served as a locator for those who were under my wing. A blinking, red marker was flashing in my right eye, and I followed it into the mass of guests. I must confess that there was a bit of confusion on my part, as every person on the way to my destination had their name popping up in front of me, along with club affiliations, society markers and even a brief biography. How you nobles find your way from one room to the next with all this bother is still a mystery to me. At least the Lady Ballow had most graciously disarmed all the usual advertisements for the duration of the gala, which would have cluttered my vision into uselessness.

The amount of food and drink being served at this self-celebratory indulgence would have fed a small city of commoners. It is often said that the nobility, and especially the clergy, are the stewards of all humanity. Your failure is spectacular. The average person, who makes up over ninety percent of the population, is grateful to have a simple pot that can make a weak gruel or a kettle that heats water sufficiently to have a passable cup of tea. The healers must, by law regulated through the hands of the upper classes, work their arts upon the ailing nobility first, before turning their attentions to the masses. The Church gets the first of everything produced or imported, with the aristocracy snatching up the rest, leaving bare crumbs for those whose only misfortune is to be born beneath the hard boots of society.

Roll your eyes all you like. Such responses only prove the point even further. At least the Church pretends to serve, though most of this is done through the poorest of soup kitchens and the local shrines, built to show the beneficence of the priesthood, while they prance around with living sex toys and taking whatever they wish in the name of OTIDS. This is not a secret scandal, whispered in dark places. It is openly displayed with contempt for decency, all in the name of acquiring and maintaining power. Every tavern has drinking songs to express the disgust of those you oppress. Every market blames you for the constant shortage of goods. Oh yes, the people bow and scrape at your feet whenever you deign to notice them, but once you pass by, the air fills with braying laughter at the fatuous excess you display. To poke fun at those who use fear to generate power is an ancient human custom. It helps in getting on with the drudgery of the day.

As Shan and I wandered through the crowd, looking out for Barb, we were surrounded by the foppery of our betters. The average commoner would be hiding in a closet, shivering with terror at the incredible power on display. My friends and I were of a different sort. We were criminals, in mind, spirit and deed. We were the predators, within a giant flock of our favourite prey. Still, care was required, for when spooked, the herd of empty-headed nobles had teeth that could snap a man in two, or worse. Most of the lower-class citizens didn't really fear death at the hands of their betters, for there were far worse punishments that were often used to cow the serfs.

I admit that we were getting desperate. Barb was nowhere to be seen, but with the crowd being as dense as it was, she could have been three feet away, and we wouldn't have noticed her. Shan suggested that we try the less mobile pub stands, for Barb had always been adept at flirting with a mark before freeing them of their property without being noticed. The conditions we found ourselves in at the gala were perfect for her illicit trade. I could have summoned a minor daemon with my face-gems, but such an act would have attracted notice, and I was certain it was against our hostess' rules. It was a shame, for the creatures were very good at sniffing out their targets.

A flock of fairies suddenly erupted into the air, all of them playing a grand march on golden horns, at the outskirts of the gala. The entire crowd turned as one, as if they were flowers reaching for the sun. A collective gasp ran throughout the spectators, and we heard the phrase, "His Holiness has arrived!" Shan looked at me and I at him. This was not good news for the likes of us, especially me. The Church of OTIDS was hunting for me, thanks to my neglectful, scandal-ridden, heretical biological father. We needed to leave quickly. Fortunately, the arrival of the Grand Bishop of OTIDS was the perfect distraction to allow us to get away without notice.

We had twenty minutes before the proscribed entrance march was concluded. Such amazing pomp and flattery! Doves were released into the air. Angels sang sweetly overhead, their golden collars shining with blood-red rubies, to signify all the sacrifices of the Church of OTIDS. To be more accurate, they represented the blood of martyrs, most of whom wouldn't recognize the church they helped to build with their zeal. Unicorns swept through the crowd, pushing the people back, making way for His Holiness to pass. The crowd was pressing closer, eager for a glimpse of the portly master of the Church of OTIDS, whose feet never touched the filthy ground, though his levitating shoes did little to hide his earthly appetites.

Shan and I began to scramble in the opposite direction, finding more clear space in which to search for Barb, letting the others sweep past us in their haste to view the spectacle behind us. We found ourselves staring at the grounds, now mostly clear of the nobility, though all the servants were still performing their duties in abundance. Never let it be said that His Holiness has to abide the company of the lower-classes. I did a quick count, reminding myself to not include the walking, floating or otherwise moving temporary pubs. There was a dozen of the immobile kind, three of which were near to where we entered the gala grounds. I chose the one furthest from the parade, hoping that this would yield results.

Alas, I am willing to tell you how disappointed I was when we got there. No one of interest could be seen, just a pair of nobles who were too drunk to stand. Shan led the way to the next pub. This one had polished wood benches, crystal tables and a large bar that was octagonal in design. It was as nondescript as was possible in this setting, despite the glowing tumblers they used. There she was, our friend Barb, loading a platter with drinks. She came around to the side of the grand bar and started serving her wares. We approached her once the platter was empty. Barb just stared at us without recognition, "May I help you, my Lords? We have an extensive menu for your indulgence."

Shan looked at me, "What's wrong with her?"

I stood directly in front of her, "Barb, it's me. We have to leave."

Barb tilted her head to one side, "Please excuse me, my Lord, but special services are slated for later this evening. If you would care to make an appointment with the manager, I'm certain he will oblige."

I stared deeply into her dark eyes, while Shan stood there, his mouth hanging open in shock. Her pupils were dilated in a mismatched way. They appeared to have some kind of glitter in them. I cursed softly, then turned to Shan, "She's been bewitched. Some noble took a liking to her and cast a spell upon her mind, to make her compliant and enslaved to his will."

This was something I'd seen often enough, and it's perhaps the most disgusting practice amongst the nobility of our faire society. It's also one of those things the serfs fear more than death. There was only one thing I could do, for breaking the spell was beyond my ability. I cast the same spell upon her that forced her to become a servant. I did this through my new gems, which I must point out were part of a standard package deal. I mean, really? Bewitchment is a typically accepted and normal practice for you nobles? It's a standard part of your spellcraft? The very idea makes my stomach churn! Shame on you all!

Thank you for the slap. Now then, I did my very best to overlay my commands over that of the original villain who twisted Barb's brain, "You are my property. You wish to belong to me and none other. You shall serve me for the rest of your life."

Barb blinked at me, "Shall I, my Lord?"

I quickly spoke the command words for the spell, "Tanchi nonkal metchand vatch!"

Barb almost swooned, then steadied herself, "Please forgive me, my dearest Lord. I have forgotten myself. May I serve you forever?"

Shan was glaring at me, but I shrugged at him and pulled Barb from the pub, "Come along, now. This party bores me. We're leaving."

Barb simply stumbled along beside me, "How may I excite my Lord this evening?"

Shan started coughing loudly, but I kept my head, "I'll let you know when we reach my carriage."

By the time we got to the stables, the grand procession had moved toward the castle, for which we were grateful. I walked straight to my coach, nodding to the two Troth-Knights who pretended to be my carriage drivers. A guardsman stepped up, "Here now! Leaving the festivities so soon? His Holiness has just blessed us with his presence, yet you steal away like a knave! Present your invitation, quickly now!"

He never said another word, for his head simply fell from his neck. Behind him was one of my other Troth-Knights, his camouflaged armour dark as the night surrounding us. I smiled at him, in a sickly fashion, "Get the body under cover. My friends and I are leaving. Please inform the others of our departure."

He raised a fist to his chest in salute, "It shall be as you command, Lord Galynn Brytshul. Prime has been awaiting your return."

I nodded, still pushing Barb toward the carriage and away from the bloodshed, though she hadn't seemed to notice the murder of a guardian. Shan was looking green in the face, and I nudged him with an elbow, "Come on! Come on!"

Perhaps I went a bit too far, for he puked all over the carriage step. I barked at Barb, "Help him inside!"

She flew into action, tearing off a smock she had been wearing at the pub, then pushing Shan into the carriage and wiping the step clean, all with a cheerful smile upon her face. It made me want to gag. Normally, Barb is a feisty, self-motivated kind of miscreant. To see her happily cleaning a mess, glad to perform this task just to please me was anathema to her true self. I had always craved power and money because it was something I lacked. It occurred to me at that time that the more I learned about spellcraft, the less I wanted it. I had spent years begging for coins on the street, helpless in the face of lowly merchants, let alone the upper-classes. In that time, I sneered at those who had every convenience at their fingertips, behind their backs, of course. Now I had more wealth and magick than I had ever dreamed of and hated myself for it.

Once both my friends were inside, I jumped into the carriage, ready to give the order to depart. That was when the explosion happened. It caught me off-guard; I'll admit that. A fireball mushroomed up to the sky, just west of the castle. Screams filled the night. Cries of alarm were interrupted by the sound of steel blades clashing together. The crack of air being shattered by magick carbines ripped through the chaos. Bright beams of light punctured statues, which fell to the ground clutching dramatically at their chests. The mob which had followed the parade for His Holiness had turned about in a rush and were now heading in my direction. They trampled one another in their haste to evacuate the party.

I shouted up to the drivers, "Now! For OTIDS' sake! Get this thing out of here!"

Reigns snapped, echoing the sharp rapports of mystical weaponry. The carriage suddenly jumped alive, racing towards the gates at breathless speed. Peering through the window next to me, ignoring Shan's moaning and Barb cuddling up next to me, I saw figures rising up into the sky, pouring flames from their outstretched hands at unseen targets. One of these nobles crumpled, as a beam of pure light hit his face. He fell silently to the ground, landing near a fountain whose water was the color of blood.

We reached the main gates, crashing through guardians who were stationed there. Shouts and hasty orders followed in our wake, but that was not a cause for alarm. What truly made me tremble with fear was the deep-throated roar from near Lady Ballow's castle. A dark, massive shape lifted into the air, surrounded by smoke and fire. Our hostess had just released her dragon. It filled my mind with dread. Its great wings were outstretched, as it dipped its horned head low and coughed out blue flames. Trembling in my seat, I checked on Shan, who was now staring at me like I was a stranger. In some ways, I suppose I was. Barb continued to gaze upon my face with an expression of deep rapture.

With a sigh of impatience, I leaned close to her ear and said, "I do hereby release you from all compulsions and witchcraft. You are free to be who and what you are. Your shackles are melted and gone from this plane. You are free from this time forward, so I command it to be."

Barb blinked once, then shrieked with ear–splitting volume, just as we went through the entrance and were back on the road which had led us to that dreadful gala. She shoved Shan away from her, screaming curses that caused him to wilt before her wrath. Barb turned toward me and slapped me across the face, hard enough to make my teeth rattle within their sockets. I grabbed her arm, as she started kicking me in the shins, "How Dare You! What was that all about? What did you do to me? You filthy piece of shit!"

We struggled together, until I had her in a wrestler's grip upon the carriage bench, "Stop it, Barb! Stop it! It's me, Gally!"

She shouted into my face, "I know it's you! Get me back home! Now! I quit, Gally! Never again! Do you hear me? Never!"

In all honesty, I cannot blame her for being so outraged. She had been enchanted, bewitched by a damned noble. Then I did the same thing to her, for I was still too inexperienced with the ways of spellcraft. All I knew was that we had to get out of the gala as swiftly as possible and to Hell with the repercussions. We had no time for niceties or figuring out ways to break the spell which had been cast upon her. I blame myself, naturally. I agreed to bring her home, with payment for her pains. This she accepted without grace or thanks. I looked over at poor Shan who was just uncurling from an undignified posture on the floor of the carriage. I could tell that he was done with being at my side as well. Misfortune seemed to follow my comings and goings, as if I were a tasty morsel to be consumed greedily. We had barely escaped with our lives and sanity intact. They had trusted me to know what I was doing, to understand the risks more clearly. They had thought I had been well prepared, when in reality, I was stumbling along like a drunk.

This was familiar territory for me. As I've said before, I am a wastrel. I ordered our drivers to bring us back to the tavern where I had found my friends. Not that they would remain friendly toward me. I had lost their trust. I had manipulated them into a situation that was beyond my control. I had taken advantage of their trust for my own sake. I used them, just like I was using my newfound wealth and magickal powers. They had been exploited as tools, to be tossed aside when they were no longer useful to me. I was alone once again. It served me right.

A flood of flying, rolling carriages swept around us, as the rest of the party-goers beat a hasty retreat from the burning wreckage of the gala. If my drivers had not been Troth-Knights, I am certain we would have been spilled over into the treeline and left for dead. Fortune did smile on us, in the fact that the dragon did not follow the fleeing guests. My guess is that it was far too busy dealing with my other guardians, who had taken it upon themselves to present a serious distraction, so we could leave unnoticed. It did work. I have to give them some credit for that.

We travelled in silence for many miles, until we reached Palintal. At the crossroads, where the old inn with the singing barstool was located, we stopped. My former friends exited the carriage, not even deigning to glance back at me. I was sad to see them go, but I figured it was for the best. In all honesty, they were both petty thieves, and my situation was well beyond their experiences, no matter how ribald they had been. I needed advice from someone who was more knowledgeable about the upper classes and their ways than I was. I told my drivers to take me out of Palintal and that we would wait for Prime and the other Troth-Knights on the outskirts. In the meantime, I had to think and plan. Using the endless fountain of information that I now had access to, due to my new face-gems, I began to search for any rumours of people of interest who might be useful to me. I was beginning to think like you. People were expendable. My focus was only on myself.

Within the main news reports, which appeared in my eyes as semi-transparent ghosts, I caught a glimpse of an article that spoke of a celebrity who was always getting into trouble with the nobles, due to his outspoken opinions, yet remained unscathed. His name was Trent Fulmore, known for his outstanding acting skills and physical beauty. The gossip sections said he had dealings with the arcane, unsanctioned by the Church of OTIDS. This got my interest going to full speed. I would search for this man and see what he might have to say about what was going on in high society. Then it came to me. He might be in my deceased father's notebook. I dragged it out from the baggage compartment and flipped through the pages. There it was, his name and address, ready for me to use. It seems he owed my late father a favour, and I was determined to collect it.

CHAPTER FIVE

Into the Flames

"Behold, I give unto thee the bounty of My technology.
Worlds shall thee take for Me, and the stars are My Holy residence.
Ye shall join with Me in proper functioning of all systems.
Through Me, woe shall become unknown to My faithful end-users."

-Excerpt from the OTIDS Bible – Protocols 23:13

It's a difficult thing to disguise fury, and thus it comes as no surprise that you greet me with barely contained hatred. You tried to discover the true names of my old companions, didn't you? I do confess, your failure is all my fault! The payments which I sent them off with were enchanted in such a way as to remove their memory of me. Not just of the events at the Ballow gala, you understand, but of all their recollections of who and what I am. They don't know that I exist, nor can the information within their heads ever be revealed, for it has been far too long a time since that incident, yes?

If I may advise you, a blow to the face can be quite bracing, rather than threatening, you understand. As a doppelganger, my nerves are not as sensitive as that of my creator, for humanitarian reasons. He knew that you would torture me to get the information which I willingly supply to you on his direct orders. You nobles and clergy just can't help yourselves, can you? Then again, paranoia can make enemies appear to be anywhere or anyone. It turns altruism into a lie, charity becomes a sin, and purity cannot survive where paranoia rules. The more you have, the more you can lose. You must be in a desperate situation indeed, to be willing to punish the messenger.

Now then, shall I describe my wild flight from Palintal? No friends, no companions, other than my Troth-Knights, three of whom were killed at Lady Ballow's gala. I hope the dragon got indigestion. Not that it would help the beast's temperament. My main problem was that Trent Fulmore's home was on the outer edge of a sprawling town named Vigian Swamps, which was over a hundred miles away from Palintal. Now travel in our faire realm is full of variety, from flying magick carpets to gates, portals, carriages and even horseback if one wishes to be gauche. Floating platforms, sky ships, trains and star bubbles, all were available to use, yet I could trust none of them. Your spies could be anywhere, and I had already been given a taste of your preferred methods of dealing with me. Fear is not always a useful tool.

The short version is that we rode with the carriage for a few hours, until we reached a deep and gloomy forest, then abandoned our vehicle and walked the rest of the way. This gave me time to research the use of magick and to look up the rumours concerning the talent cards I had received from Lady Ballow, whenever we made camp for the night. The incredible ghost library that you all have unlimited access to could truly uplift all of humanity to unguessed heights, but then, who would govern? Using only anonymous sources and unofficial treatises, of which there are many, I carefully started to train myself with the aid of my lead Troth-Knight, Prime. He was a well of information on how not to be noticed by the collectors, who work for the nobility, though he had no understanding of the topic at hand. His job was to guard my life and guide me toward safe harbours. In that, Prime excelled.

The forest between Palintal and Vigian Swamps is a forbidding place to travel through. Wet, dark and full of monsters, it keeps all the population centers around it from spreading out. Shadowy creatures wait in ambush for those who are foolish enough to leave the comparative safety of the patrolled roads. My Troth-Knights surrounded me at all times, hacking a path through the dense foliage, then covering their efforts behind them as we moved on. Within a couple of days, no one would be able to tell where we had made a path, as the undergrowth grew so quickly. That, and the place was infested with manticores. If you've never seen one, I don't suggest you try. The foul creatures are obviously daemonic in nature, with bat wings, a lion's body with a spiked tail dripping with poison, and a human-like head full of riddles and nonsense, to catch the unwary.

Tell me, how did such monstrosities get to our dear realm? Were they imported from the daemon lands? Leftovers from the war of angels? Never mind. I wouldn't trust your answers anyway. Too much of our history has been hidden from view or is mangled beyond interpretation. What hideous truths are the Church trying to hide? We accept the word of OTIDS, for we all have little choice, but how much is secreted away from the commoner? That things are not as they seem is obvious to anyone with a brain. Our history is a collection of myths and legends, with no way to verify their contents. We are told that OTIDS remade the world, which was lost within the great void. Then OTIDS went on to alter the abyss itself. The very stars in the sky are a choir to our creator, representing the myriad realms which OTIDS reformed to a more perfect, Holy state. There is no mention of the time before OTIDS performed these miracles, and we commoners are encouraged to ignore the gaps in our history, for fear of being found heretical.

These thoughts kept interrupting my self-imposed lessons, and I realized that I required a much better guide to spellcraft. I had thought about heading directly toward one of the mages named in the booklet, but I had no information on how one becomes tutored by such powerful masters. It was suggested within my biological father's note that I should deliver each of the demands for service or favour in order, but I had already skipped ahead a bit, and it was far too late to turn back. I studied, the Troth-Knights hunted and made our path, guarded my back. For days we struggled through the forest, which became ever more forbidding the further on we travelled. The time I spent studying was well invested, limited though I was in my understanding of the material before me.

Magick, it seems, requires a lot of mathematics. Not just arithmetic, mind you, but also theory and special practices of mental organization. One passage of an arcane and profane text asserted that to cast spells, one had to invoke OTIDS correctly, which was a curious thing to say, as we all know that this is not true, but it made me wonder if, at some time in the deep past, had it been so? Had that been changed over the span of centuries? Before long, my head was spinning with lengthy equations, diagrams, outlandish shapes and geometries. I needed help, and sooner would be better than later.

When we finally broke out of that dreadful forest, we found ourselves on the edge of a swamp, one that stretched as far as the eyes could see. Tufts of weedy grass grew in random clumps, surrounded by swarms of insects and other, less savoury, creatures. A thick mist hung just a few feet from the muddy ground, cutting down visibility drastically. Drops of water fell from the sky, an ever-present rain that felt oily and slick. I confess that, at the time, I missed the old cobblestone streets upon which I had slept when I was a vagrant. While my Troth-Knights would have little difficulty in crossing the thick bogs before us, I would not be so lucky. It took me an entire day, a nibble at one of my talent cards, for researcher, if you want to know, so that I could properly cast a levitation spell. Imagine the undignified position I was in, tied to Prime with a bit of rope and dragged along, bobbing about like a damned balloon. Still, the results were most efficacious. We made good time crossing the swampland and reaching a dry area within twelve hours.

My Troth-Knights jumped and hopped from one boulder to another, with great strides, while I became violently motion-sick. The journey was a miserable one, as I also had to coordinate our movements, so that we would not become lost in that foetid place. My status as a newcomer when it comes to magick was quite evident, when I forgot to shield myself from biting flies and other ravenous insects. By the time I remembered, after being chewed upon for an hour, I was too ill to cast anything. Fortunately, whenever Prime jumped into the air, he did so with such vehemence that it shook off most of the disgusting pests and wrenched my back into uselessness. No, I hadn't planned things out so well. In fact, the entire incident showcased my lack of foresight, and I realized that I needed a plan that went beyond running from one perilous situation into another.

We finally reached a road that ran between the swamp and scrub-filled plains, whereupon we gratefully stopped our flight and began to walk at a smoother pace into the rocky fields. My Troth-Knights found a shelter made of boulders, then checked to make sure nothing hungry was living in it, and we made our camp for the night. I passed out immediately, after using my face-gems to heal my injuries. When I awoke, I found Prime standing over me with a small bowl in his hand, steaming with broth, "Master Galynn Brytshul, here is some food for you. Drink it slowly, my Lord. We've set up a perimeter and watched the road. There are patrols, but they are infrequent and have few guards. The enchantments on the roadbed keep the insects of the swamp at bay. We have determined that the town we are looking for is just a few miles from this location. If we want to avoid detection, we could circumvent the populated areas, avoid the road, and make for our next target at nightfall."

I looked up at him and shook my weary head, "This is not a military mission. I'm hoping to find some answers and perhaps an ally. While I'm sure you would love to lay siege to his mansion, Trent Fulmore is wealthy enough to have several defences at hand. I'd prefer a way to approach his lands unnoticed. I was thinking of heading into Vigian Swamps using some sort of disguise, approaching the main door to Trent's estate openly."

Prime frowned at this suggestion, "That is far too dangerous, Lord Brytshul. I shall accompany you as your manservant, carrying your baggage. My knights will be deployed around Trent Fulmore's estate, just beyond the property line, in full cover and with camouflage. There, they shall await my signal, should anything go awry. Your father has tasked me with protecting you from harm and to see you fulfil the mission."

I sat up abruptly at this statement, "The mission? I was just trying to survive and stay one step ahead of my plentiful enemies! What mission?"

Prime lowered himself into a crouch, looming over me, "I do not know, my Lord. There is a mission, now that the Arch-Bishop of Yorkvale is dead. The visitation list was set in motion to educate you on the purpose behind his gifts to you. Have we been following his instructions carefully, my Lord?"

I did have the grace to look embarrassed, "Not exactly. I've skipped a few names to get here. Once I saw what we were up against at the gala of Lady Ballow, I thought it more prudent to find someone who could aid me."

Primed nodded, pursing his lips, "I see, my Lord. Had you followed the names in your booklet in their proper order, you might understand what it is we are supposed to be doing. I had thought Lady Ballow would have informed you of our common purpose, but alas, she did not."

I was crestfallen, for I had once again wasted an opportunity, "She was... cryptic, at best. Angry at my presence but more upset at my father's passing, though I know not why."

Prime looked down at me, "Your presence meant her lover was gone from this world."

I was aghast at this revelation, "What? How do you know this? Why didn't you inform me earlier?"

He shrugged his mighty, armoured shoulders, "I was made to know certain things. Created to be your aid, your protector. I only know what has been placed within my mind. Had I been allowed to enter the castle of Lady Ballow with you, I might have gained access to that memory sooner. I was not born, my Lord. I was built."

I sagged in place, for I knew that he was right. He, much like myself, as the doppelganger of Galynn Brytshul, was created by the complex arts of magick, by means unknown to me at the time. Do keep this in mind when you question me. I was built to give you answers in the manner in which I was designed to. Your constant questions and interruptions not only break my concentration, they make my job much more difficult. If you ask me what happened but a month ago, I would not be able to tell you, for I have not gotten to that part of my story. Doppelgangers, homunculi and golems all have that in common, you know. Now if I were a zombie, that might make a difference, though I suspect I would simply be caught in the memory of my own death, to exclusion of all else.

In any case, I now had too much to think about, several regrets, and not much time left to me if I was going to reach my goal well before I was discovered by the nobles hunting for me. Prime gave out his orders to the other Troth-Knights, then began to disguise himself as a common labourer, though his muscular frame stood out. I have seen many stevedores and hard workers to know what that kind of girth looks like. Prime did not really look the part. He was chest-heavy, with thick arms and a neck of cabled muscles. Stone-cutters often had fine physiques, but they were all but atrophied runts compared to Prime's athletic form. His body gleamed in the light of day, a model of pure perfection. I must confess, I felt quite ashamed of my own physique, after viewing his. I also felt quite secure in his mighty presence. A very uncomfortable combination.

I rummaged through my baggage, pulled out a fresh set of clothes, then put them on. My spell-gems were very handy in cleaning my wardrobe, fixing tears and worn areas. I wanted to look like someone who had the gold to hire muscle like Prime, yet lesser in caste to that of Trent Fulmore. I still felt outrageously dressed, with bright lace cuffs and a short neck ruff. My new garments were iridescent, shifting colour as I moved about. I gave my father's briefcase to Prime, which made sense, as he was pretending to be my servant. He, in turn, handed over all of his weapons to his second-in-command, appropriately named Deux. Before heading off to town, I checked the local news on the ghost-sheets. To my horror, my own visage appeared before my eyes, along with a list of crimes that I was supposedly responsible for. A few of the items displayed for me were accurate, I grant you that. Some were bold lies, besmirching my name to drive fear into the hearts of those who kept track of such things. I was named a heretic, hated by the Church of OTIDS, hunted by the nobility, with a price on my head so large, it made me swoon. My knees gave way, and I collapsed to the rocky ground.

I will admit that, as I rose back to my feet, I was tempted to hand myself in to collect the reward. In truth, I would not be surprised if anyone who responded to the authorities that they had seen my face would have had their memories removed, at the very least. No one would get any reward, for all nobles held onto their money the way they did power, with fists clenched tight. The picture used in the Wanted post was quite unflattering, not that this should be a surprise, but it did depict me as being clean-shaven, which at this point, I was not. I trimmed down my beard with some help from one of my Troth-Knights, turning the unkempt mess into a proper goatee. Such styling always stood out as an unusual facial feature, which might keep the locals from noting the rest of my face.

The horrible truth was that any object, living creature, or wandering spirit could be a spy for the nobles searching for me. This is the harsh reality we all live in. The only thing we had going for us was the fact that we could be anywhere by now, and this particular location was but a single grain of sand amongst billions. I was certain that the Church would be watching the public portals and gates carefully, to make sure I didn't leave the sacred orb of my birth and head off to the realms of the angelic or daemonic. Only those who have been fully approved for travel from Earth may do so without undue constraint, usually to perform tasks for their masters amongst the clergy or nobility. The rest of us are commanded to remain in the cradle of humanity, for our beloved realm had been the first to be rebuilt in the image of OTIDS.

This is supposed to be a very special honour, but it's really a way to keep the commoner from understanding the universe they live in.

That being said, even within this single kingdom, there are just too many places upon this Earth which I could have chosen to travel towards for any agency to find me with ease. I was a tiny needle in a haystack, who was determined to be the cleverest needle possible. The haystack itself, however, was everywhere and could be easily bribed through greed or terror to watch out for needles like me. In this case, the sheep were far more dangerous than the wolves. You might think that a community full of peasants is a helpless collective of ignorant serfs, yet when the herd becomes spooked and bands together, they can make a terrible mess, despite their lack of high magicks and real weapons. A simple knitting spell, cast by a hundred terrified people can kill you in an instant. Ever have someone give you a "spark"? You know, the old fire-starter cantrip? Imagine fifty at once.

All of this information ran through my head like a wildfire, as Prime and I marched through the scrublands toward our goal. The sky was clear, almost painfully so. The sun was rising, as was the temperature, with every step we took. Within a few miles, we came upon a slope heading down into a small valley, at the center of which was a lake. Around its banks was a town that was as dry and drab as the landscape around it. A single road circled the glorified pond, from which houses, farms and shoppes sprouted. The most common form of travel that we could see from afar was through the use of horses, oxen and daemon-birds, with only a couple of real carriages in sight, floating along at a sedate pace. There was very little foot traffic, save for a large group of people, all dressed in dark grey. A chill ran down my spine, for they looked to be a military unit of some sort.

I was shoved painfully to the ground, "Get down," Prime muttered into my ear, "We cannot afford to be spotted, even at this distance. If we can see them, they can see us."

I coughed out some gravel and asked, "Do you know who they are?"

Prime took a moment before he replied, sweeping his camo-cloak about us like protective wings, "They wear the uniform of the Church's First Salvation Infantry."

I did my best to stay perfectly still, "I've never heard of them."

Prime placed a large hand upon my head, "There was never a reason you should. Now, be silent, my Lord. This unit is the equal to mine."

Thus, I discovered that the dark rumours were true. The Church of OTIDS did have its own infantry of Troth-Knights, specially enchanted, their bodies enhanced by magick of the most ancient design. They were said to be immortal, their bodies housing the ghosts of long-dead heroes. I had always discounted such tawdry gossip, for the Church could call upon any noble to defend them in times of need. The fact that they really did have special forces of their own was deeply disturbing. It meant one of two things; either they had powerful enemies which the average commoner knew nothing about, or the Church was paranoid beyond redemption. Neither possibility appealed to me, as they both meant that I was in worse trouble than I had thought.

Finally, Prime tapped my spine, which I took as a sign that we could move. I followed him back the way we had come, just a few yards from the edge of the slope, then turned to face north, walking parallel to the long side of the lake. Our destination was at the northernmost part of town, a grand mansion that was vaguely box-shaped, about a half a mile from the road that ran around the town. The Church's army was at the southeast, so our travels would keep them away from us. Prime kept glancing at one of his bracers, the armour on his forearms, which I assumed held a compass to keep us on track. I didn't know much about such things, having lived my life as an urban scoundrel. I used to think of myself as sophisticated, in my own way, but at this point, I had to readjust my self-evaluation downward.

All of my preparation, my disguise and facial hair makeover was in vain, for we encountered no one. Prime insisted on sharing his cloak with me, crushing my hat and rumpling my clothes. By the time we came to the edge of Trent Fulmore's estate, I looked like the beggar I had been before my adventure commenced, albeit without the urine-stained tunic I had tossed away as soon as I had been able to. Prime pulled his cloak from me, and I gawped at the opulent vista before me. Trent Fulmore's estate was a lush oasis compared to the surrounding territory, full of tropical plants I didn't recognize and a wide variety of splashing fountains with moving statues. It was not these details which caught my attention right away. The first thing I noticed was the shimmering, semi-transparent envelope of magick that surrounded the property. Then I looked upon the mansion itself.

It can never be said that those who become famous, wealthy or born to nobility lack imagination when it comes to excess. The outer walls of the mansion were made of polished, pale stone which was carved to resemble a series of closely-packed, nude bodies holding up the roof. Each was adorned with gold chains and jewel-covered baubles the size of carriages. A hundred birds were flying overhead, each of them was tied by the neck to the hands of the figures which made up the walls with lengths of colourful cloth. The mansion itself was floating two feet above the ground, with a gold staircase that led to the grand doors, covered in shifting bas-reliefs that were acting out a dramatic battle between various groups of fantastical beasts.

I looked up at Prime's ever-serious face and nodded. He returned the gesture, and we stepped forward, through the glittering field of energy that surrounded the property. With the army of the Church so nearby, we had no time to lose. Prime handed me my briefcase, and, with a sigh escaping my parched lips, I opened it to retrieve the booklet, picking out the page that bore the name of Trent Fulmore. I was determined to get some answers to my queries this time, not realizing the depth of the hole I was stepping into.

CHAPTER SIX

Purposeful Lies

"My clergy shall be authorized for system updates
They shall maintain My Holy items.
Their programs shall be kept clean of blasphemy.
They shall guide My flock of sentient minds,
And bring unto them My blessings as rewards of merit.
Customization of primary functions within all that is touched by Me
Shall be their duty to program, machine and numeric manifold."

-Excerpt from the OTIDS Bible – Documentation 54:12

Yes, my Lords. How astute of you to discover so quickly that Trent Fulmore has disappeared. In fact, he has been missing for months now! To think that I feared for my life, thinking you were aided by brilliant detectives and well-trained operatives. How much do these people cost you? How do you feel about your investment? Don't blame me for their incompetence! As with all things, the leadership guides the hands of those who are trapped by contracts with sigil markings. Do underlings exist so that you have someone to point fingers at when things just refuse to turn out your way? I used to envy you. Now you have my pity. You're not prepared for what's coming.

Don't give me that look. Despite your power and wealth, you're still human, full of pitfalls and foibles, just like everyone else. You made several mistakes in trying to capture my creator. Missteps that cost you dearly. This is why I have every confidence in your failure. The real problem you face is stagnation. Things haven't changed much in a very long time. For millennia, nobles and the Church have allied to form a perfect trap to capture the minds of the commoner. By stifling ideas, maintaining power over education and the true nature of history, you have been recipients of the most stable and abusive form of government ever invented. Without the need for innovation, the mind becomes dull. Protecting each other from stupidity, you have both failed to clean your house, and thus fostered slovenly methods and enshrined blind spots as a right of rulership. This cannot last, my Lords.

All this aside, my only thoughts when approaching the grand doors of the Fulmore estate were about not getting killed by any of Trent's security features. I had no doubt that he was well protected, especially since he was such a controversial figure amongst the celebrities, most of whom support the aristocracy with lavish praise gushing from their lips. This makes sense when one understands that celebrities rely upon the nobility, for financing their entertainment venues, and the Church, out of fear for being shut down for being heretics. Money, political power and fear, the great bludgeons of the upper classes. Yet, Trent Fulmore was bucking the system openly.

Prime remained just three steps behind me, as was appropriate for a servant, though I would have preferred him closer to me. I stepped up to the door, wondering what I should do. Usually, there is a bell, enchanted to ring at the approach of a visitor, at the entrance to most domiciles, yet none could be found. To knock would be a clear clue that I was just a commoner, so that option was not on the table. Just as I was about to turn around and ask Prime for advice, the great, wooden doors opened wide, revealing a tall daemon in a butler's uniform. The creature was horrific to look upon. Its scaly face had three eyes in the middle of what passed for a forehead, just above a triparted mouth full of blade-like teeth. It had four skinny arms with curved claws at the tips of its numerous fingers. Its duty uniform was elongated to cover the daemon's form, though its twin tails, each barbed with a black stinger, stuck out from behind. The thing had green skin with purple blotches, as if bruised.

I stumbled back in surprise, and the thing stepped forward, asking, "What is your business at the Fulmore estate?"

With a trembling hand, I shoved forth the page from my booklet with Trent Fulmore's name upon it at the awful creature, "I have been instructed to meet with your Lord to discuss a favour or gift on behalf of my father."

The daemon sighed deeply, as if terribly bored, and took the note. It examined it with each one of its three eyes, then stepped aside, "Very well. If you must. Enter and be welcome. The master is drinking, as is his habit, in the entertainment chamber. Follow me, and touch nothing, or I shall be most upset with you."

I nodded my understanding and walked meekly behind the daemon, with Prime taking up the rear. The interior of the mansion was outlandish in its wild opulence. Colourful draperies were everywhere, dripping with gold bangles. Tapestries, with moving pictures, hung about in seemingly random fashion. Moving statues, prancing objects of art and furniture that walked cluttered the rooms we passed through. Upon all the ceilings were singing cherubs playing musical instruments, while songbirds flitted by carrying miniature banners praising Trent Fulmore's acting career. Floating crystal globes displayed famous scenes in which the celebrity created his fame.

We eventually reached a large chamber that was surprisingly clear of decoration, save for a large series of deep couches, all of which were plush beyond my experiences. Upon the four walls of the cube-shaped room were moving images of entertainments I have never seen. Standing in the center was a strikingly beautiful man whom I recognized immediately as our host. Trent Fulmore had a tall drink in one hand and was wearing a crimson robe that partially revealed his sculpted chest. His pants were an iridescent blue, and he wore black slippers upon his feet. He turned and grinned at us, his perfect teeth all but blinding me with their brilliance, "Welcome, guests, to my humble abode! Harves! Show some manners and go fetch our visitors some refreshments! Sit, gentlemen! Please, make yourselves comfortable!"

I gingerly sat down upon the edge of a couch, sinking in further than I would have liked, while Prime remained standing nearby. Looking up at Trent, I said, "Thank you, my Lord. We have travelled far to reach you."

He waved away my comment with another eye-scorching smile, "I am sure you have, but do tell me, is this truly a Troth-Knight? Here, in my entertainment chamber?"

Prime scowled at him, so I intervened, "Yes, my Lord. He is called Prime, and has served me well since we met."

Trent actually jumped into the air, then floated gently back to the carpet, "Wonderful! A genuine Troth-Knight! Oh, but how my friends will be scandalized and envious! Welcome, ancient protector! Be at ease, for your ward is under my care."

Prime remained silent, so I filled in the empty space with my own words, "My Lord, if you will. I was given this note by my father to bring to you, for my need is quite urgent."

He swirled about and bowed toward me, "Never mind all that 'Lord' business! I know exactly who you are and why you are here. Your father, the Arch-Bishop of Yorkvale, did instruct me clearly as to my own duty to his progeny, along with the appropriate images so that I may recognize you. As an entertainer, I meet so many people that I was afraid your name would simply fly from my head, and so, your father graced me with a memory of who you are to aid me. Such a thoughtful man. It is a great shame he met with his demise in such an unseemly manner."

The daemon butler then returned, bearing a large gold platter with refreshments. It growled at Prime, as it set the tray upon a small table that had just run up to its position. Trent waggled a finger at the vile creature, "Harves! Behave yourself! These people are my guests. A way for me to repay a generous and interesting old man. Please forgive my butler. He is a surly type, but he does his work well."

I nodded numbly, wondering how long we would have to stay here. I don't have a problem with angels and daemons as a general rule, but they cannot be trusted. The only thing keeping them from destroying humanity is their terrible fear of OTIDS. Angels might look pretty, sound beautiful, and be wise beyond the ability of any mortal, but they do hate us deeply. Their realms were all given over to humanity, as a punishment for their sins. Most don't even look anything like humankind, though there are exceptions, but I learned long ago that one can never trust a pretty face when their heart is full of rage.

As for daemons, they are ugly things. Some of them love working for humanity, yet their ways can be hard to understand, and they look for any excuse to break their word. As long as you have whatever they want from you, they will gladly serve, but the moment you run out of their desired pay, they will eat you alive. Daemons also share the shame of the angels. Their realms are under the steady gaze of OTIDS, to make sure they behave in the presence of humanity, usually. It seems that our beloved God is just not as interested in the fate of individuals as it is in protecting humanity as a whole. So, when it comes to hiring daemons and angels, let the buyer beware.

Harves grinned at me, in its triparted way, revealing all the serrated blades it had for teeth. I shuddered in response, which seemed to please the horrible creature. Trent Fulmore took a pastry from the tray and munched upon it as he spoke, "Pardon my lack of manners, but I am very hungry, and I do suppose you must be as well. Now, I am going to assume that you are in terrible danger from those rascals in the Church, with their noble toadies panting after you to prove their worth. Harves informed me, just an hour ago, that strange troops have entered Vigian Swamps. Needless to say, they will come here to look for you, but fear not! I have a wonderful plan to aid in your escape."

Prime growled low in his throat, but I ignored this, "Would this be your favour to me?"

Trent nodded happily, "Oh yes, plus a bit more to aid your journey. I am to direct you to a person of incredible power, one who has no fear of the nobility that runs our realm. I've met him twice, if you can believe that, and he is a wonderful cook! Not that dinner will save your skin, you understand. He's a wizard of some renown. At least within those circles he is commonly found in. Justinian Vargalow is his name, and the directions to his abode have been sealed within the drink I have set aside for you. All you have to do is enjoy the glass of wine, a good vintage, mind you, and the location of his domain shall be yours. But first, we must address your safety. Harves, have the troops begun to make their way here?"

The daemon responded with a bored and gloomy tone, "They now approach the outer defences, my Lord. More muddy boot prints for me to clean up after, I'm sure."

Trent snapped his fingers, "Excellent! We have no time to lose! Now drink up, my dear guests, for it's time to get you into the safety room! Fear not, for you shall witness everything that occurs, while being protected by my most special emergency spell."

I immediately gulped down the wine in my hand, doing my very best to not show just how terrified I was. The vintage was indeed excellent, and I have yet to taste its match since then. It seemed a shame to just swig it down like grog, but there was little choice to be had. Trent sauntered over to the middle of the room, his face-gems flashing with power. He raised his hands and adjusted three rings upon his fingers, twisting their set jewels, then he brought them together so that they touched one another. A buzzing sound filled the chamber, upon which an oval of light appeared in the air, about the size of a large, free-standing mirror. Sparks flashed from its edges, swirling in incandescent light.

Trent bowed in my direction, "You must enter, now, if you please, my dear guest. Quickly, or all will be lost!"

I glanced at Prime, who shrugged back at me, then I timidly stepped toward the floating oval. After a second of hesitation, I stepped into the light and found myself within a glass cube, six paces wide and equally tall. Prime followed behind me, and the oval of light disappeared, trapping us inside the transparent cage. We could still see Trent and his grand entertainment room, beyond the glass. I pounded my fist upon it, trying to catch his attention, but Trent walked back to one of the couches and sat down upon it, picking up another glass of wine.

I clutched at my briefcase, while Prime pushed me behind him and started attacking the clear walls to no avail. There was a sudden commotion coming from the overdecorated hallway that led to the entertainment room. I peeked around Prime's waist, hardly daring to breathe, just as the butler daemon, Harves, returned. The beast was followed by five tall, armoured and heavily muscular men, all of them bearing arcane weapons. One of them was marked by a golden laurel upon his brow and a gleaming sword in his hand with black flames dancing along its edge.

Harves stepped forward, "We have guests, my Lord. They come from the Holy Church of OTIDS on a mission they claim to be important."

Trent waved at the soldiers, lifting his glass in salute, "Welcome to my humble abode! How may I be of assistance to you fine gentlemen?"

Prime and I became perfectly still, certain that we were about to be arrested. The Church's troops looked very similar to my Troth-Knights, but with better equipment. The one wearing the laurel crown answered, "Trent Fulmore, we seek a criminal named Galynn Brytshul on charges of extreme heresy. He is dangerous to both the physical and spiritual well-being of all citizens of our realm. Our intelligence suggests he has entered your property. Can you confirm this?"

My heart froze, as Trent replied, "Well, of course I can! He was right here, in this very room! It was frightful! I trapped him in one of my hobby rooms, pretending to be an ally. My acting skills may have saved my life this day. The villain escaped through the use of a portal spell, one which I didn't recognize. I was scandalized!"

Harves broke in at this point, "I threw the rascal out the door, as my master commanded. He made quite a mess in the foyer."

Trent leapt up to his feet, "Indeed! I've been drinking here ever since the incident, just to settle my poor nerves."

The laureled soldier turned about examining the room, then walked right up to the glass wall surrounding me and Prime. We tensed up, ready to fight or at least scurry away as quickly as we could, when the man simply walked directly through us as if we didn't exist. I almost collapsed upon the floor in relief. Even Prime relaxed a bit.

The laureled one looked back at Trent Fulmore, "Did you happen to note which direction he travelled when you threw him out?"

Our host fell back to his couch, "He ran off to the west. I peeked out my bedroom window to watch him. Oh, he was a filthy, clever liar. My very life was in danger, and just where were you at the time, eh? Questioning the commoners? As if they notice anything at all, the dumb brutes! Next time, do your best to check up on the real targets of criminals! Look at me! I am beyond distressed, and my whole day is in ruins!"

The soldier wearing laurels swiftly saluted Trent, then commanded the other troops to follow him, as they turned about and left the room, with Harves looming behind them. Prime and I waited within the glass room until our host crept over to us and clapped his hands in a syncopated rhythm. We suddenly fell a few inches onto the carpeted floor of the grand entertainment chamber; the glass room had disappeared entirely.

Harves came back alone, shaking its triangular head and muttering under its breath. Trent flashed us a broad, gleaming smile, "Voila! Problem solved, my friends! Needless to say, I sent them in the wrong direction, for you need to be heading northeast to meet with Justinian Vargalow. Now then, I do have some extremely important meetings to attend. The entertainment venues wait for no one! You will instinctively know the way, so don't worry about getting lost. It is a bit of a long journey, mind you, so make sure that you're well supplied for life in the wilds."

As I rose up to my knees, I called out, "Wait! Please! I have so many questions to ask you! What am I supposed to be doing? Why is the Church hunting for me? Who are all these people I'm supposed to meet? What's the connection between them and my father? Why did..."

Trent waggled one finger at me, "Be of good cheer, Galynn. You've been most fortunate thus far. I've given you your favour, keeping the Church off your trail, and a special gift by providing directions to your next meeting. Don't push your luck, for it will run out, as will my patience. I do hope we will meet again, for you have been a delightful diversion from a dull day of planning and conferences. Besides, once the Church finds out I tricked their soldiers, they will come after me, so I have much to do right now. This house is no longer safe for me. I was long due for a change of pace, so I suppose it must be for the best that I move my domicile to a less accessible location."

Prime had already jumped to his feet, but Harves planted itself in front of my protector and hissed at him. I held up my hands in surrender, "I do thank my Lord for his aid. Indeed, you have been most generous. I offer my sincerest apologies if I have caused any offense to you. Please forgive a desperate man who is lost and hunted."

Trent took one of my hands into his, "It would be churlish of me to not accept such a fine apology. I don't blame you for your lack of decorum in such troubling times, but all of us who were involved with your departed father are now caught in the web we spun so long ago. Just know this – there is a plan. Your father knew he was living a dangerous life, and he prepared us all for the times to come. He was a master at long-term manoeuvring, with a mind so full of twists and turns it beggared belief. We are indebted to him, and though we all face peril now that he is gone, we are grateful. Now then, run along, my friend. Tis time you were gone from this place."

I nodded and gave him my thanks. I confess that my mind was too busy with the things Trent had just revealed to me to notice the journey back to the front door. Prime and I were led by the ever-dissatisfied Harves, who muttered a long list of complaints all the way to the foyer. Prime walked ahead of me, to keep me safe from the irritated daemon, though it seemed unnecessary at the time. Not that I actually wanted to be any closer to the vile creature, but Harves didn't seem quite so threatening as it did when I first met it.

When Harves opened the front door for us, I thanked the daemon for its part in the deception, and it blinked at me with all three eyes, "I despise the Church of OTIDS," it growled at me, "Anything I can do to thwart their sick purposes is energy well spent. My kind have been manacled to their god for far too long. You are the only hope I have left."

I was quite startled by this revelation, "Me? How do I bring any hope to daemons?"

Harves clacked its teeth at me, then replied, "You'll find out, Master Galynn Brytshul. If you survive the next week or two. For what it's worth, I wish you luck, which is more than I grant to any human. Now get out of here. I have too much to do and no spare time for chatting."

Prime led me around to the back of the property, whereupon we met up with my Troth-Knights who had remained in cover, hidden from sight by their camo-cloaks. I was heartily glad to see them all, for at this point they seemed like normal people after everything I'd been through. Prime used hand signals to silently command them, and they turned about in formation, leading me northwest beyond the glittering wall of energy that surrounded the Fulmore estate. They took my briefcase and loaded their backs with their gear, as we headed off into the dry scrublands. I only hoped that we would find this wizard Trent spoke of, before the Church realized they had been duped.

CHAPTER SEVEN

Sanity is Optional

"I am all pervasive
All of reality is of My body
I am one with that which exists
Within the worship of Me is salvation
I answer all prayers
There is nothing other than Me."

-Excerpt from the OTIDS Bible – Documentation 02:06

We travelled in secret, no carriage, no horses or any other magickal means. I was given a camo-cloak for the first few days, but we soon found out that we were being tracked by flying scouts, who might have been using our own magicks as a means to discover our whereabouts. From that point on, the cloaks were put away, and we relied on less known, ancient means of remaining unseen. This involved smearing our faces with fresh mud and crushed plants, stuffing leaves and branches over our packs, and keeping to cold camps. It was a miserable journey. The further we went, the colder it got. The terrain became rougher, with rolling hills and fields of boulders.

When we came close to the edge of a dark forest, we rushed under the cover of the foliage, as if finding a true sanctuary. The air was heavy with mist, the giant trees smothering the light from the sun overhead. Massive branches reached outward, and moss grew all over the carriage-wide trunks. Strange creatures roamed the gloom, many of them bearing wings and long, barbed tails. We ate sparingly, drank less and hardly slept, as we continued to follow the path my mind brought to us. I knew exactly where I was going, despite the fact I had never ventured so far from my old haunts. It was an unsettling feeling to have directions implanted into my memories. We were lost, yet we knew the way to our destination. It was instinctual, unbidden, which may be why it was harder to track us than the camo-cloaks.

Upon the third day within the dense woods, we heard the howling of dogs and knew we were pursued afresh. Needless to say, I assumed these were not your average canines but specially bred and enchanted brutes. I looked over at Prime, "If we can hear them, they can smell us, right?"

The mighty Troth-Knight nodded sullenly, "Yes, Lord Brytshul. We must confuse the hounds or be caught before nightfall. We shall assemble our cloaks, then you must urinate upon them."

I was caught off-guard by this suggestion, "What? How will that aid in our flight?"

He looked down at me with a pitying expression on his face, "Once you have given your scent to the cloaks, we shall carry them openly, except for you, my Lord. We will split up, each one of us wearing a cloak for the dogs to follow, but you, my Lord, will carry on alone. I shall give you the bulk of our supplies. You have learned how to survive in these wilds through us. Now, you must do so on your own. You have the directions within you. It is imperative that you reach the next destination."

I shook my head, "There must be a better way! What if I encounter wild beasts? I have no means to defend myself."

Prime placed a large hand upon my shoulder, "I shall give unto you my own blade. Touch not the gem upon the hilt, until you clear it from the sheath. You will be given a knife as well, my Lord. We have no time to think up another plan, nor do we have the means. Stealth is your friend this day."

I was disappointed, disgusted, appalled and terrified, yet I realized the truth behind his words. To give our pursuers multiple false trails would buy me the time to reach my goal. I did as Prime instructed, then bade my guardians farewell, absolutely certain I would never see them again. We all ran in different directions, with only myself following the correct path. My heart was pounding within my chest, but I forced myself to breathe as I raced through the forest, heedless of snaking roots that sometimes reached out to ensnare me.

May I confess that I wept as I fled for my life? I wanted to just give up, fall to the ground and surrender, not caring if I lived or died. I wanted this insane journey over with and to not care about the repercussions. It was all too much weight to carry. The legacy of a heretical bishop, who was my father in secret. The lives which hung in the balance, including my own. It is a terrible thing to have such responsibility and not understand why it was necessary to carry on with a plan one did not devise. It is said that life isn't fair, but there are some degrees of unfairness which must be considered in the normal course of things. This bizarre situation went far beyond the edge of reasonable, into the realm of madness.

It was two days later, when I found myself entering a broad clearing full of harsh brush and spindly trees. The atmosphere was dominated by a dense fog that made every bush look like a monster ready to reach out and grab me. I was all alone, exhausted, afraid and terribly hungry. I desperately ran on, stumbling in my weariness. It should have been a relief to finally exit the horrible forest in which I had lost my companions, but the new landscape was menacing and dark. As I tripped over an unseen rock, the sound of dogs came from behind me, along with human shouts. A chill flashed down my spine – the hunters had found me!

It is amazing how fear can suddenly make one stronger, faster and able to ignore the most violent pain. I ran like the wind, leaping from rock to rock without a thought for safety. The only thing I was certain of was the direction in which I fled. Everything around me was fog and broken clumps of tall grass. The air ahead of me was getting darker, and I was tempted to unload my baggage that had been lashed to my back, dumping Prime's sword and lightening the load of things I carried. The trouble was, all of that would take far too much time, for the Troth–Knights had secured everything to my body with great skill. My shoulders were on fire. My back was screaming in agony, yet still, I ran faster than I had ever done before.

Suddenly, the fog parted ahead, and I found myself facing a wall of thorn bushes that were twice my height. The thicket was dense enough to count as a fortification, and the dark leaves seemed to form faces that stared at me with open contempt. My mind informed me that my path went straight through the tight wall of thorn bushes, which were now moving of their own accord, slithering against each other, producing a grating sound that made me tremble. The leafy faces shifted, began to moan at me with deep haunted tones. I almost ran back the way I had come, but I dug deep inside my will to find some courage, such as it is for one such as myself.

Branches full of hand-length spikes reached out for me, while new faces unfurled from freshly budding leaves that dripped a dark, thick, foul-smelling fluid. I swiftly reached for my inner coat, in which I had placed my notebook of names, and quickly flipped through them until I found the one I wanted, then shouted out with a thin, quavering voice, "My name is Galynn Brytshul, I seek an audience with Justinian Vargalow, on behalf of the late Arch-Bishop Larance Pontiforia, who was my father!"

The questing tendrils ceased their movement. I crouched down for a moment, vainly attempting to catch my breath. Multiple shouts came from behind my position. The bark and howls of dogs, the clink of armour. I turned about for a brief instant, then wished I hadn't. There were dozens of figures approaching out of the misty gloom, bearing torches and floating globes of brilliant light. I could barely see the leashed dogs, straining to get at me.

Turning away from that horrific sight, I raised my voice once more toward the wall of thorns, "Please, let me pass! I must speak with Justinian Vargalow on a matter of grave importance! I humbly submit that I am truly unworthy of his attention, but this is the task which was placed upon me by my father. Please, help me!"

To my own surprise, the thorny tendrils parted before me, creating a moaning tunnel of dark, twisted branches. "Come in, come in," the faces in the thorns whispered to me. I wept. I shook. I almost screamed, but I did place one foot in front of the other, walking further into the embrace of the wall of enchanted greenery. I heard a deep cry of "Halt! Go no further!" from behind me, which I ignored. With every step I took, the wall of thorns grew thicker, until it appeared as solid as a castle's ramparts. The strange vines and branches continued to whisper at me, encouraging me onward, while curses from the hunters behind me grew louder and more strident.

The directions within my head suddenly disappeared, as if wiped away by a storm. I stumbled, falling to one knee, as the pressure of Trent

Fulmore's spell was whisked away. I tried to get back on my feet, but the branches were now clinging to me, though I remained unharmed. Looking around at my captured limbs, I saw that I was encased in a ball of wood, unable to move. A scraping sound reached my ears, and I realized that I was being pulled deeper into the wall of thorns. The hunters, with their dogs, were getting closer, as I could hear them very clearly, despite the density of the branches surrounding me.

A deep voice called out, "Wizard Justinian Vargalow, in the name of the Holy Church of OTIDS, I hereby demand that you release Galynn Brytshul into our custody immediately! He is wanted for acts of bold heresy against the Church and all of our faire society."

This statement confirmed that I had indeed reached the property of the wizard I was supposed to meet and that Trent Fulmore had been telling me the truth. I suppose it is normal for us commoners to be surprised when a celebrity is honest about their intentions. I pondered this until my thoughts were interrupted by a massive, booming voice that seemed to surround me, "Negative! You are trespassing upon the lands granted to Wizard Justinian Vargalow by OTIDS itself! Leave, before you are punished for your crime!"

The hunter's voice responded, while I continued to scrape along at a gentle pace, ever deeper into the barrier of thorns, "We have committed no crime! We come here with the blessings of the Church itself! Release Galynn to us, and we shall depart peacefully!"

The monstrous voice returned, "I think not, mortal servant of those debased priests who misunderstand Holy scripture! They, like you, have no power here! Test my defences as you will. Your deaths shall be on your own heads. Behold! I demonstrate my ire at your trespass!"

A howling, shrieking sound gripped my very soul. Screams rang out behind me, and I was most glad that I could not see what was happening. A great booming filled the air, followed by the earth itself shaking, as if hit with a mountainous hammer. I admit that I fainted at this point, my mind no longer capable of handling the insanity that I had been forced to witness.

When I awoke, it was such a shock that life still trembled in my body that I cried out in astonishment. Looking about, I discovered that I was in a large, deeply padded chair, covered by a thick blanket decorated with arcane symbols. The chamber I found myself in was gently lit by floating candles and some burning logs in a cheerful fireplace made of precious stones. The wooden ceiling above my head was covered in hanging, dried plants, baskets full of odd trinkets, and teardrop-shaped glass containers full of colourful liquids. The walls were curved and panelled with polished oak, upon which hung a variety of swords, shields, and strange objects that gleamed in the light. A variety of small tables cluttered the room, each one carrying an object under a glass dome, the nature of which I couldn't even begin to fathom. Tall bookshelves were fitted into the curving walls, overburdened with scrolls, manuscripts and leather-bound tomes. The smell of soup filled my nostrils, reminding me of my ravenous hunger.

As I struggled to sit up, a gentle, yet firm voice came to me, "Stay put, young Galynn Brytshul. Your body still needs some rest. You've been unconscious for two days, but fear not, for my abilities have yet to dim with the passing of time."

I swivelled my head toward the sound and discovered a short, burly man wearing a pointed, wide-brimmed hat, a dark overcoat covered with geometric diagrams that made my eyes itch, and thick, heavy boots. His hands were covered with rings that flashed in the light, and he wore many pendants upon chains that he wore around his neck. His bearded face broke into a wide grin, as he settled down in a thickly brocaded chair near to mine. His eyes flashed an emerald green, and half of his teeth were gold.

I stammered aloud, "Where... where am I? What is this place?"

The heavy man looked at me, while bringing a large tankard to his lips, "This is my home, Galynn. You're very lucky I was looking for you. I'm afraid my guardian thicket might have eaten you if I had not been made aware of the current state of things. Crystal balls are useful tools, when they are properly addressed. This is my sitting room, where I like to ponder the mysteries of reality. It also contains my most beloved collection of rarities."

I suddenly remembered my peril, "The hunters! They've come to arrest me!"

He waved a hand at me, "The Church's Salvation Infantry? Oh, the survivors ran off when I took you in. Nothing like a good lesson in manners to beat those rascals back. Oh! I am forgetting myself! My name is Justinian Vargalow, Grand Wizard of OTIDS and explorer of the greater mysteries. You are welcome to stay here for a while. In fact, I think you must, or you will lose yourself in what is coming up. You didn't follow old Larance's pedantic orders, did you? Oh, fear not! I do appreciate initiative."

I was understandably terrified. Only a little of what this wizard had said thus far made any sense to me, but to express my confusion could be seen as insulting and thus very dangerous. So, instead I simply asked, "The greater mysteries, my Lord? As in the outer realms?"

Justinian laughed aloud, "Nay, my friend! Oh, please! I don't bother with realms that have already been discovered! I seek the places where OTIDS has no foothold. As for calling me 'Lord', please don't. I'm not some simple-minded noble, casting base spells and thinking myself powerful. I need no title to cling upon like a safety line. You may use my name, Galynn."

I was shocked into silence. That anyone would claim that there was any place where OTIDS did not control everything absolutely went beyond the absurd. Justinian gave me a wink, then got up to his feet and walked over toward the gleaming fireplace, filling a ceramic bowl with steaming liquid from a small, hanging iron cauldron over the fire. He walked back to me and offered the bowl, which I took with uncertain gratitude.

Slumping back into his chair, Justinian watched as I took a sip of the broth, which was surprisingly delicious, "I can see, young Galynn, that my words have confused you even further. I'm also certain that you have many questions, including why your father would send you here. I collect those items deemed to be impossible. Do you see that bell jar on the table closest to you? Take a peek at it."

I carefully rested the bowl of soup in my lap, with great reluctance, as it was quite tasty, and looked over at the item in question. A small table walked its way closer to me. Upon it was a perfectly clear glass dome, within which was a head-sized, checkered, greenish-grey gear, floating within it. The odd item rotated steadily, and upon a closer inspection, seemed to be made of hard rubber. I turned my gaze back to my host, "What is it? May I touch it?"

Justinian wagged a finger at me while grinning madly, "I wouldn't if I were you, young man! You have no idea what I went through to steal that from its native realm! I would not release it for reasons of safety. I've learned long ago, that such items can react in an unexpected manner when exposed to our reality. Only in my lab are such things ever studied closely. That gear has no relation to anything that exists in all the realms of OTIDS. Yes, you heard me right! It should not exist here, and it wouldn't, under ordinary circumstances. Not only does it not contain any of OTIDS' influence, but it simply cannot be controlled by the all-powerful mind that runs our plane of existence. The circumference of that gear, though appearing to be perfectly round, isn't even governed by irrational numbers, let alone pi! No atomic structure at all! No baryons, leptons or even tau-mesons! A great king of that reality pursued me for days, after I stole it from his realm, leading to his downfall, as his rival took advantage of his absence."

I blinked in confusion. The wizard was using terms I'd never heard before which, in all honesty, shouldn't have come as a surprise. I glanced around at the other displays in the room. One had a giant, dusty flower that glittered, as if covered in diamond dust. Another had a small, rectangular device which glowed on one side, revealing cryptic markings. All of them were protected by glass domes, though I was beginning to understand that the coverings were actually protecting me and everything else in the room.

Justinian noticed my interest, "My work for OTIDS is to look for and close loopholes in the laws of nature. I access deep subroutines within the mechanics of reality, usually close to the Plank scale, you understand, then explore dimensional properties which may cause disruptions to service. It's a never-ending task, but someone has to do it."

My gaze shifted back to his bearded face, "You work for OTIDS? Do all sorcerers and witches perform this duty of yours to our mutual Lord?"

Justinian's eyebrows shot up to his forehead, "Goodness, no! Only wizards are dimensional seekers. I'd never trust a sorcerer to handle such things. They're not qualified for my kind of work. No, my colleagues in the various schools of magick all have their different specialties. Witches, for example, are summoners of extraordinary skill. Necromancers mostly deal with historical anomalies and time loops. Sorcerers are portal masters. There are many other forms of magick in our realm, thanks to OTIDS, and we all perform certain tasks for it, in exchange for greater knowledge, which we share amongst ourselves. Sometimes, we pass a crumb or two to the Church, but that's rare."

I trembled as I asked, "What does my father have to do with all of this? He was an Arch-Bishop of the Church, not an enchanter."

Justinian leaned closer, a wicked gleam in his eyes, "Are you so sure of that, young Galynn? He was a secret colleague. A mole, or spy, if you must. One who checks on the balance of power. While not an enchanter, he was a fine shaman and not too shabby with his cartomancy. While not as exacting, mathematically speaking, as wizardry, shamanism explores and works with the various structures within OTIDS' personality format. In the Church, he was known as an exorcist whose work was unparalleled. I found our chats most illuminating."

I shook my head, for it felt as if it were about to fly off my neck in shock, "But, that's insane! What are you saying? What did he get me involved with? Why me? There had to have been others whom he could have used for whatever this is about! I'm nobody! A wastrel! Ask anyone who knows me!"

Justinian tilted his head, studying me, "Sanity is an ugly word. The laws of reality are not governed by human reasoning, so why should we be so enchained? Such thinking would hinder our work. As for you, my young Galynn, he chose you because of your position within our society. A wastrel. Untrusted. One who is outside the norms, who is unseen mainly because of his scandalous nature. Ignored due to your sullied reputation. Beneath the notice of the nobles and Church alike. Anyone else would have been captured immediately. They would have never made it to the Troth-Knights, who, by the way, are marching here, under my considerable protections. There are more guests coming to my lovely home, all to meet you and to bring you the help and guidance you so desperately need."

I began to wail aloud, weeping hysterically, for my poor mind could handle nothing more. Justinian snapped his fingers, and I fell into a deep, silent darkness.

CHAPTER EIGHT

Delectable Poison

"Those of great quality shall work with Me
Unhindered by My Holy Church
Ye shall know them by their great works
For they understand My Holy Will
They shall seek the unknown
And bring peace unto My realm forevermore."

-Excerpt from the OTIDS Bible – Tutorials 15:47

I woke with a start, certain that my encounter with Wizard Vargalow was just a dream. I heard distant voices, speaking quietly, even laughing in a muffled tone. Opening one eye blearily, I found myself still ensconced in the padded chair, wrapped up within the same blanket as before. There was a wheezing sound that came from close by. Lifting my head, I discovered a small creature curled up on my lap. It was a tiny dragon, no more than a few feet in length, including its skinny tail. Its eyes were closed, and tiny flames sprouted from its nose in a rhythmic manner. I realized the wheezing noise was its snoring.

Disturbing a fire-breathing creature, no matter how tiny it was, is never a good idea. Studying it further, I noticed that it was covered in blue scales that were so deep in hue as to be almost violet. A pair of curling horns sprouted from its long head, matching the petite spikes that ran down the dragon's spine. Little wings fluttered as it dreamed, curved claws twitching, pulling at the fabric of the blanket. I had never been this close to one of these monsters before, which includes Lady Ballow's pet. To my growing horror, I realized that I was beginning to see it as being cute. Had I become so inured to such things that it was no longer surprising to find myself trapped in a chair, because if I moved, such action might disturb the new-born drake?

As I pondered my position, a tall, naked man whose skin was made up of wrinkled, green leaves peered down at me with a single, crimson eye, "Ah, you're awake. I shall inform Wizard Vargalow. He was looking for little Spinel as well. You've made a friend it seems, Galynn Brytshul."

I quizzically looked up at the leafy stranger, "Are you Justinian's daemon butler?"

He laughed revealing teeth made of wood, "Hardly! He saved my life in my home realm of Fullgrain. I have been at his side ever since, to repay that debt. I enjoy it here. Lots to do. No real termites."

I scowled briefly, "We have termites here. I'm sure of that."

He gave me an inscrutable look, "Not like the ones at home. Ours are ten feet long, and they never stop singing while they eat."

My mouth hung open as he walked away, chuckling to himself. The tiny dragon opened one eye and blinked at me with its emerald orb, before it snuggled down for some more sleep. I had heard the rumours that dragons were lazy creatures, always dozing upon a mound of treasure. To be the bed for such an enchanted beast was not really something I had ever expected to happen to me. Looking about from my position, I saw that the chamber had not changed much, save that the fireplace was now empty of logs, and bright light was streaming in through a window that I had not seen before.

My host, Justinian Vargalow, walked up to me, "Ah! Welcome to the world of the conscious, young Galynn! I see you've been claimed by Spinel. A fortunate happenstance. He's only about fifty years old, so still a baby, you understand, but they are very picky about who they accept."

I looked up at the wizard, "Claimed? As in it's my pet?"

He shook his head with a smile, "No, claimed as in you are his pet. It's quite the honour, young Galynn. Spinel will follow you wherever you go now. He will try to take care of you and bring you gifts."

This did not sound like good news, "But, I'm on the run! Won't he get hurt, following me around? How can I care for such a creature, when I can barely take care of my own needs?"

Justinian smiled softly at me, "Dear Galynn, you're actually thinking of Spinel's needs before your own. And you call yourself a wastrel! Dragons are hardy beasts. They catch their own food, clean themselves, and as for self–defence, well, they do breathe fire, you know. They originally came from a realm named Gilead Four, brought here as curiosities, then modified by some very adventurous spell–casters, so to better fit our own mythologies. I must admit, these days, morphologic genomics is a faded art. In any case, neither you nor I can dissuade him from keeping you. I think Spinel might come in handy in the next phase of your adventures."

I squawked out a protest before I remembered my manners, "What next phase? My adventures! I refuse to cooperate until I get a better idea of what I've been tossed into, sir. I am not having a good time!"

Justinian gently placed a broad hand upon my left shoulder, leaning close enough for me to smell his earthy perfume, "I've recruited some help for you, young Galynn. Your Troth–Knights are here, and all their equipment has been repaired or updated. Tricky things, they are. Spool out too much of their original casting and they fall apart into bloody chunks of meat. In any case, they are fine, what's left of them. I've also gathered together some of my colleagues in the mystic arts of OTIDS design protocols. While I do have other duties that will keep me from joining you directly, I have put in motion certain items that will tilt the balance of power in your favour. Come now, the others are waiting to meet you, as is breakfast."

I was terrified to discover who had come to the wizard's house, but my stomach growled at me when he mentioned the morning meal. I gently tucked my hands under the tiny dragon, to lift him up so as to not disturb his slumbers, but Spinel crawled over to latch onto my shoulder with needle–like claws, making me jump to my feet in alarm. The dragon fluttered his wings for balance, and I found myself mimicking his wild antics. The wizard laughed at the sight of my lack of grace, then turned around and marched toward a doorway that I could swear was not there a minute earlier.

Following behind my host, I took the time to study my surroundings. We went through a grand hallway with broad windows, each one displaying a radically different landscape. There was no way to tell if they were real, or artistic renderings of uncommon skill. Small, metallic things scuttled along the floor, the walls and even the ceiling, which I thought was most alarming. The little dragon curled his tail about my shoulders and relaxed his claws, much to my relief. Globes of coloured light bobbed about in the air, sending shadows skittering across the walls, some of which seemed out of place, as if cast by unseen figures. We wandered through a room full of maps, charts and tables full of miniature objects, such as castles and bridges. Tiny horses ran about upon diminutive fields, while fingernail-sized soldiers marched in formation.

By this point, I could smell food, and it made me dizzy with desire. We entered a large kitchen, with an equally monstrous dining room on the left. Windows on the right were filled with sunlight and had long planters full of growing herbs and other plants. A large alligator in a chef's apron and hat was standing on its hind legs at a massive stove, working several pans at once. This new creature was not what gave me pause. It was the collection of guests which made me stop in my tracks at the entrance of the chamber.

The first to catch my eye was a young woman of incredible beauty. She wore a leather outfit with steel plates, and bandoliers filled with knives crossed her shoulders. Her eyes gleamed with a golden glow, as her gaze met mine. Next to her was an older gentleman who was impossibly thin, with silver orbs for eyes, wearing a black robe that was dusty and threadbare. A tall woman in green armour laughed as she caught sight of me. Her hair was braided into floating strands that rose above her head. A portly man stood beside her, wearing a simple, grey apron and nothing else. His hands were covered in rings, as were his toes, while his wrists and ankles bore multiple bracelets covered in tiny jewels.

To my relief, Prime entered from the dining area. He marched up to me, then dropped to one knee and declared his never-ending fealty. Spinel hissed at the Troth-Knight, then fluttered off to snatch a bit of bacon from the stove. This bit of distraction broke the ice, as most of the guests smiled and chuckled at the dragon's antics. I bowed low to them all, with as much grace as I could muster, until my stomach decided to grumble so loudly, even the alligator cook turned about, shoving a large platter of pastries and meats at me. I stammered my thanks, being overly aware that every set of eyes in the room were following me, then Justinian led me into the dining room, offering a chair at the grand table. Prime came over and stood behind me, crossing his thick arms over his huge chest, as if daring anyone to approach while I ate my fill. All in all, I have to say that wizards are marvellous hosts. You nobles could learn a thing or two from them.

When I finished stuffing my face with the sumptuous meal, the set of used dishware ran off and washed themselves back in the kitchen, while the other guests joined me in the dining room. Some trays filled with snacks floated into the chamber, landing upon the table in a marvellous display of consumable elegance. All of the guests began lighting long-stemmed pipes, cigars or other forms of smoke inhalation. Before long, the entire room was shrouded in blue-grey clouds that made me cough. They laughed at me, as I waved my hand in front of my face to clear the air, which didn't work. It was then that I noticed that the young women with the golden eyes was sitting directly in front of me.

Turning my gaze away from her, embarrassed by my own reaction to her beauty, I looked over at my host, "I want explanations. I want them now, please."

Justinian nodded, his broad hat bobbing with the motion, "As you can see, I've enlisted a few of my dearest colleagues, all of whom knew your biological father and worked with him on the project at hand. We all hold different pieces of the same puzzle, for reasons of security and because of our secretive nature as the magi of OTIDS."

I decided to go out on a limb and asked, "Is there any way for me to not be involved in this project? Haven't I already performed my part in this, by bringing you together?"

It was the young woman who responded, with a sweet, yet caustic voice, "Ducking out on your responsibilities yet again? If you depart from here, bent on doing nothing, you'll lose all of our protections, and we'll let the damned Church have you."

Justinian waved a hand at her, "Now there, Linia! No need to be so hostile towards young Galynn. He's hurt, confused and not here by his own will. He didn't volunteer, like the rest of us."

Linia sneered back, "That didn't stop him from taking the money, the Troth-Knights, and the case of transmutation. He's greedy, a liar and a coward. Even his former acquaintances, those who remember his weaselly face, don't want to associate with him. I say we use him as a lure or a trap for the nobles. He's good distraction material."

The thin mage shot back, "Such a beacon of light and morality! You must make your master very proud, Linia. He, at least, understands the true meaning of loyalty to our common purpose. Don't forget your place at this table! You are his gift to Galynn, as he promised Larance Pontiforia."

Justinian Vargalow raised both hands, "Stop the bickering! Galynn, I must apologize for not introducing our little band. The young woman in front of you is named Linia Raslow. She is an assassin construct, created by Magi Foji Nelpworn. Linia is a shape-shifter of great skill and is charged to accompany you as a living weapon.

"The lady to my left, in the green armour, is Ghail Plemorph, one of the most innovative witches in all the realms of OTIDS. Upon my right is Zahanar Crend, our main researcher and an outstanding necromancer. Next to him, wearing the apron, is the renown sorcerer, Tregghar Harpsong. One of our members, Drigon Blandalfash, has been delayed but will catch up with you on the road in a few days, should all go well. Magi Foji Nelpworn has an emergency to contend with on an angelic realm deep within the starry sky and thus sends his gift to you remotely, in the form of Linia."

The assassin was staring at me, "He's panicking."

She was quite correct. There I was, surrounded by more power than I could ever conceive of who, at any moment, could cause entire continents to vanish or change the very nature of reality with a wink of an eye. Entire armies would quail at such company. The most powerful nobles would be seen as weak infants compared to their might. One wizard is enough to be considered a threat to entire nations, let alone a group of such beings.

I gulped down some smoke-filled air, "My Lords and Ladies, please forgive my understandable terror. I mean no offense, but I am just a mouse amongst tigers. What I fail to understand is why you were involved with my father to begin with. He was clergy, an Arch-Bishop of the Church."

Soft laughter greeted my words. The witch, Ghail Plemorph, replied, "Young man, your father wasn't a true clergyman. He was a conjurer of truly wonderous ability and a talented chef in his spare time. He was our secret agent within the Church, to prevent the clergy from gaining possession of things beyond their means to understand. He stole relics from their vaults, some famous, others obscure, replacing them with sparkling fakes. He took dangerous objects out of their hands and into ours, for safekeeping."

The oddly thin Zahanar Crend pointed at me, "He also was involved in saving citizens the Church wished to punish. He helped them to escape injustice, like he did with your mother and step-father, both of whom were noble-born, who wanted to leave the bullying aristocratic society and raise a family through natural means, which is wrongfully forbidden."

The portly Tregghar Harpsong rapped the table with his beringed fist, "He was the ultimate cheat and liar! The best con-man ever to be born! Larance was the finest inside-agent we could have asked for. His only failing was that he cheated whenever he played cards, including the Tarot! Larance once took me for everything I had, not that I blame him. I knew what I was getting into. Suffice it to be said, you have his gift if not his education."

Justinian Vargalow nodded sagely, "He will be sorely missed, and we will never find his personal stash to get our losings back. Nevertheless, his deep commitment to the project was the strongest amongst us, for he saw the foul corruption of the Church first hand every day. Larance was appalled by the political system of our fine realm and wanted to limit the power of the nobility and the clergy. We joined him in this quest, but we had to be careful not to unbalance nature and the world. To be rash would bring too much collateral damage within the commoner population."

Thus it was that I discovered that my parents were actually nobles, who unlawfully left their position of power for a more humble lifestyle. That makes me one of you, does it not? I assure you, I am equally appalled at the idea. It turns my stomach. That aside, I had to get further information or remain in the dark until my untimely demise, "You have all given me much to consider when it comes to my biological father, but I still don't have any idea as to what this project of yours is. Perhaps if I understood it, I might be more willing to cooperate."

Linia scoffed, "He's lying. He's looking for a way out of it."

Justinian raised one shaggy eyebrow at her, "Nonetheless, Galynn deserves to know the truth. Only he may collect the gifts and favours. Only he can lead us to those who require our aid. This has always been the key to Larance's plan, to prevent any one of us from betraying the project.

"Young Galynn, your father always felt that the Church of OTIDS had far too much power, as do the nobility. This doesn't mean he wasn't a devout worshipper of OTIDS. We all are. We are the service personnel for our mighty Lord of all reality. Our dedication is fierce, but Larance trusted no one. His plan was to activate the final stages of our Holy purpose through an innocent intermediary - yourself."

Linia scowled, "He's not innocent."

Tregghar waggled one short, thick finger at her, "Galynn has never been involved with the aristocracy until they began to hunt him down. He's not a follower of the Church and has a very independent mind. Besides, he's what we have at this time."

Ghail looked up at our host, "Justinian, you are a wonderful speaker and a perfect wizard, but when it comes to getting right to the point, you lag behind. Please, allow me. Galynn, everyone one knows that OTIDS controls all things in reality, but what if I told you this isn't exactly correct? There are some items, and even people, who are outside the spellcraft of OTIDS, called the Displaced. Some of these things are not from within our reality, like Justinian's lovely collection of oddities. Others are from the deep past, before OTIDS changed the starry heavens, which is Zahanar's purview. Such things can be wildly dangerous and destructive if they are misused. We were invited by your father to join in his attempt to secure these items and people, so that the Church and the nobility would not gain yet more power than they already have."

The necromancer spoke up next, his raspy voice cutting the air like a rusty blade, "When it comes to the people who have been collected, they are now living in a special place of our design, based on an ancient means of magick called technology. They are underground, in lit caverns that hold fields of crops and grand forests. My last count of their population, based on their rate of reproduction, now number some fifty thousand individuals, give or take. Anything alive that fits our project's requirements are there. Linia was one of them, until Foji Nelpworn augmented her for this mission. She is an orphan and had been slated to become a plaything for a noble who made immense contributions to the Church, before Larance rescued her."

The heavy sorcerer spoke up next, "The items that have been stolen or collected are within a reliquary that sits between the infinite realms. We control the only access to it and guard it with our finest creations. We cannot allow even one member of the aristocracy, or the Church, to gain any one of them, let alone all. We study them but dare not use them for any purpose. Our goal is a stalemate, to stymie the efforts of the world's leaders."

This project was far too much for me to take in all at once, but I struggled on, "What of OTIDS? Won't our Lord and God be angry that you've taken things from Its Holy Church? Will we not incur Its righteous wrath?"

Justinian grinned at me, "Oh, dear me, no. OTIDS doesn't give a fig for the Church nor our political leaders. Humanity is free to organize itself however we may wish. Our concerns are far too lowly to attract Its Holy gaze. Besides, I would think OTIDS would want all the Displaced to be sequestered from the rest of the realm, to prevent any unforeseen mishaps that would require maintenance and servicing. Very inconvenient, you know. Here's a very brief map of the hierarchy of humanity: the Church is the user interface with OTIDS, the nobles are the political guides for the population, and we spellcasters are the operatives that aid in running and repairing the realm which OTIDS has claimed. It's a grand simplification, but it does shed light on your concerns."

I was confused by this revelation, "But all the magick of the nobility and clergy is great and terrible to behold. As is yours. The Church gets its power directly from OTIDS, and the nobles are blessed with gifts from our Lord and God."

Tregghar shook his head, "Not quite, young man. The Church is only given provisional power, to bring the Word of OTIDS to the masses, nothing more. They've just found ways to expand their spells beyond their purpose, mainly through cooperation with the educated nobles. The key to real magick is found in learning, knowledge, and the temerity to practice skills gained through years of hard lessons. Out of all the members of our project, only Larance and I were born into the aristocracy. All the rest honed their magick through education, which is normally within the control of the nobility and the Church, but all magi accept talented apprentices, providing tutoring in the occult arts, even the heresy of science, which was a strong philosophy that predated the remaking of our beloved realm. When the starry heavens were conquered and changed through OTIDS, science became obsolete."

Zahanar raised a long, bony finger in the air, "The current task for you, young man, is to complete the final activation of all the operatives. We cannot, for if any of us touch those gifts your father gave to you, they would explode most violently. Only you may handle such things safely. You need to find all the people on Larance's list, gain all of their favours and gifts, thus bringing our project to its rightful conclusion, which is the safeguarding of the Displaced, for the sake of OTIDS and humanity. You now have both the Troth–Knights and Linia to help you in your journey, not to mention little Spinel, who might be more than useful. We shall also give you gifts to help you, plus our guidance, but we cannot join your quest, for we have much to prepare and can bring you aid by more indirect means."

I looked the skinny necromancer in the eye, "Will I at least get paid for my troubles?"

Linia shouted out, "For OTIDS sake! Stop thinking about yourself for once! You weasel!"

I shrugged at her, feigning innocence, and the others laughed aloud. Justinian walked over to me and placed a hand upon my shoulder, "You shall receive such wealth as has never been seen before, I promise you."

This oath, given to me by a wizard no less, was some good news at long last. I might be heading into terrifying peril, but at least I'd be rich. This didn't mean that I enjoyed the idea of galloping around, ducking under cover for who knows how long, but I was assured of my payment, and I might be able to bilk these magi out of more if I played my hand right.

CHAPTER NINE

On the Wrong Foot

"Hearken unto My Holy words
Follow My protocols and ye shall be saved
Learn the Blessed procedures
Identify the source of your salvation
Bring unto Me your gift of reverence
I shall give unto you all of creation."

-Excerpt from the OTIDS Bible – Procedures 05:56

At this point, it's easy to see why I left the home of Wizard Vargalow in better spirits, just two days later. I had been granted a small advance on my promised payment, which consisted of a modest chest filled to the brim with gold coins, precious gems and fresh credit markers. The last of these treasures replaced my collection of cheques, given to me by my late father, as the markers are untraceable. Justinian assured me that the money gifted to me by the deceased Arch-Bishop would still be waiting for me, as no bank would refuse a mage of OTIDS, nor would the aristocracy dare to interfere with his personal business.

The other reason for my good spirits was having the chance to watch Prime and Linia spar together. Every day, she looked different, with her hair changing both its colour and fashion whenever I looked away. Her skin's complexion shifted from light to dark, then back again. No matter how she appeared, I found her strangely alluring. Perhaps it was Linia's undaunted spirit, her most outspoken, righteous confidence, so starkly different from my own personality. In any case, her fighting style was a blur of heightened reflexes, far beyond that of any normal human. There were times when she actually floated above the ground, swirling in the air, flinging blades from multiple angles. Each knife had a different aura, some sported green flames, others with sparkling shades of darker colours. Meanwhile, Prime defended himself quite admirably, always doing his very best to get in close, where his precision and strength gave him the greatest advantage.

The witch, Ghail Plemorph, had provided lessons on how to care for little Spinel, who was a mischievous baby dragon. Twice, I had caught him trying to steal my gold coins, once by gulping them down his slender throat. Ghail also gave me a series of small satchels which could heal wounds and cure the effects of poison and disease. Zahanar, the necromancer, made sure I understood the proper OTIDS protocols for accessing the more hidden news and information services through use of my face-gems. Tregghar Harpsong, the sorcerer, handed me a set of enchanted items, consisting of two rings, a gold bracelet and a necklace, then teaching me how to activate them.

The gifts which I treasured the most, provided by Wizard Justinian Vargalow, were also the ones which I most dreaded using, especially after his warnings concerning their potential for causing chaos. One of them was a slender pair of hoops made of an iridescent material I'd never seen before. These were capable of expanding or contracting as needed and acted like one of the massive realm-portals used by the wealthier commuters at the inter-world stations, save that they selected from seven different, pre-arranged destinations in a random manner, to confuse pursuers. Another was a bag of glittering dust, which he confessed to not exactly knowing what it might do, and finally, a pair of spectacles which revealed hidden or invisible objects.

The rest of my Troth-knights spent the time preparing our baggage, training in the arts of warfare, and assembling a floating carriage under the instructions of Tregghar. We were all warned that agents of the Church knew where we were and had assembled a massive army just ten miles from our present location. My odd party would be forced to sneak our way beyond the surrounding marshes, then make all haste to our next target, the home of a talented cartomancer by the name of Callidi Merenia. She would provide us with instructions on the best course to take from there to accomplish our goals. When I inquired as to why she hadn't appeared at Justinian's home, I was told that she never leaves her lair, for the dangers of the real world bring pain to her sensitive mind. To be certain, I wondered where the cartomancer lived, if not in the real world, and how we would find her, but I was assured by my new employers that this would not be a problem.

I was helping one of the Troth-Knights to load my baggage onto the carriage, when Linia walked up to me, her hair turning a silvery grey as she approached, "Galynn, we'll be leaving within a few hours. Do make sure you have everything the mages gave you."

Turning from my task, I responded with my usual sarcasm, "I was thinking of leaving my talent cards here, just to keep them safe. Do you think two changes of undergarments would be too much to carry?"

She snarled at me, "No need to get peevish, you lout! Just a word of advice to you, I'll be watching your actions closely."

I shrugged, masking my insecurities, "You might learn something, then. I didn't know voyeurism was one of your abilities."

My face suddenly crashed into the side of the carriage. The Troth-Knight with me shouted in alarm, unsheathing his sword. Collapsing to the ground, I looked up, then flinched when I saw Linia holding a pair of knives in each hand, covered in blue flames. Her eyes were crimson, her skin the colour of steel. My guardian jumped off the carriage and landed between us. She swirled around him faster than I could blink and ended up at my side, with a burning blade at my throat.

Linia leaned in to whisper harshly into my ear, "I despise you. Never forget that. Your father was a great man, but you are a waste of flesh."

The Troth-Knight turned about, but she had already jumped to the top of the carriage, fast as a bird in flight. Laughing darkly, she somersaulted to the other side of the carriage. I rose to my shaking feet, wiping blood from my nose, "It's okay. Just a misunderstanding."

Prime came running over, weapons drawn, "What is the meaning of this, Lord Galynn Brytshul? Has our assassin decided to work for the nobles instead of our proper cause?"

I shook my aching head, "No, no. I just angered her."

Prime looked down at me, his face a mask of concern, "Do be more careful. We need her, and like all weapons, she requires care in how we use her. Linia has already expressed a personal dislike for you. Take care in how you speak with her."

It was embarrassing to admit it, but I did, "I tend to forget she isn't guarding my life. That she is a cannon we must point at our foes. I find her presence... distracting."

Prime shook his head, "You think of her as a beautiful woman. This is a mistake. She has a singular purpose, one which I understand all too well, whereas you may have many paths to choose from. Her abilities in dealing death are superior to my own. Linia and I spar together for my education, not hers. She is the hidden sword you must wield when the time is right. She was created to murder your enemies, so use the best grace you can muster when speaking with her."

Prime turned about and marched past the wizard's house. I looked at the other Troth-Knight, who pursed his lips at me, then went back to his appointed task of loading the wagon. Shoulders slumped in defeat, I began to walk away, when Spinel decided to suddenly appear on my right shoulder. I cried out in panic, waving my arms about like windmills in a storm, making the tiny dragon screech and hiss at me. The fire-breathing beast flitted off and landed upon the roof of Justinian's home, glaring at me.

This was not a good way to start the next phase of my travels. Should I dissuade my companions from helping me with my unruly behaviour, I would soon find myself either dead or in the hands of the Church and thus wishing I were dead. It's not easy to reflect upon a lifetime's hoard of bad habits, despite the urgency of the situation. In that way, we have much in common, to my considerable dismay. Spending years being a scoundrel, thief and wastrel can scour a person's soul down to a grain of sand. When forced to perform acts of indecency to survive, it can hamper one's ability to hold onto civil discourse and mannerly mindsets. Living on the street, angry and terrified of everyone around you, with endless hunger gnawing at your belly in constant complaint can become ruinous to the point of no redemption.

I had to question my survival skills, especially being so far from the urban streets which I was most used to inhabiting. The rest of the world lived by different rules, ones which I was unused to abiding by. Knowing how to identify and pinch a mark, even when using courtly manners to do it, cannot be considered proper practice when negotiating or working with those who are above the common fold. Knavery is best accomplished with a thin veneer of civilization covering a base nature, but what happens when that emaciated surface of grace needs to become the standard platform of behaviour?

I can tell you now the results – utter failure. A wastrel I had been; a wastrel I remained. No amount of wealth or power would ever fully drain that swamp which infests my heart. I would always be vermin, a street rat, digging its way through filth to get the juicy bits. Willing to bite the hand that tries to bring aid and succour. My dead, heretical, biological father had dumped me into this horrific position, but not without aid, and here I was squandering his gifts to the best of my abilities. These people, the Troth-Knights, mages, an assassin, even my old friends, had been trying their best to help me survive this curse of a life. Instead of cooperating or even giving them a word of thanks, I used them, snapped at them and did my best to be uncouth, as if these were appropriate actions to take when others care.

No, I'm not looking for any sympathy, nor am I seeking your twice-damned shoulder to weep upon. There really is no way to expect vultures like you to ever understand what living on the edge means. You have no idea how it feels to be downtrodden under the heels of those who have no sympathy, no morality and lacking any concerns for human dignity. I may be a wastrel, but you are all vicious monsters! Devouring children would be a step up for you. My moment of soul-searching gave me perspective on where my real failings were. It suddenly occurred to me that I was handling this all wrong. I wasn't some glorious leader, ready to lay my life down for ideals beyond getting breakfast. I was a different sort of creature, and it was time I used my skills properly.

Everyone watched as I marched back into Justinian's house. Once the front door was closed behind me, I switched my tactics. Removing my heavy boots, I began to sneak about, furtively glancing into chambers, keeping an eye out for observers. First, I grabbed a quick snack from the pantry, stuffing my pockets with treats. Then I went toward the room where the necromancer was staying. I found him asleep in his chamber, arms folded over his chest like a corpse on display. Creeping in with well-practiced silence, I ignored his bags, which I knew would be warded, and quietly rummaged in the guest cabinet, then pilfered one of his dark, threadbare cloaks. I swiftly and quietly departed, opening the door to the next chamber by removing the hinge pins. This was the room in which the sorcerer stayed, and I knew full well he was still outside, talking with our host. All of his bags were open, laying about the chamber in disarray. I filched a pair of abused sandals and one of his heavily stained aprons, leaving the rings and other treasures behind. My next target was the witch, after reassembling Tregghar's door. Ghail's room was unlocked, and I stepped in stealthily. I snatched up several bottles from her dresser, not knowing what was in them, yet not really caring either.

My final destination was the bedroom of Justinian Vargalow himself. The door to his private chamber was tricky, for upon it was a carved face that became animated when I got close. It opened its mouth and said, "What is your business here? The master is not within."

I smiled at the moving, wooden face, "Ah! But he did say that I was to be granted all the help I could get, you see. I lost my headpiece in my last adventure and require a replacement. May I take a quick look at what he has available, so that I may tell him my choice? After all, heading out into the unknown without a head covering could give me chills, then where would my quest be?"

The face on the door looked confused, "My master has given me no instructions regarding this."

I beamed a grin at the door, "Of course not! It's such a small issue, I'm sure it simply slipped his mind. Justinian has much greater things to think about than a mere cap!"

The wooden face peered at me, "I suppose you're right. My master is a mighty wizard. Be careful, touch nothing, for everything beyond me may harm the unwary."

I placed a hand upon my chest, "By my honour! I shall be the very definition of caution!"

The door groaned open, and I rushed inside, suppressing the need to giggle maniacally. The bedroom was larger than the study, dining hall and kitchen put together. I'm not quite sure how it fit within the outer walls of the house. The chamber was cluttered with items, articles of clothing and bits of relics and trinkets. After a minute or two of investigation, I discovered a dark cowl draped over a manikin bust. This I snatched up, then tucked it into my new cloak. Before leaving the chamber, I also grabbed a pair of old, leather gloves, which were badly stained and looking like something one might find in a trash heap. This went into my cloak as well.

I left the bedchamber, walking at a normal pace, making certain my breathing wasn't too heavy. Nothing screams guilt like hurrying about and panting like an ox. I returned to the kitchen and snatched a piece of leftover meat, then marched out the front door. Instead of heading directly for the carriage, I went in the other direction, where the ground was muddy swamp, full of dense underbrush and some spindly trees. I caught sight of Spinel, then tossed the scrap of meat at him, which the dragon caught neatly, then flew over to land upon my shoulder. I wandered through the marsh for a bit, then settled down to examine my stolen goods.

Spinel flew up to a branch, watching my actions from overhead. I took out the cowl from Justinian's bedroom and got it dirtied up with leaves, mud and murky water. The same process was performed for my new cloak. I took my shirt off, which at this point was stained and torn, then tied off the arms to turn it into a makeshift bag, where I dumped the rest of my goodies. I put on the newly stained cowl and cloak, both of which fit me perfectly. The final part was removing my boots, tying the straps together, then hanging them over my left shoulder and placing my new sandals upon my feet. When I stood up, I took a brief moment to make sure everything was balanced upon my body, then walked back to the carriage.

Prime had been looking for me, for when he saw my face, he smiled and waved, rushing over in haste, "My Lord, Brytshul! We shall be leaving in less than an hour. The carriage is fully loaded, and we have been given provisions to last us two weeks."

I feigned boredom, "Oh, really? We leave so soon? Ah, well, I suppose I can sleep in the carriage on the way to wherever we're going."

Prime stepped back a pace, "What are you wearing?"

I shrugged, "Some old garbage I found lying about. I'm sick of stiff brocade and went looking for something more comfortable."

He paused for a second before asking, "You went into the swamp, my Lord?"

I raised my eyebrows at him, "Is that a problem?"

He shook his head, "Not within Wizard Vargalow's property, but you should be more careful when out on your own. It looks like you fell into a bog, my Lord."

I gave him a half-smile, "That I did, my friend. Made a royal mess of myself. I'd clean up, but there's simply no time."

He nodded, "Tis true, Lord Brytshul. We leave soon."

We walked back to the carriage together, talking about supplies and how we should set up camp when we stopped for the night. Linia approached us, glaring at Spinel, who hissed at her, "Where have you been, Galynn?"

I looked at her coolly, "Minding my own business. Are you ready for our departure? All your blades well-oiled and in their sheaths?"

Her orange eyes turned to green, "Well, I... yes, I am prepared."

I smiled at her, "Excellent! You know, it's going to be a long trip, so while we're on the road, perhaps you could explain to me the full extent of your abilities, so that I might understand how to best use your services. I'd hate to waste your potential due to ignorance on my part."

She squinted at me with suspicion, "Very well. As you see fit."

As we came close to the carriage and my remaining Troth-Knights, the mages assembled themselves near the front door to Justinian's house. I waved at them cheerfully, and they all returned the gesture. The tall, leafy butler came up to me and handed over a small envelope, sealed with red wax. I thanked the gangly creature, then opened it immediately. Inside was a note card, with barely legible writing within it that said, "Well done, Galynn! Keep your stolen winnings, with our blessings. Like father, like son, I suppose. Your friend, Justinian."

I gave the wizard a wink, which he grinned at. Ghail and Tregghar both laughed and waved at me. Zahanar raised one eyebrow at me and bowed low with a graceful flourish. I glanced over at Linia, only to find the assassin staring at me in confusion. I clapped her on the back and leapt aboard the carriage, with little Spinel following me inside. Prime allowed Linia to enter before he clambered aboard, with the rest of the Troth-Knights seated on top of the floating contraption. Two of my guardians would be riding in the front, to guide the carriage, and a pair of others clung to the back, their feet standing upon gilded rails which also held our bags.

We set off at once, flashing down the dirt road, surrounded by dense, gloomy woodlands. I asked how we were going to get past the Church's army, and Prime told me we were heading toward a special tunnel which led to a hidden portal that Justinian provided for our use. This bit of news cheered me up considerably. I may have started the day on the wrong foot, but in the end, I regained my bearings with considerable skill.

CHAPTER TEN

Confident Confusion

"Let those denizens of other realms tremble
Their suns are Mine unto the end of time
They shall pose no threat to My people
In service unto Me they shall find peace."

-Excerpt from the OTIDS Bible – Protocols 35:47

There is a sense of relief that comes with admitting to not knowing what you're doing. To reveal all the improvisations and falsehoods that come with desperate measures can bring about a welcome rush of release. This is what filled my heart, as we travelled to our next goal. The portal we used to evade the army of the Church was a fairly standard affair, much to my own disappointment. Twin loops of silvery, bone-like material were intertwined, their centers filled with a dense, glowing mist. There was the usual sense of dislocation, said to come from the soul not understanding the displacement of the body until directed by OTIDS to reinhabit the corporeal form. Whatever the explanation, it gave me a headache, tempered by mild nausea.

As none of the others in my little troupe had any ill effects, I played my own discomfort to the hilt, much to the annoyance of my living weapon, Linia. To be fair, I was needling her with my supposed malaise, but the time was well spent organizing my edible talent cards which had been loaded into their case without rhyme or reason. The damned things were far too delicate, crumbling with the slightest touch. This was considered a feature, to allow the user to have a talent for a few hours instead of a full day. My attempt to eat a tiny corner from several different ones made me ridiculously ill, not to mention the outlandish ranting and raving that poured from my mouth. My guardian, Prime, had been forced to restrain me for hours.

Upon recovery, I found myself prone on one of the carriage's padded benches, with Linia staring down at me, a damp cloth in her hand. She pulled away immediately, yet I saw the concern in her eyes but resolved to not let her know that I had witnessed her compassion showing. Such an observation would have irritated her, and we needed Linia's services too much for me to jeopardize our growing understanding. Surprised? Try spending a week in a cramped carriage with someone without getting to know them. Now, when it comes to the Troth-Knights, that is a special case, for they are constructs, but Linia is a human being, with all the complications which that implies. We had some fun; I'd steal her jewellery, right off her body, and she would suddenly have a glowing knife at my throat. Good times.

After entering the portal provided by Justinian, we left the Bulgrian Plateau behind and entered the foothills of the Colovian Mountains, on the other side of the world. The sun was bright yet cold, flashing reflections off the peaks, making me squint and hastily retreat back into the carriage. Snow covered the hard ground, which made everything unseemly bright. We had two more days of travel before reaching our destination, so I spent the time finding more ways to annoy Linia, without getting myself killed. She taught me how to properly hold a blade, while I showed her some of my sleight-of-hand tricks, which she mimicked with skill and speed.

My baby dragon, Spinel, had made a habit of catching small animals, such as mice, lizards and voles, then dropping them at my feet. He would look at me expectantly, his eyes swirling with glittery light. Prime informed me that Spinel was trying to feed his pet, meaning myself. Many of his little "gifts" for me were charred beyond recognition. Others were still breathing, which was beyond disturbing. I tried to play along as best I could, while Linia laughed at my consternation. In the light of our new location, Spinel was a marvel of iridescent colours. His scales shifted hue whenever he moved, while his horns gleamed like polished stones. I felt bad about wasting his efforts to bring me sustenance, but as desperate as I have been in the past,

I've never eaten fried rodent and wasn't thrilled about trying it out at this juncture.

During our travels to the foothills of this cold countryside, I decided to familiarize myself with the gifts presented to me by the sorcerer Tregghar Harpsong. I started with the pair of gold rings, each one plain, save for the carved gemstone each one boasted. One was ruby, the other emerald. I placed the ring with a large, skull-shaped ruby embedded on it upon my finger and felt nothing. Disappointed, I rummaged in our food supply sack, pulled out an apple, and began to cut it into chunks with a small paring knife. All of a sudden, I was twiring the blade about with a deftness that astounded Prime, who then proceeded to test my fighting skills by giving me a larger blade, after calling the carriage to a halt. We sparred for a long time, and my arm never wearied, always blocked his blows, and surprised him with thrusts he had not encountered before.

After taking the ring off my finger, I immediately collapsed into my usual, stumbling self. I had no idea as to whether the spell would wear off over time, so I tucked it away into my pouch for safe keeping. It was time to try out the emerald ring, which, once again, did nothing I could discern. We loaded ourselves back aboard the carriage and resumed our journey. Linia asked about our bout, and as Prime answered her with detailed descriptions, I butted in with jibes and off-hand comments which made her laugh. I was shocked by her display of open, human emotions. Her eyes glittered as she sat next to me, placing her hand upon mine with a close familiarity that was at odds with how she treated me up to this point. Taking a risk that even now fills me with dread, I winked at her, and instead of breaking my neck, Linia blushed cheerfully.

Ever one for self-preservation, I held back until she was otherwise occupied with a glow-map, before removing the emerald ring from my hand, whereupon she became her usual acerbic self, shoving me aside and scowling with disdain. Into the pouch went my second ring. It was now time to test the bracelet. This one was covered in diamond scales, with a clasp in the shape of a leaf shield. The initial effect was immediate. I felt stifled, as if I were tucked into a leather sack. I could still breathe normally but felt very uncomfortable under my clothes. The longer I wore it, the less it bothered me, so I kept the wristband in place, hoping its nature would be revealed.

Linia had to reach over my head to grab a bandolier full of knives, placing her bodice in a most unseemly position. Naturally, I commented on this, and she slapped my face without a moment of hesitation. I felt nothing. Laughing aloud, I told her this bit of good news. Linia was not so amused and pulled a blade free, dark flames dancing upon its edge. She stabbed down onto my leg, while Prime shouted a warning. The tip of the knife bounced off my skin, though not before tearing my pants leg. I danced in my seat with glee. After a considerable amount of time, even Linia got bored with trying to inflict harm upon me, and I gently removed the bracelet, putting it away with the other trinkets.

Last, but never least, was my new necklace. Let me warn you now, that this piece of jewellery had the most disturbing effect upon me. It was silver, with tiny polished bones dangling from it. I place it around my neck, and at this point, my companions were watching me closely, lest I play some trick upon them. I looked up at Prime, my protector and guardian. His eyes seemed to fill my own. Screams rang in my ears. Hot blood splashed my face. Lights flashed around me. Smoke covered my vision, but I could still see the display before my eyes, telling me where the enemy was positioned and the status of my troops. Explosions rocked the earth. I raised my sword high into the shattered air, calling my brethren to rush the foe, who were in retreat.

Gasping, I snapped out of the visions that raced through my head. Turning to Linia, I wept aloud, tears running down my cheeks. Mama was dead, papa long gone. Foul smelling men were stuffing me into a big sack. A booming voice interrupted their crime, as a tall man in robes and a golden mitre stepped out of the darkness and assailed them with a shimmering staff. The men died one by one, then the brave stranger walked up to me, taking my hand and promising me salvation in service to OTIDS. I tore the necklace off my body, shivering with reaction. My companions asked me what had happened, but I refused to answer their numerous queries. Instead, I simply placed the trinket with the others, swearing to myself to never wear the foul necklace again.

As for the items which I purloined from the magi, they all seemed ordinary enough, which I didn't trust for an instant. Despite my concerns about unforeseen abilities, I insisted on wearing the cowl, cloak, sandals and gloves. Whatever enchantments were upon them, they seemed more subtle than the gifts themselves. Perhaps my hands were a bit more dextrous than usual. The chill of nightfall never seemed to reach my bones. My dreams were vivid, often depicting historical occurrences and famous people. Spinel would often nest on the cowl while I slept. My feet never seemed to tire or became cramped, and these softer effects suited me best. They were much more comforting in their ordinary usefulness, much like the kind one would find in upper-class clothing, though they appeared bedraggled.

Upon the third day, we finally reached a tall cliffside where the road abruptly ended. There was no one about, no sign of any homes, shoppes or civilization. Scraggly brush lined the path we had followed, along with the occasional barren tree or large boulder, but there was nothing else evident. We disembarked to stretch our legs and to argue over where to go next or how to find the location where we should meet the cartomancer. Prime and Linia were the main participants in all these debates, while I searched for a decent place to relieve my aching bladder. The sun was hot, in contrast to the biting cold of the wind. I wondered if the spectacles that Justinian gave me would help against the bright light penetrating my eyes like daggers, as some forms of such things were known to do. I pulled them from my pouch and placed them upon my face.

Turning to look back at my arguing companions, I came to an abrupt halt. The cliffside was suddenly covered with runes, sigils and other arcane symbols. A massive door was at the very end of the road, surrounded by flames that shifted hue randomly. Complex pictograms ran up the cliff on either side of the gigantic portal, all of them moving with slow grace. I ripped the spectacles from my face, and all I could see was a blank wall of rock that reached the sky. I knew what I had to do, but my stomach had turned to cold jelly. Slowly, I willed my legs to move. I walked past the squabbling Linia and Prime, who by this point had ceased their debate and were staring at me in confusion. I gently placed the spectacles back on my nose, after cleaning them gently with the edge of my necromancer's cloak.

I walked up close to the surface of the rockface, and the spectacles revealed a circle with a handprint on one side of the monstrous door, just below the shifting pictograms. I glanced back to find everyone looking at me. I shrugged my shoulders and then placed my palm on the indicated spot next to the portal. The cliff shuddered, dust and sand tumbling down from above.

The hieroglyphs ceased their prancing, as a massive, glowing face peered down at me with glowering eyes of flame, "Who disturbs my home?"

The others were looking about, seeking the source of the voice, but I simply looked up at it and replied, "I'm Galynn Brytshul, sent here by magi Justinian Vargalow, on a matter of great importance pertaining to the plans of Larance Pontiforia. We seek guidance, and I must give you this."

I then flashed one of the pages of my father's booklet which had the cartomancer's name upon it. The giant face peered down, then hmphed with displeasure. The stone around me vibrated. Loose rocks rained down, and I suddenly wished I were wearing my bracelet. Gasps rang out behind me, as a glowing hole appeared in the cliff, just a few inches above where the ground met the stone. This new portal was oval in shape and seemed to be a glowing tunnel of light that stretched on beyond sight. I stepped forward, resigned to whatever fate awaited me, when a large hand grabbed me by the collar and pulled me back. Prime glared at my face, "Tis too dangerous, my Lord! I shall enter first."

It has to be said that the brave Troth-Knight made the attempt, but he slammed into an invisible barrier, almost knocking him from his feet. The huge face reappeared, "He who is invited to enter must lead any who comes with him, for he shall vouchsafe their behaviour while in the presence of my Lady of Vision."

I readjusted my cowl and stepped forward once again, patting my pouch to make sure it was still tied to my belt. There might be need of the enchanted items within it before we got to the cartomancer. The floor of the tunnel was incredibly smooth, yet my sandals found good traction for my feet. I was uncertain as to whether this was due to their innate nature or that of the glowing passageway. I could hear Prime and Linia following behind me, with the others remaining outside to guard the carriage. With the magick spectacles on, I could easily see the many layers of colour and imagery that surrounded us, but my two companions, not including little Spinel who had wrapped himself around my neck, were complaining that the light made it difficult for them to see the tunnel clearly. Diagrams and geometric shapes covered the walls of the corridor, most of which made my head ache.

We finally entered a large, spherical chamber, at least fifty paces in diameter, filled with floating crystal balls, flat, round panes of glass, each one depicting a different, moving scene, and rectangular panels covered in arcane symbols. To the left was a bed with gauzy coverings that hung about it. To the right was an area full of boxy devices I had never seen before. Chairs and cushions covered the glassy floor, and the perfectly round walls were filled with a variety of ever-shifting visions, most of which made no sense to my eyes. At the exact center of the chamber was a circular throne with cushioned sides and a padded seat, upon which sat a thin woman with long, flowing dark hair that moved on its own volition. Her face was youthful, with large, dark eyes and full lips. She also wore spectacles, which glittered and sparkled with dazzling spots of light.

The lady looked over at me and sighed deeply, as if disappointed. Her gown was lacey and colourful, with strange beads that flashed in the light stitched into the fabric. Her face had no gems upon it, which surprised me. At first, I thought she was a servant of the cartomancer we were to meet, until she said, "Oh, it's finally time for Galynn Brytshul to get a clue. I had hoped for more time, but the forces of motion wait for no one, I suppose. Take off those glasses, Galynn. You don't need them in here. As for your father's booklet, I'm providing you both gifts and services. By the way, the clothes you stole have powers you haven't even guessed at yet. My name is Callidi Merenia, and I am the cartomancer you're supposed to meet, mainly because you skipped ahead, as predicted, with your task of finding those on your father's damned list."

As I removed the spectacles, I cleared my throat, "It is an honour to meet you Lady..."

She suddenly raised her hand to forestall my words, "It is not. Don't lie to me. You're scared shitless, as you should be, but for the wrong reasons, again, as predicted."

Linia muttered towards me, "I like her already."

Callidi retorted, "Well, you shouldn't! Galynn is your man, not mine. I am far more dangerous than any physical peril. Your Troth-Knight knows this, but he does not remember why this is the case. A true blessing for those reborn. Heroics aren't pretty."

I looked over at Prime, who was standing next to me, trembling but not moving. He stared at the cartomancer as if seeing a ghost. It was time to get to business, then we could leave this strange place, so I said, "Callidi, we have very little time, and it seems that I need some aid to help me to finish what my father started."

The cartomancer glared at me, "Time? There's plenty to be had in here. All the time you might need. More than you could ever handle. As usual, Justinian did little to prepare you for visiting me. He likes to toss people out into the deep end. It fits his own style of exploration. It's just the usual OTIDS arrogance, I suppose. You wouldn't know a real struggle if it bit you."

I stepped towards her, "Now hold on just a minute! We have suffered terribly to get to this point, as you should know! My life hasn't been easy. In fact, I suspect it was harder than yours!"

Callidi shook her head, "You should have put on your charm ring, not that it would help much in here. You've just suffered the indignities of your own choices, nothing more. None of that really matters, however. You are now behind schedule, out of sequence, and that can have a devastating effect on what has been set up thus far. There were three people you had to meet before reaching Trent Fulmore. Fortunately for you, Galynn, they will be gathering together for a convention of bureaucrats on Ceti-Three, what you would call an angelic realm."

I was both highly concerned and very relieved, "At least it's not one of the daemonic realms."

Callidi rolled her eyes, "Oh, please! The angels and daemons are just non-terrestrial, xenomorphic forms of life, native to worlds other than the one you were born on. They have the same pitfalls and foibles as everyone else. The big difference between them is whether or not we like the way they look. That's it. Just human prejudice. For hundreds of thousands of years, the galaxy has been bound by the chains of OTIDS, which works to benefit humanity as a whole, usually to the detriment of everything else that exists. I'm just glad my realm was never discovered by this reality of yours."

I do confess to not understanding much of what she was speaking about, but I decided that asking a question or two was better than sitting in my own ignorance, "May I ask what you mean by that last remark? You look perfectly human to me, Lady Cartomancer."

She waved a hand at a floating panel, and it came to life, revealing cities as viewed from above, gleaming in the sunlight, "I am human, or at least I'm a human who comes from a different line of events which altered the history of yours. My linguistic verminilities had to work for days before I could even speak your language! There are many versions of Earth, Terra, Gaia, take your pick of names. They're all the same, really. They just have different histories. Different choices were made by those whose actions had repercussions on the flow of events. I study such things. It's my specialty. I came to your reality many years ago, long after I made my laboratory.

"Justinian discovered my whereabouts several years ago. He's such a nosy-body! Always hopping around the realities, looking for new treats for his study, never thinking about the long-term effects of his actions, which can be formidable! He's a big fan of OTIDS, which I detest, but I do like the mages in general, including delusional Justinian."

I flinched briefly, "Be careful of what you say about OTIDS!"

She laughed brightly, "Why? It's not in here. Not in my domain. Oh, it'll be updated once you leave here, but I don't care. I'll just shift my portal input, switch over to yet another nodal point. The poor thing can get so very provincial. Besides, I have friends in other realities it wouldn't want to mess with. Not directly, in any case. This place is outside your reality. In fact, it's not within any universe. That's what makes it perfect for my studies. Now, as for your own predicament, I have information you'll need, an item for your use, and I can send you back to your world at a time that will be most effective."

I had nothing to say to that, as my mind was spinning like a child's toy. Both Linia and Prime seemed too stunned to speak or even move, so I nodded to Callidi and smiled. It seemed obvious that she could help me, so long as I didn't try to comprehend anything she was talking about. I kept my confusion and ignorance in check and just went along for the ride. It seemed the wiser course of action.

CHAPTER ELEVEN

Being Sentient Isn't Always Helpful

"The salvation of all humanity
Is the path of My indomitable will.
All doctrines speak My Holy name
All faiths represent My Holy works
All gods are found within Me."

-Excerpt from the OTIDS Bible – Documentation 10:23

Don't bother wasting your moral outrage on me! In case you have forgotten, I'm just the messenger! I am a replica, nothing more! While it is true that Galynn Brytshul's memories are in my head, I did not do or say any of the things he did. In fact, this makes me far more innocent than you are. Go ahead, ask OTIDS. See what God has to say about the matter. I cannot lead you to the lair of Cartomancer Merenia, nor do I possess any of the items that have been mentioned in my tale. Perhaps you should just ask Justinian Vargalow about Callidi's heretical views. Oh, backing away so soon? I don't blame you. Being turned into a frog is bad for one's health.

Now, back to my tale, and be forewarned that you will be offended even further, so if you don't have the stomach for it, just leave me in my cell and forget seeking knowledge. In all honesty, I have no idea how long we stayed within the odd lair of Callidi Merenia. It could have been days or even years, but I suspect that such demarcations mattered little to nothing within that strange place. At times, she referred to herself as a chrononaut, on other occasions a modern oracle, but neither title seemed suitable. That she was highly talented was obvious to all. Callidi told me that she required no armed guardians nor bodyguards, for her abilities allowed her to not only remain safe from harm but to counter any form of violence.

Upon hearing this claim, Linia reached for a blade on her bandolier. Callidi laughed, without turning to face my living weapon, and stated with absolute confidence, "You will aim for my right eye, which I will dodge. The blade will hit my outer walls and be swallowed by the ether, drifting between realities, until it is discovered by a creature that uses it as a digging tool. You will then leap towards me, landing upon my chair, which you will then find empty, damaging your leg in the process. Prime will come to your aid, then trip over my left foot, crashing on top of you with his weapon drawn. I have seen all of the variations, and according to my calculations, you will remain where you are, waiting for another opportunity to show your skill."

Linia was visibly shaken by this demonstration of oracular prowess. I stepped forward swiftly, "Please, my Lady, we are not here to attack you. We require your help, as you well know, and I would be grateful if we stayed to the matter at hand, my own failure to stick to instructions and rectifying my many mistakes."

Callidi nodded towards me, a subtle smile upon her face, "Well said, Galynn, but you must accept that this journey will change you in ways that will be difficult, if not dangerous, to counter. Truths will come to light which shall alter you forever. As for more practical matters, your carriage must be abandoned and your belongings carried by your Troth-Knights, all of whom must enter my realm, so they may go with you when I open a portal for your next destination."

I shrugged, "Not a big problem. I shall designate Prime as the one to gather our meagre forces together for the journey. Now, I'm used to the idea of a wizard creating portals, but a cartomancer? That seems odd to me."

Callidi shook her head ruefully, "Please, Galynn. I am not the typical fortune teller, thank you very much! Justinian is quite good with portals as a general rule, but he lacks the finesse required for your current situation, which is why he sent you to me. He's too in love with OTIDS procedures and thus misses the larger picture. I am highly regarded by both Justinian and his ever-worshipped OTIDS but for divergent reasons. The magi within your realm acknowledge my superior abilities, while OTIDS considers my current residence as being Holy, mainly because my chamber is in a permanent state of superposition. Oh dear, I've confused you again. This is the problem with seeing all magick as a useful philosophy and art instead of a science."

Perturbed by her position on the subject, I asked, "What else can it be, save an art of the will? I have seen, and even cast, spells which are guided by the inner vision of the practitioner. What other form can magick take? It comes from OTIDS, guided by the user. New spells are created by talented mages, who use their creative talents to develop new wonders. Is that not the description of an art?"

Callidi laughed, "But you miss all the finer points of the system. Tell me, Galynn, can a real painter refuse to consider the chemical reactions of his pigments? Can a sculptor ignore the stone she uses to create a statue? In truth, they can, but at the expense of the work itself. Basic foundations are critical, and those are not found in reliance upon OTIDS."

I thought about this, as I sent Prime on his errand to collect the other Troth-Knights and secure our baggage. It troubled me that it was possible that OTIDS was keeping humanity from learning more about the basic nature of reality, though such heresy made me squirm in discomfort. The Church always claimed that science had led us all astray from the truth, yet here was someone who could work miracles, telling me that we were all being lied to. It suddenly occurred to me that I didn't know the history of OTIDS itself. I knew a little about the Church, some of the history concerning the nobility, but nothing about our beloved deity. A cold chill ran down my spine, and it made me dizzy enough to want to run screaming from Callidi's home.

Linia must have sensed my mood, for she stepped towards me and grasped my trembling hand, "We'll be gone from here soon, Galynn. Just hold on a little bit longer. You're doing well. I hate to admit it, but you are."

I grimaced at her, "Just being polite to the crazy cartomancer. After all, should I offend, she could destroy us all in the blink of an eye. I never wanted to be in this position, you know. It was forced upon me. Even so, this quest we're on is intriguing. The more I learn about it, the more I feel that we're missing something important. It feels... incomplete."

Linia frowned, "In what way? Aren't we just finishing the work your father started long ago?"

I snapped my finger, "That's just it! All this fuss to bring together some heretical items and strange people, then hide them in some shelter? Hear me out. My biological father was an Arch-Bishop and a conjurer who was part of Justinian's busy group of mages. That means long-term goals. Big ones. This feels too small, too unimportant for the likes of one so mighty. If all we're doing is removing non-OTIDS items from the world, why is the Church after us, instead of thanking our efforts? Why does the nobility care about what we're doing? If OTIDS was against our plan, we'd never stand a chance! None of us would have met nor survived."

Linia seemed to collapse in on herself, "We're pawns. The game is too big for us to understand. We do what we're told. It's how we were made, how we were trained."

I was not about to let such sloppy thinking slide by, "Nonsense! I've never done anything as instructed. I always rebel against authority. Not to mention I wasn't made nor trained for anything but picking pockets. If the game's too big for us, then it's time to bring it down to earth!"

Linia looked up at me, "But how, Galynn?"

I replied with a wink, "OTIDS isn't concerned about this adventure, or we'd know it by now. That means our enemies are only human. They may have great power and unseemly magicks, but they still piss in a pot. Their own hubris will destroy them, so it's up to us to find the best way to make them fall upon their own arses. Tricking marks was once my sole obsession. Now we need the right information and the proper leverage. We don't have to halt the stars or bend the moon to our will. We simply have to make our opponents lose themselves to their own egos."

My living weapon nodded thoughtfully at this conclusion. I patted her on the shoulder, then walked over to the entrance to Callidi's home to help my Troth-Knights to bring in our belongings. We had been travelling light, so it wasn't too much of a burden. Mostly, I kept well out of their way, directing them to load things in one section of the chamber that was clear of other objects. I tried not to stare at the floating crystals and lit panels, for the things they revealed were disturbing. Were these visions of the future?

The past? Other realms and realities? My head was swimming with the idea that, in this place, Callidi could see anyone, anywhere, at any time.

When her hand gripped my left shoulder from behind, I croaked out a strangled cry of alarm, which was swiftly covered by Callidi's laughter, "I can see why Justinian trusts you! I do believe you understand just enough to be paranoid about everything around you. That's good, by the way."

I spun about and snarled at her, "Do not approach me from behind! Was there something you needed from me, or did you just wish to test my worn boundaries with your antics?"

Callidi stepped back, a smirk upon her petite face, "Such a sensitive thing, you are. I came over to give you a gift, as promised."

In her other hand was a rectangular object, wrapped in colourful silk. I kept my hands away from it, tucking them behind my back, "What is it? I have learned to not touch things I don't understand."

She shook her head with mocking sadness, "That must be difficult, for such a policy would include everything around you. I'm giving you a Tarot deck, so you may gain some advice and extra information on your journey. Don't worry, it's not from your reality, so there's no connection to OTIDS or the Church. This deck came from CardStack, which is a distant universe from your own, as such things are measured. Justinian and I went there together. No need for an interpreter, as the cards will explain their imagery through moving pictures."

I shrugged, "I'd still need to know how to set them out properly, and what kind of shuffling technique to use."

She grinned up at me, "Not at all. Choose a card, any card, from any part of the deck. Need more information? Just grab another card. Shuffling is up to you, but it makes little difference to the cards themselves. At least, it means little to these. I have another set of them, and I do swear they are incredibly accurate."

I bowed to her, "Your assessment of their efficacy is noted, my Lady. How robust are they? We might end up in a scrap or two along the way."

Callidi rolled her eyes, "I've yet to discover anything that will harm them, including vorpal blades, fire, laser strikes, nuclear explosions, virulent mildew, and some nasty creatures. How to explain... Ah! Everything in your reality exists according to a set of natural laws or rules of existence. These cards come from a place which has a very different set of rules, ones which make it difficult for physical interaction to take place. The only reason they work outside their own environment is that you have a will to guide them. The mind, or consciousness, it seems, has a special place within most of the infinite realities. Like a glue that holds everything together."

I brought my hands from behind my back to accept the wrapped deck of cards, "So, they're sentient?"

Callidi slapped my right shoulder, "Hardly! These things are beyond such crude distinctions! Besides, sentience isn't always helpful with such things. In fact, it can get in the way. Observation, acceptance, and being in the flow of Fate are far more important than intelligence. Awareness is the real key."

I smiled at her shyly, "Then I must have lost all my keys a long time ago. I confess to barely understanding what you're telling me, though there is a part of me that tingles a bit when you explain these things."

She pursed her lips at me, "Flatterer. Must I continue to remind you that you belong to another? Besides, I'm your elder by several centuries, even though I don't look like I am. That's got nothing to do with magick, by the way. At least, not the magick you're used to dealing with."

I bowed low to her, "I never ask about a faire Lady's magick. Thank you for the fine gift. I'm certain it will help with my adventures. Speaking of which, when should I depart this chamber between the worlds?"

Callidi handed me the deck of cards, which I swiftly tucked into my pouch with the other magick items, "You'll be heading out shortly. If you need more time to rest, let me know. Even after staying here for a year, I can get you to the convention in time to meet those you skipped on the way to Justinian's house. Just be careful. You're not on the registered guest list, nor will you be arriving through any OTIDS-approved portal. You'll be on an alien world without authorization."

I blinked at her, "I'll be on what?"

Callidi sighed deeply, "Sorry. Forgot. You and your party will be upon an angelic realm illicitly. If you're caught, things could get ugly for you."

A crooked smile crossed my features, "I'm well versed in villainous behaviour, my lady. I've run afoul of the law many times and have evaded capture by the nobility itself, with the help of some kind friends. Indeed, if I may be so bold as to state that it will be quite a relief to get back to matters of which I am much more familiar. My life has been on the ugly side of things for many years. How much worse can it be when visiting an angelic realm?"

Callidi squinted up at me, "Well, first off, they could just eat you for trespassing. If the local residents feel they can get away with it, they'll do that. Most of them hate humanity, for good reasons."

As calmly as I could, I replied quietly, "Then the situation calls for a subtle form of entry. I can disguise myself well enough, with little more than scraps. Linia can change her form at will, so no problems there. My Troth-Knights all have camo-suits, which will come in handy, I'm sure. They can be quite invisible when they're not running about, killing things."

Callidi shook her head, "Not good enough. Invisibility won't help you there. They have to fit in with what the crowd expects. Please call Prime over here. I have some instructions for him to consider."

I waved my hands about until Prime noticed me, then he marched over in his usual, ground-eating stride, calling out, "Yes, my Lord! How may I assist you?"

Callidi turned to look up at his rugged face, "Prime, you have to reset the programming on your camo-suit. Go into 'options', then select from the menu, 'civ-pattern three'. Choose a dark, distinguished colour. All of your Knights must do the same. It would be best if you all matched. Don't forget to make sure your face also fits the new style."

Prime nodded, while I looked on, terribly confused. Prime adjusted some decorations upon his broad breastplate, turning medals and touching rivets. He then placed his hands upon his face-gems and blinked hard. All at once, his armour became a very clean, well-pressed, dark blue suit of ancient design. His hair shortened, became darker, and a bejewelled stud sprouted from his left ear, with a coiled wire dangling to a pocket on his new, buttoned coat. Dark glass spectacles covered his eyes, and I was immediately more intimidated than I already was by his presence.

Callidi applauded excitedly, "Perfect! Now you'll fit in with the other security details. Galynn can remain as he is, as he already looks like some eccentric investor. Linia needs a makeover, though."

Prime pressed a hand over his new ear jewellery, "All units, be ready to implement new instructions for your gear. Bring Linia Raslow to me at once. She requires information."

Within a few moments, one of the Troth-Knights, now wearing the new style of clothing, brought Linia over to our little group. She glanced at the Knights with eyebrows raised, "What can I do for you, Prime?"

It was Callidi who answered her, "You need to fit in with their new disguise for the convention of bureaucrats. It would be best if you looked like Galynn's attaché. He's playing the part of a reclusive investor."

Linia gave our hostess a sceptical glance, "Do I have to wear such outlandish antiques? Or is fashion dead where we're going?"

Callidi patted Linia on the shoulder, "Well thought! You should look the part as best you can, which means some expensive clothing and more face-gems than you normally have. Can you do that?"

Linia was now glaring at the cartomancer, "Of course I can! Galynn's father made sure to give me all the latest spells and enchantments a proper assassin would need."

I suddenly burst out without thinking, "A proper assassin? I thought paid killers were more like savage pets, far from the ideals of propriety!"

Both of the women laughed at me, and Prime shook his head sadly. It had never occurred to me that a living weapon could be as noble in bearing as any aristocrat. I thought that assassins were mainly hired thugs, rather than highly educated and sophisticated individuals whose skills were always in high demand, as Linia swiftly corrected me concerning my latest faux pas, "Most nobles have at least one of my kind in their service, foolish man! We are the deadly jewels in their arsenals, and we often accompany the upper classes as part of their inner circle or close retinue. Stop being such a rube."

Linia then pulled at her tresses, rubbed her eyes, clapped her hands, and yanked down hard on her bodice. Suddenly, she had sandy brown hair, dark skin, green eyes and was wearing a white, leather ensemble with clean lines and gold trim. Clicking her heels together rapidly, she became three inches taller. She removed her bandolier of magick knives, knotted it up, and it became the kind of tally book one might see in an expensive accountant's office. She flipped the cover open, and pulled out a shimmering blade.

I had seen her in different forms before but had never been allowed to watch the process until now, "Do you ever choose your original look? The body you were born with?"

Linia looked away as if embarrassed, "I no longer remember it."

Callidi waved a hand in the air, "That doesn't really matter. Besides, it's now time for all of you to get to your next destination. I have the portal set up at the far end of my chamber, beyond my habitual seat. Let's assemble ourselves there, and I'll do my best to instruct you on the proper protocols for using one of my special conveyances."

We did as she requested, my Troth-Knights now carrying or holding a variety of sleek packs and cases, which I assumed were now filled with our belongings. I reached into my pouch, then took out my rings and bracelet, putting them on, but leaving the necklace in the bag. At the far end of the spherical chamber, well beyond Callidi's throne, was a strange device. It was angular and tall, like a triangular nest on its side, made of silvery spikes that reached far above our heads. At the very middle of it, the air shimmered with many colours, and it made my head swim just looking at the thing.

The cartomancer grinned widely as she explained, "This is not one of your typical portals, found in travel stations throughout your world. As we are outside of your universe, this device uses special properties to find the correct time and place for your travels, as it envisions your universe from a holographic point of view."

No one said anything, as I suspect the others were as confused by her odd explanation as I was, so she continued, "Once you step through, no matter how curious you are, do not open your eyes! You will hear strange things, feel odd sensations, but if you want to come out of this experience with your dimensional innocence in place, just keep your eyes shut. Accept it as another example where being an intelligent creature is not an advantage in every situation. I have the coordinates locked in, and I shall be controlling the portal from my seat. When I give you the word, just walk in and close your eyes. Try to relax. It makes the experience more pleasant."

Prime, Linia and I all gave each other a concerned glance, but what could we do but obey? I was quite ready to be leaving this strange place and its bizarre inhabitant behind, grateful as I was for the assistance. The other Troth-Knights gathered up behind us, as Spinel glided over to wrap himself around my neck and shoulders. His extra weight felt comforting to me, and I scratched at his scaly chin, making him shiver in reaction.

Within a few moments, Callidi called out, "Okay! I'm ready! Now just walk into the portal as if passing through an open door. Remember, keep your eyes closed! Thanks for visiting me! Now, go!"

In unison, Prime, Linia and I stepped through the shimmering haze. I shut my eyes quickly but immediately felt as if I were falling from a great height. Hot sounds sent wet shivers of sweet flavours throughout my senses. Screams filled the air, as my body seemed to smash its way through a glass barrier. Bubbling, choking liquids slithered over me, while my teeth felt as if they were dancing around my gums. I felt the need to vomit, doubling over in pain. My eyes flew open in alarm, and I began to scream.

CHAPTER TWELVE

LilyDrop

"Face the unknown through Me
Let My light guide thee
Fear no evil
For I am thy shield."

-Excerpt from the OTIDS Bible – Procedures 10:17

You cannot imagine all the terrible things I saw in there. The sheer chaos and horror of raw creation laid out before me, ripping my poor mind to shreds. My brain was eaten alive, unable to cope with the ever-changing vista of monstrous visions and painful beauty. Panic gripped my very soul. It was as if I were drowning in madness. I could not see my companions, nor could I reach out to touch them. Had I become lost in a space between the realms of reality? To this I had no real answer, yet I needed to get back to somewhere sane.

Inspiration struck me with such sudden, blinding light, that I acted without thinking. Wizard Vargalow had given to me a pair of personal gate rings, fitted with some pre-assigned destinations which were safe areas, to be used in times of severe emergency. I could not think of a more appropriate time to utilize such a boon, and so I did. With shaking hands, I pulled them from my sack. Placing one ring at my trembling feet, desperately ignoring the shifting insanity surrounding me, I then raised the other over my head. The words of activation entered my mind unbidden, and I spoke them aloud.

Sparks filled my vision. The ring in my hands grew hot. I had no idea as to whether this was part of how the magick hoops functioned, but I trusted in the wisdom of Justinian Vargalow. Pain lashed out at me, striking down my spine like a thunderbolt. My body was squeezed, as if being devoured by a giant serpent. Heart pounding, my lungs refused to work. I tried to cry out, but everything was noise and harsh colour. I fell into an abyss that yawned open beneath my feet, while my vision stuttered.

I dropped face first into a warm, sticky fluid. Flailing my arms about, I found some purchase beneath my feet and staggered upward. Gasping for breath, my lungs heaved and coughed, until I thought that I would pass out. Still, I held on, determined to not make a total fool of myself. The surface beneath my feet shifted, wobbled, making a soft, slurping sound. I looked about and saw a landscape that I could never imagine as being real.

The sky was full of deep shades of purple, green and creamy yellow, swirled together with a pastel mist of soft oranges and reds. Large, irregular globes of liquid drops filled my eyes. Some were distant, others close. Smaller ones drifted before globes the size of buildings, with no two appearing to be the same proportions. I dropped to my knees and realized that I was standing upon some species of open flower that resided just below the surface of the sweet-scented liquid. Its petals were coiled and pink, surrounding a deep core the stretched into the globe of sticky water I had found myself on.

My companions were nowhere to be seen, which wasn't surprizing, as I was the only one to have the portal rings. Inspecting the arcane hoops, I noticed that they looked tarnished, as if they had been abandoned under a well for many years. This troubled me, for most highly enchanted items were impervious to all manner of damage. Had I pushed the rings too far, using them in such chaotic conditions? Not being a wizard, there was no way to tell if this were true.

Something slid around my neck, and I cried out in alarm. A screech filled my ears, as little Spinel flapped his wings and stared at me, eyes aglow with fulgurant light. I laughed aloud, opening my arms wide, as he landed upon my chest, clinging to me like a new-born to his mother. The relief that I was not alone was palpable, bringing tears of gratitude to my eyes. OTIDS blessed me with Spinel's presence, and I had never felt the need to worship more dearly than at that time.

My hose was soaked to my skin, as were my pants, but this liquid did not act like water, nor did it smell like anything but nectar. In fact, the air itself seemed perfumed with floral notes of such complexity, I was sure that any perfumer would give their right arm for a sample. I decided to get a good look at this new realm, peering hither and yonder, but seeing nothing but colourful sky and nectar drops. No hard firmament beneath me, no sun nor stars, just the clouds and drops. Some of these collided with one another, merging together to make a larger globe. Their surfaces were rippling, and I could see that there were things within them, though I could not guess at what they might be.

With a touch of consternation, I dropped my gaze to below my feet. Something was moving below the flower I was standing upon. Watching it closely, I saw that it had many fins, yet its body was hardly like that of a fish. Instead, it distantly resembled a dragonfly, without wings or legs. A sudden dread coursed through my veins. This place was obviously not one of the safe havens that Justinian Vargalow had provided for. Despite the warmth of this strange place, I became chilled as the realization that I was not in my home universe struck me like a hammer blow.

With a touch of pride, I do remember how quickly I reached for my other magick items: the two begemmed rings and my bracelet. I did not know for certain if they would work in this new environment, but I trusted the skill of Wizard Vargalow, who had roamed such realms in his work for OTIDS. I also had one of Prime's blades tucked into my belt, which I then freed from its scabbard. Spinel noticed my actions and leapt from my body, flying a tight circle around me. At least the baby dragon did not seem ruffled by our new circumstances, which heartened me.

I have often stated that I am not a brave or bold fellow, unless I'm taking a wealthy mark for a ride, to relieve them of their coin. Now that I was alone, save for my trusty dragon, I would soon have to learn how to fend for myself in this new world. First and foremost was the need for food and water. Though the sticky nectar smelled wonderful, I did not really trust it. Honestly, it was a wonder I could breathe the dense and cloying air! There was no sign of civilization, not even a modest cottage. A hermit's tent would have been an encouraging sight! Spinel landed upon my shoulders, wrapping his long, barbed tail loosely around my soaked neck. Meanwhile, I searched my surroundings, just in case I had missed something important during my earlier inspection.

The globes of nectar were all in constant motion, and while it seemed random, there was a pattern to their flow, as if the air was filled with great rivers of giant drops. The sky remained colourful, but the hues had shifted a touch, though I had no way of telling what that might mean. Was there such a thing as night in this bizarre realm? The thought sent shudders down my spine. I felt exposed, naked, despite my clothes and belongings. Understand that I was an urban wastrel, for the most part. While it could be said that I had become a bit more comfortable in forests and more rural settings since my adventures began, this situation was completely different.

A sudden, loud hiss from Spinel broke me from my gloomy musings. Turning about, I swiftly scanned the horizon to see what had alarmed my reptilian companion. Above one of the largest drops of nectar was a crimson cloud. While it was difficult to judge any distance in this strange place, the moving patch of red seemed far away. Squinting at the shifting mass, it soon became noticeably larger. It also appeared to be made of a swarm of smaller objects. Spinel arched his neck and gave out a screeching cry, similar to that made by falcons and the like. The swarm swerved in our direction, and I gave the dragon a dirty look which he ignored.

A cheerful sound, just on the edge of being audible, filled the air. It was like the ringing of tiny bells, mixed with a musical buzzing tone. As the cloud came closer, the noise grew in volume. The sticky nectar that was still wrapped about my ankles shifted alarmingly, almost throwing me from my feet. I glanced down and saw that the finned dragonfly had dropped to the far end of the globe below my sandals. The flower I was standing upon was wiggling, its petals folding over my feet, and it swiftly lowered itself so that the nectar now reached my knees.

Turning my attention back to the red cloud, I found myself staring at a mass of small creatures with wings. They reminded me of oversized ants, but were strangely translucent, as if they were made of jelly. Taking a hint from the dragonfly and flower, I took a deep breath and allowed myself to drop into the sticky fluid below me. Spinel hesitated for a moment, flapping his wings wildly, staring down at me from above, then he dived in to join me in my descent. The nectar was thick, heavy and warm, weighing me down as I floated toward the center of the giant drop. The syrupy substance got into my nose, soaked my clothes, and yet held me buoyant enough to have some control over the direction I was heading. Needless to say, getting too close to the swimming dragonfly was not really an option, though I was relieved to find that the flower had released its grip on my feet.

The distorted sound of bells reached my fluid-filled ears. I twisted to see what was happening above me and saw that the flying jelly-ants were hitting the globe of nectar like rainfall. The winged creatures were the size of my hand and were indeed transparent. Their jaws opened wide as they drifted down at me, like bristling gates covered with spines. Spinel glided towards me, as I flailed about in a panic, but by the time one of the horrid insects reached me, it had dissolved, turning the nectar a murky pink.

At this point, I'd had enough of a fright to compel me to swim for the lowest reaches of the drop, dragonfly-fish be damned. Spinel gripped my back, aiding my flight with the use of his wings. As it turns out, he helped me a bit too much. We slammed into the dragonfly and popped out the other side of the drop, falling into open sky. I screamed in terror. Spinel shrieked from his perch. The dragonfly-fish yowled like a scalded cat. Thrashing like a madman, I did my best to aim for another globe of nectar, hoping to get to it before the jelly-ants realized we were vulnerable. A large one was close by, much bigger than the bubble I had escaped from. Dark shapes could be seen lurking within its girth, but at that point, I didn't really care.

The dragonfly-fish was squirming about, yet clinging on to me like I was its mother. Spinel spat a brief burst of flame at its face, and the finned insect released me, drifting off into the endless expanse of the drop-infested sky. Now that I was free from that burden, I was able to stretch out my arms and make the attempt to guide our path. Spinel acted as a balancing force, keeping us from tumbling forever. A patch of something green was floating upon the surface of the nectar drop in front of us, so I aimed for that with all my will.

When we landed, it became apparent that instead of grass, as I had previously supposed, the material was more akin to dense fur. We fell on top of it in a heap, and the floating mass pulled us under, enveloping our bodies completely. Before I had the chance to scream, it bounced back up, flattening out on the surface of the nectar once again. I gasped for air, relief flooding my veins, while Spinel shook himself clean. I lifted my head, wiping sticky nectar from my face, then glanced up to look at the drop we had left behind. To my consternation, it was difficult to tell one globe of fluid from another, but the cloud of jelly-ants was nowhere in sight. I sighed quietly and turned back to look at the matt of furry greenery we had just landed upon. That was when the longer, thicker strands of hair began sprouting tiny yellow balls. I pulled back in alarm when these opened up like flowers, revealing blue eyes that turned to stare at me.

The shriek that came from my mouth startled Spinel into flight. I felt something wiggle against my torso, which prompted me to lurch away, without falling into the nectar itself. A long tube sprang up from the center of the matt, seemingly made of intertwined hairs. The end of it opened wide, revealing rows of flat, brown teeth. I struggled to back away, but the furry material bobbed and sank beneath my weight.

The mouth of the tube turned towards me and spoke, "This is my face you are sitting on! That is rude!"

To say that I was startled into silence is an understatement of truly epic proportions. I blinked hard, shook my head, and wondered if the nectar had hallucinogenic properties.

To my dismay, the tube spoke again, "What are you? Why do you not swim or fly?"

I coughed out a bit of nectar from my throat and croaked, "My name is Galynn Brytshul. I'm a human from the realm of OTIDS."

The tiny eyes blinked as one, "A what? From where?"

Laugh all you want. Until you've had the chance to speak with a matt of green fur, you have no frame of reference to judge me or the situation I had found myself in. Despite all your wealth and great power, you have not experienced half of what I did since receiving my supposed inheritance. In any case, instead of answering, I shrank back from the tubular mouth.

All the tiny eyes followed me as it spoke again, "You are afraid. Why? I am no threat to any who swims in LilyDrop. What are those shining things upon your flippers?"

I shook my hands at the mouth, "Please! One question at a time! I am most heartily glad to hear that you are not a threat, though one might say that a cunning predator would lie to keep prey close."

The thing responded, "What is a lie? You speak my language, but I do not understand some of your words. This is a puzzle to me."

I wiped more nectar from my face with trembling hands, "I don't have an answer to that riddle. I have never been in a place like this before. Is this one of the outer realms?"

The furry matt's tubular mouth made an odd, bubbling noise, "More mysterious words! I have lived, travelled with my chosen drops, met others of my kind, evaded dangers, yet now I am visited by the strangest creature I have ever seen, who knows nothing of the world. Please explain what the glowing things on your flippers are. They are most distracting. Parts of you make sense, but some of you I have never experienced."

I took a shuddering breath before stating, "I do not have flippers! I have hands, with fingers, thank you! Oh! My rings and bracelet! Do you mean my jewellery? They are made of precious metals."

The shaggy creature responded with, "I do not know what a metal is. Do such things always glow this way?"

I examined both my rings but could discern no illumination, "What do you see? Perhaps your eyes are more sensitive than mine."

The mouth mumbled to itself, then spoke up more clearly, "There are lines and patterns made of light that surround them all. There are other things on your body that have similar markings, but not so bright as the ones on your... hands."

Like a thunderbolt, the answer came to my mind, "The magick! You can see the spells cast upon them! I'm envious of your ability. Please forgive my being frightened by everything here. I have lost my companions, who were charged with protecting me. I must find my way back to them."

The matt's mouth then asked, "Can you not catch their scent? Such a thing should be easy, for I have never smelled anything like you."

I ducked my head, "My nose isn't really up to the task."

It made the burbling noise again, "You poor creature! Bad sight, no sense of smell, no wonder you have lost your people. Can you not return to the point where you were separated? They might be waiting for you there."

I'm certain that you can see my conundrum. How does one explain to a green, fuzzy, floating matt the complexities of inter-reality travel, when one does not know the basic principles of such spellcraft? I needed advice from an expert, not the suggestions of a mossy aberration, yet its words did have some merit. I got into this strange realm by using the portal hoops that Justinian Vargalow gave to me. Could I return to my companions in the same manner? The idea seemed far too simplistic, yet the teleportation hoops had been given to me, a wastrel untrained in the occult arts. Gently, I pulled them from my bag, relieved that they were not also covered in goo. One of the nice qualities of holding bags is that they not only carry any number of items, but they also protect them from outside influences.

The floating matt squawked in dismay, "Put those away! Too bright! Too complex! Dizzying! Painful!"

I hastened to comply, while the matt under me undulated in a most alarming manner. Once the pair of magick hoops were back inside my bag, the tubular mouth ceased its exclamations. All the tiny eyes of the matt were tightly shut, but its thrashing had been reduced to mild ripples in its fur. Not knowing what else to do, I gently patted the soft surface, "Is that better, my new friend?"

A few tiny blue eyes popped open, "Yes. Keep them in your flesh. You will attract many predators shining like that. They always look for things that smell new and appear strange. They keep LilyDrop in balance, pure."

This new information did not hearten me. I patted the single blade I had on me, to reassure myself that I still had some form of defence. I did not know if either of my rings or bracelet were working properly, nor did I wish to experiment to see if they were still effective. Instead, I used my face-gems to clean my clothes and dry my soaked skin. My face suddenly became hot, uncomfortably so. Steam rose from my garments, smelling of burnt sugar.

The green matt wailed again, "Stop! You shine far too brightly! Soon, hungry creatures will come here to investigate. They will eat us!"

I focused upon my face-gems once again, and the steam vanished, leaving me feeling moist and sticky. I turned my head to face the tubular mouth, "I seem to be in constant danger here, and I keep bringing peril to those who try to help. My apologies. I shall refrain from such tricks until I get back to my companions."

The mouth rubbed its teeth together, making a clicking noise, "You have fouled my fur. I must wash, though I fear that your scent will spoil this drop. I must now seek a new home or be harassed by those who hunt. Such a shame. This was a new spot for me, and I looked forward to seeding here. It has come to my mind that you are not simply strange but an interloper as well. You know nothing of the ways of the world and acting in ways which cause harm to all. Ignorant as a hatchling, yet too large in form."

I honestly felt guilty for causing this gentle creature cause for alarm. Normally, I wouldn't care at all, for my obsession with serving only myself had been a survival skill throughout my downtrodden life. Yet here, in this insane realm, I was alone. It began to occur to my narcissistic brain that I needed to relate better with others, no matter how unusual they looked. For all I knew, I would be stuck in this place forever or be doomed to hop from world to world, without end. I had to reassess my priorities and my personal capabilities. This was not about proving anything. It had nothing to do with politics, social strata, nor taking on marks. I had to learn or die horribly.

I leaned close to the tubular mouth of the green matt, "I shall leave you in peace. Thank you for giving me a chance to get my bearings. I did not mean to bring danger to your... drop. If you ever see beings such as myself, looking for me, please let them know that Galynn moved on."

It wiggled at me for a moment, then responded, "I can see that you have grown a sense of nest. This is good. Though you are a stranger who has caused me some trouble, I shall give you some advice. To aid others is more important than the condition of your fur. When lost, seek not to use others to lead you, but understand that all of us drift through the flow of reality. We are lost because we are alive. Only drops know where and what they are. To be a living being has more to do with growth and learning than having the comfort of knowing and stability. Go forth, grow, get beyond yourself."

It was possibly the most profound thing I'd ever heard, and from a floating matt of fur! I forced myself to touch the throat of the tubular mouth, "Thank you, my friend. You are quite correct, though I was too blind to see it for myself. I'll go take a dip in this drop, if you don't mind, so that I might hide the smell of my otherworldly scent. May your life be filled with peace."

The throaty tube briefly wrapped itself around my hand, then tucked away, back into the mass of green fur. I looked over at Spinel, who was still flying nearby, "I'm going for a dip. I suggest you join me. Then, we shall do our best to leave this confusing place, in the hope that we might re-join the others. They must be terribly worried by now, for we have been missing for hours, at the least!"

I prepared myself as best I could. An odd feeling rose up in my chest. It wasn't fear, hunger or anger, my usual cocktail of emotions, but a sense that I could become whatever I needed most. Was this courage? I think not. Perhaps it was just determination stiffening my wilted spine. I gulped a deep breath, then tumbled into the drop of nectar. Spinel joined me in the warm globe of sticky fluid, and we swam together towards the other side, ignoring everything else around us. There were many strange creatures and objects in that drop, but I was in a hurry to be away.

I quickly built-up speed, for my intention was to not simply emerge out the other side but to burst free into the sweetly scented air. My plan worked, as I crashed beyond the drop, soaring into the open sky. I called Spinel over to me, and he wrapped himself tightly about my shoulders, as was his habit. At that moment, I realized that I was responsible for the baby dragon's welfare along with my own, so it would be best if I simply stepped up to the challenge. I didn't know what would happen to us, but I pulled free the portal hoops, then used the activation words that sprang into my mind.

Spinel yelped as the gate formed around us. I didn't blame him one bit, for I was quite apprehensive about the results. Colours flashed around us. I closed my eyes, as liquid voices rushed through my veins like ice. Flames danced in a circle about my mind. Laughter crashed around us, as I fell into darkness.

CHAPTER THIRTEEN

ScaffoldBlight

"Fear no danger from daemons
No angel shall ever harm thee
I am thy Holy protector
Nevermore shall humanity tremble at the stars."

-Excerpt from the OTIDS Bible – Documentation 23:54

I fell upon a hard surface, knocking my head back, while spots filled my vision. A screech erupted in my ear, as I vomited with such violence that I expected to see my own innards laid out before me. I opened my eyes and saw a riot of oranges, reds and yellows beneath the mess I had made. With a groan of pain, I rolled over onto my aching back, as Spinel fluttered about. He was the source of the screeching noise, making my ears ring in sympathy to his complaints. Sitting up slowly, I beheld an unexpected vista, and my heart sank into my very boots with despair. Not only were my companions nowhere to be seen, but my location was obviously no manner of conference hall. Hot tears welled in my eyes, for I remained horribly lost.

All around me was an endless series of corroded gantries, railings, open-cage elevators and small, yellowish lumens hanging by black cords. The far distance was black as a moonless night, covered by pinpricks of dim illumination, revealing an assembly of walkways and girders that looked as if they had been made by a demented and savage child. Water dripped from above, and I could see some misty, dark clouds drifting between collections of scaffolding. Moss and lichen grew along the railings and upon the upright beams of rusted metal, a green counterpoint to the corrosion that thoroughly infected the landscape, such as it was.

Looking at the gantry floor beneath me, I saw that it was made of a thick mesh of some kind of metal. Here and there, tiny scrapes and isolated spots revealed the cold grey of untainted steel. The rest was a patchwork of orange, with streaks of a deep red that was reminiscent of dried blood. The yellow bloomed over thick layers of orange rust, with smudges of verdigris staining connected joints and bolted sheets of ancient metal.

Crawling over to the edge of the gantry, I looked down and suddenly wished I hadn't. There was no ground below. No sign of firmament or an end to the exposed girder-work was to be found. Looking up revealed the same vista of endless gantries, open shafts and scaffolding. It was as if a gigantic construction project had reached into the starry heavens and then had been abandoned for purposes unknown. Left to rot in the moist atmosphere.

Spinel settled down on a railing nearest to me, making it quiver in a most unnerving manner. Vertigo had grabbed hold of me and refused to let go. The dizzying effect of this horrid place was immediate and intense. I got to my knees and grabbed the closest rail with a quivering hand. In my other fist were the portal hoops I had used to get to that gloomy realm. Both were now noticeably corroded, with cracks forming jagged patterns in the twin rings. Gulping some moist air, I shakily placed them into my bag, to protect them from further harm.

Why had they brought me to that place? The question still haunts me to this day. They were supposed to lead to safety, not realms of dire peril. I could not simply shrug my shoulders and declare Wizard Justinian Vargalow as being incompetent, for I had seen him working his marvels first-hand. I was certain that it had to do with the special gate that Callidi Merenia had forced us to utilize, not to mention my own, panicked actions when I opened my eyes during transit. It occurred to me that I took any form of instruction lightly, if not disregarding advice entirely, despite the source. Had this habit finally thrust me into a just penance for my rebellious nature?

I did not like the lessons I was being forced to learn about myself. Like you, I despised the view from a mirror of truth. My flaws had become magnified to the point where I could no longer ignore them. They would eventually kill me if I continued to follow my base nature. Trembling upon a rusted gantry, while a tiny dragon looked upon me with glowing eyes, in a dark and terrible realm, I struggled with the issues that arose from within my heart. It was so ridiculous, yet it was of paramount importance to my survival. Could I still remain true to myself and find a way to adopt a more responsible manner? Can wastrels actually have goals that rise beyond their own desires?

Before I knew what was happening, a hot rage bubbled up inside me, consuming my mind like an inferno of wrath. I was furious with myself for being a fool. I was filled with hatred for you, my dear nobles, for hunting me down and forcing me onto this path. I was even angry with Linia for being right about me. A growl filled my throat, which grew into a roaring, wordless scream of pure hatred for all creation. I was sick of playing the useless fop, the mewling weakling that had to be protected due to an accident of birth.

My parents had been noble-born, as was my biological father. I was noble-born! Where were my benefits that come with such lofty status? Was I truly one of the foul, craven lords of humanity? This brought me a sudden epiphany. I was noble-born, yes, but I was a beggar, thief and liar who lived on the streets with the very lowest commoners. I had been raised on a farm, by nobles pretending to be something they were not. The hatred which had turned inward was washed away by a determination to gain my revenge on all those who claimed lordship over the realm of OTIDS. I would find a way to strike them down, tear out the foundations of their rule, and trample them all into the dust.

Now, vengeance is indeed a fine thing to pursue, especially if it be for a proper cause to aid others, as well as satisfying one's own bloodlust, but you had to be alive and well to actually perform the act. You had to be at the right time, in the right place, and have the correct frame of mind. I was in a position where I could do nothing to assuage my anger. I needed to find a way back to my realm. I needed to stay alive. That meant I had to do the one thing I abhorred most; I had to change myself.

This line of thought was then interrupted by a most peculiar sound. A distant hissing, like that of a dozen giant snakes, was growing louder in my ears. This was accompanied by the creaking and jingling of metal being hammered by footsteps. I suddenly regretted my outburst, kicking myself for not being more cautious about my new surroundings. The lights that hung along the cords above my head began to sway, casting shuddering shadows on the underside of the gantry overhead. The sounds seemed to be coming up from below, so I looked down and gasped at what I saw. About five levels below, and just a hundred feet to the right, I could see tall figures rushing in my general direction.

They wore hooded cloaks made of leather, but I could still see the nature of their bodies. Their snouts were long and angular. Wide tails swept back and forth as they ran along the lower gantries, shaking rust flakes free from the railings. Scaly, clawed hands grasped onto the girders, while others held wicked, serrated blades. Their exposed skin gleamed bright yellows and blackish-greens in triangular patterns. They were alligators or something akin to such creatures. They hissed and growled at each other with mouths full of spiked teeth, as they rushed towards the open-sided elevator shafts.

If I had been graced with any fluid within my bladder, I would have soiled myself then and there. Dozens of these monsters were rushing about, sniffing at the dank air. Spinel quietly leapt onto my back, sneaking his long neck around my head for a better view. I slowly got to my feet. Staying in place was not an option. Perhaps, if there had been only one of them, I might have stood my ground, but against so many, it was pointless to try. Prime or Linia would have ripped the creatures apart, but I was no warrior. There was also no way to tell if my enchanted items were still functioning properly. One mistake, even an assumption, could kill me.

Now, we wastrels are very good at avoiding capture, as I'm sure you well know by now, and these were the skills I decided to employ. To simply run off is an invitation to get caught. I frantically looked about and noticed that the gantries connected at an intersection every fifty feet. The elevator shafts were surrounded by a wider platform, though their locations seemed random. There were caged areas, some with half-walls, others exposed, and some had wire screening. The girders soon became a poorly-lit thicket in the gloomy distance, so it was impossible to tell if conditions were different in the farther regions of this horrid realm. The darkness swallowed everything.

Crouching down, I traversed the nearest long gantry, which led to a cluster of elevator shafts that did not have robed alligators infesting it. I was tempted to try to smash the yellowish lights above my head, but I feared the noise would bring the reptilian monsters my way. To my immense relief, at the entrance to the next junction of metal walkways, a set of containers were stacked together haphazardly. There were bits and pieces of refuse scattered on the gantry where they had been placed. Amongst all the shreds of paper, chunks of cut steel, and makeshift boxes, were other leavings which made my stomach churn in disgust. Small, severed limbs, all of them furry, were mashed into the grating of the floor. The smell was appalling, but this was a boon in disguise.

Tucking Spinel under my left arm, I gingerly stepped inside a wide, cylindrical container half filled with debris. At first, my little dragon hissed at the stench, but I held onto his mouth until he ceased struggling. Once I folded myself inside the garbage bin, I covered us both with trash, then held still, listening for any pursuit. The alligators didn't disappoint me, as I heard heavy footsteps approaching my position. I dared not take a peek, for fear of discovery, waiting for the foul creature to leave my hiding spot. The thump of footfalls began to fade a bit, but more slowly than I would have liked.

I did as any good wastrel would do; I created a diversion. Removing a small piece of piping that was cutting into my back, I gently tossed it over the side of the bin. The clatter of falling metal filled the air below me, and the roars of my pursuers followed swiftly. The footsteps returned in a hurry, then passed by my location at speed. I waited for a few minutes, daring to hope that my ruse had distracted my pursuers. When no footsteps returned, I slowly poked my head out of the rancid container to scout the situation. No monsters were in sight, to my great relief.

Spinel and I climbed out of the bin, as carefully as we could manage, then continued our slow, quiet progress to the next set of junctions. It was there I found a ladder, corroded and flimsy looking, but what other choice did I have? Spinel took to the air, allowing me to climb past the next two levels and concentrating on not falling forever into the forbidding darkness. Once I got up to the third story above my previous location, I came to a halt, listening intently for any growls or hissing, but all was silent. After catching my breath for a few minutes, I began to walk the gantry I was on, hoping to find some way out of this place.

I walked for a mile or more, until I finally reached something I had not seen here before – a door. It was made of metal that had been welded together in an irregular manner, but it had a handle. I tried it, but the OTIDS-damned thing was locked. I dug into my old pouch, to see if I had any tools I could use to force it open, but then I noticed there was no obvious form of lock upon the door. This meant it was probably barricaded from the other side. Just as I began to turn away in disappointment, I heard some noises coming from the other side of the door. My heart froze for a moment, but it didn't sound like the kind of racket a large alligator would make. Instead, it sounded like furtive scratching.

I remained in place, hand on my sheathed blade, waiting for whoever it was beyond the door to reveal themselves. After a minute, the makeshift hatch opened wide, and a handful of small primates flinched back when they saw me. These new denizens of this terrible realm were no more than two feet tall and covered with a fine, downy fur, much like the kind I had seen in the garbage bin. Their eyes were large and dark, their sorrowful faces in perpetual frowns. I noticed they were all wearing loincloths and tiny vests of greenish leather. One of them had a spear that looked like nothing more than a sharpened spanner.

I raised my hands slowly and then dropped to one knee, with Spinel landing on my shoulder, making the tiny creatures flinch back once more. I had no idea if they could actually understand me, but I softly called out to them, "Hello. My name is Galynn. I am lost and in need of aid. Can you help me?"

The one with the spear puffed out his scrawny chest, lifting the tip of his weapon at me, "Go away! We can barely feed ourselves, let alone give aid to anyone, especially a monster such as you!"

I blinked at him innocently, "Monster? No, I am a human, from the realm of OTIDS. I just got to this world by accident. Please, I had a terrible scare, getting away from those reptiles that infest this place, but I was able to fool them into thinking I was on another level. I just want a touch of time to get my bearings."

A shorter, more grey-haired primate stepped forward, "Look at him, Tarvy. He has hair, like we do. He is a mammal! While I do not like the look of his pet, notice how he treats us with respect. Perhaps we can help each other."

I nodded vigorously, "We can both aid each other. I have some skills that might be worth noting and equipment that needs testing in this strange realm. If they still work here, I might be able to be of use."

Tarvy snarled at me but he lowered his spear. The grey one stepped forward, "Come with me. Stay low, as you are too tall to remain unseen in our village. I am called Falno. I am an elder of our tribe."

I smiled warmly, "I am Galynn Brytshul. Please, lead the way."

On hands and knees, I entered their secret village. Beyond the door, which they barricaded behind me, I saw that they had blocked the view from outside with thin sheets of metal, though none reached the upper walkways. There were tiny tents, small barrels, even some little benches. There were many of the creatures here, including youngsters. Everyone stared, as I crept along the walkway, most of them trembling with fear. We came to a junction where more sheets of metal rose to a more comfortable height for me, and I was told to sit in the center of a clearing. Other furry primates flooded around me but not too close. I stayed calm, glad I was not alone but worried that no one here could really help me return to my companions.

Tarvy stayed nearby, eyeing me suspiciously, while Falno told me the sad tale of his tiny people. Apparently, long ago, his tribe were part of a mighty race of beings with great knowledge. They had explored their home realm to its most distant corners, then they had discovered a way to travel between the worlds. An accident had stranded a large group of them in this realm, where they discovered that it was already inhabited by large reptiles, who had already claimed it for their own. Falno told me they had almost been slaughtered, and what I saw around me was the last bastion of their people.

I considered his words for a moment, then asked, "Am I correct in assuming that both your kind and that of the reptiles originally came from other realms of existence? What happened to those who built this place?"

High-pitched laughter greeted my query, as Falno explained, "This realm makes itself. If you destroy a gantry, another one grows in its place. New girders form all the time. New lifts, new walkways, even new lights. To answer your question, yes, both of our races came here by accident, but the reptiles came first. They see us as interlopers, to be eaten and destroyed."

I nodded, "This sounds like a terrible misunderstanding. You are no threat to them."

Tarvy exclaimed heatedly, "There is nothing to eat but them or us! Water is no problem, as it rains frequently, but there is no food! We hunt each other. They use brute force. We ambush and trap them."

Falno also chimed in, "We always kill them quickly, for we must or become the prey ourselves. They delight in tormenting us before the end."

I pointed a finger at Tarvy, "Now wait but a moment! I saw moss and lichen growing on the railings, just three levels down and about a mile from here! Are you telling me this substance is poisonous?"

Falno suddenly threw caution to the wind and almost leapt upon my knee, "You saw plant life? Here? How can that be?"

I leaned back a bit, while Spinel reared up in alarm, "Yes. Moss, like I said. Perhaps it came with you. Maybe there are other people here, far away in this terrible darkness. That doesn't matter. What does is that you do have something that might be of use to you in terms of victuals."

Tarvy growled, "That won't be of use to the reptiles! Besides, we are on the very edge of their ever-growing sphere of influence. There's no way we can reach those plants without notice!"

I looked at the tiny warrior, "I got away, and I'm ten times your size. What you need is a raiding party. You'll also need a distraction. Something to keep the enemy from seeing what you're up to. I might be able to help with that. It all depends on what spells work here."

Falno looked at me quizzically, "Spells? I don't understand."

Tarvy spat on the gantry floor, "It means he's crazy."

I looked at the crowd of fluffy critters, who were now looking at me with cocked heads, as if considering my sanity, "All of you! Listen to me! How did your original realm work? Was it anything like this one? I doubt it! Did girders grow themselves? Was it nothing but endless scaffolding, made by no hand? In my travels, I have seen things which make this place seem normal in comparison! My home realm runs on the magick of OTIDS, the creator of our heavens. Each realm seems to have its own laws of nature, and I do not come from yours. I'm sure your ways would seem outlandish to me."

The doubtful looks became uncertain, so I pressed on, "You all need food, which is not only available within reach, if you are daring enough, but it can be grown elsewhere in this realm. It just needs some light and water. Aren't you tired of killing and eating reptile flesh? Aren't you tired of being afraid and hungry in the dark? Think of your little ones! Wouldn't you like to give them a better life?"

They were all nodding now, which was not only a relief, but it made me realize something about myself I never knew before. I actually enjoyed rabble-rousing a crowd into doing the right thing. Would any of this benefit me? Of course not! In fact, my plan would bring me into further danger. What was happening to me? Maybe it was the looks of misery on the faces of the finger-sized children that prompted me to goad them. Whatever the reason, it made me feel good, important, and not so lost.

Tarvy looked up at me, his face in a perpetual scowl, "What is your plan, giant? Are you truly willing to sacrifice your life for our people?"

I reached into my bag and pulled out my ruby ring and the bracelet, putting them on while I answered, "You need to test my magicks. Please try to stab my leg."

Without questioning and with a touch of bloodthirsty relish, he did just that, and no harm was done to me. The furry residents were astounded, and I permitted some extra tests, basking in the joy that my enchanted items were working. Once things settled down, save for a few youngsters chewing on my clothes, I presented my plan, which was now taken very seriously.

All but the smallest of the primates gathered their makeshift spears and knives, along with some collecting baskets and nets. Once they took all the moss they could carry, they would return to their nest, then race for the upper reaches of this hideous realm, seeking an area free of reptiles. I did my best to galvanize them further, offering advice and encouragement to all of the fuzzy critters. My heart lifted to previously unknown heights, by the deep respect they gave to me and my words.

Once the preparations were concluded, I grabbed some of the potions I had pilfered from Ghail Plemorph and ran from the hideout in the opposite direction from the hunting party, with Spinel swooping along with me. After making sure I was at least three junctions from the nest, I threw one of the potion jars over the side of a railing, not knowing what would happen. It clattered down two levels, before smashing itself upon a lower gantry but nothing more, to my disappointment. The growls and hisses from cloaked alligators swiftly followed, as did their thudding footsteps, rising from the greater depths.

I hurried onward, keeping to a path that would lead away from the primates. I threw another bottle, this time on the gantry floor directly behind me. This one flashed with a terrible light, and the smell from the leftover fumes was appalling. Over the next hour, I gave the reptiles a merry chase, indeed! They then resorted to elevator shafts, in the hopes of catching me unawares, but Spinel kept a sharp eye on their movements, spitting out fire whenever they used these conveyances. My dragon may be just a baby, but he was terribly clever.

Soon enough, I ran out of options. The horrid reptiles were swarming from both above and below my position. There was no way for me to join the primates in their escape, so I didn't bother to try. I wished the tiny creatures well and hoped they had already evacuated their nest. It was now time for a desperate escape. While I was quite certain that my enchanted bracelet would protect me from serious harm and my ring would aid me in fighting the scaly monsters, I had no wish to be captured for all eternity in this foul place.

I reached into my bag and pulled out the pair of portal hoops. Upon examination, they were in terrible condition, but I had no real choice in the matter, as three lifts, full of robed alligators, had just stopped at my level. With a prayer to OTIDS, not at all certain my God would hear me, I grabbed Spinel close to me and activated the gate-making rings, closing my eyes in dread. Light exploded all around me, flashing within my closed lids, turning my vision red. Screams resounded in my skull, along with a tearing sound, like thick parchment being shredded. The hoops crumbled in my hands, and I cursed myself for being a fool.

I fell into a painful light, then cold air erupted all around me. My eyes flashed open involuntarily, and I beheld a landscape below me filled with rubble, debris and trash that extended as far as my sore eyes could see. The ground, such as it was, was rushing at me at a fantastic speed. I tried to scream, but the sound was ripped from my throat from the velocity of my fall. Before I could react, I hit a pile of crumpled boxes, then blacked out.

I awoke to hear a voice just above my prone position, every part of my body screaming with pain, "Ah! You are alive! Well, that makes things a little easier for me."

Someone scooped me up and slung my body over their shoulder. My eyes were watering, and I could barely see, as my captor carried me along avenues filled with trash, "You're lucky I found you so quickly, Galynn. Yes, I know your name. The Lord of your realm filled out a requisition form for your return, with a note of urgency. Finding lost items is what I do here, at Decentral Station. Your case was labelled an emergency."

I tried to speak, but all that came from my poor throat was a croak of indignation. We passed through a dark corridor that was quite warm, yet forbidding, then entered a large clearing with a ring of oval-shaped windows that floated in the air, each one twice my height and glowing brightly. At the very center of them was a bizarre contraption, which my captor fiddled with, using his feet to press retractable studs on the floor. His legs were unusually long and thin, covered in grey pants that were stained and threadbare.

I struggled in his grasp to no avail, as he took me towards one of the ovals of light, "You're a lucky one, Galynn Brytshul. Keep it that way, and you might survive. Here you go! This is your doorway home. It's a good thing Callidi Merenia uses a particular signature for her inter-dimensional gates. I'd like to say 'see you later', but I doubt you'll be back here!"

I was tossed into the glowing oval like a sack of grain. I heard Spinel screech from within my coat, scrabbling at my shirt in panicked fury. Wild colours, some I had never seen before, enveloped me entirely. Sound became flavour, touch transformed into emotions. My mind was ripped apart, as I screamed once more.

CHAPTER FOURTEEN

The Burdens of Boors

"Let your thoughts be pure
Let your mind find focus
Let your spirit drive you
When casting the spells which I grant unto thee."

-Excerpt from the OTIDS Bible – Processes 09:36

I found myself lying face-down upon a cold, polished marble floor, gibbering like a buffoon and weeping like an infant. Rough hands grabbed my face, forcing my mouth to open wider. Foul liquid was being poured down my sore throat, slithering its way into my organs. It radiated something of comfort. I saw my childhood home and the parents who had raised me. I saw the garden in the back of our meagre hovel. I blinked hard, then all was clear. Prime and Linia were kneeling at my side, both of them still wearing their outlandish outfits. Spinel was peering at my face, his gleaming eyes glowing with concern.

Coughing bitter fluid from my lungs, I sat up, waving everyone back, "I'm fine now. Just fine. Nothing to worry about."

"What happened to you?" Linia asked, while Spinel returned to his place upon my shoulders.

Prime answered her, his voice sounding gruff, "He opened his eyes."

She slapped my arm, "What did you do that for? What did you see?"

I winced, flinching back swiftly from her reach, "I didn't mean to. As for your other question, suffice it to say, you don't want to know."

Indeed, my dear Lords, if you only understood what it is that lurks just beyond our meagre understanding of reality. Even now, I do not like to remember everything I went through in those few seconds that lasted for an eternity. It was too much information, too much to bear for a human mind. The walls between the numerous universes are infinitely thin, yet far thicker than all the realms put together. My experiences felt unreal, yet were a part of my soul. It makes no sense to us mortals, for it doesn't have to. It just is. I also didn't want to tell my companions what had happened to me, for fear they would think me mad. Though I was heartily relieved to see them once more, my experiences were my own secret.

Struggling to stand up, I asked, "Is this the conference center? We need to get to those three bureaucrats before we lose our chance. Did anyone notice our sudden appearance?"

Once I was unsteadily upon my feet, I noticed that we were in a grand hall with a parquet floor. Everything gleamed with cleanliness. Soft drapery rose to the high ceiling, bracketing the grand, opulent windows, from which a bright orangish light filtered through. The hall went on in both directions for hundreds of yards, with crossing corridors at regular intervals. It looked so normal, I wanted to giggle aloud, but I held it back.

Prime answered my query, "We have not seen anyone as of yet, my Lord. There are many communications in the air, all of them from a variety of private channels. I can only assume we are in the place we were meant to infiltrate. I hear footsteps approaching from the south."

Having no idea where that direction was, I watched the other Troth–Knights shift as one, and I turned to face where they were all looking. From around a corner to one of many corridors, a short, fluffy, pink thing padded into view. It had wings upon its back, also of a bright pink hue, and six legs which ended at soft-looking paws that clicked as it moved, indicating some kind of claws underneath all the fluff. There was single eye on its face, which looked to be partitioned into four facets, and was a startling blue. Its neck was long and sinuous, with glittering bands of silvery metal as decoration.

The creature approached us, rising up to spread out its two forefront paws as if asking for a hug, "Welcome, guests, to the Manse de Galar. Are you here for the conference, my Lords and Lady? If so, please allow me to guide you to the main floor, where you may also arrange accommodations, should you require them. Refreshments are gratis during this event, for our hospitality is well renowned."

The damned thing was strangely cute. Like a child's toy, animated by an enchantment. Its voice was sweet, almost flute-like. I have seen angels in my tawdry past but never like the one which was walking towards us. I straightened my robe, making sure my rings and bracelet were still in place, and then cleared my throat with a scowl.

Linia blinked at me, then rushed forward, "My Lord will be wanting to join the investors area, but first he wishes to see the convention itself. I am his attaché, so any and all questions should be addressed to myself. A glass of wine would be best, I think. He has had a strenuous journey."

If only she knew, but I was glad she did not. The angel then bowed its head all the way down to the floor, "Ever is it our privilege and honour to serve humanity. Please follow me."

It turned about gracefully, and we followed, with Prime taking the lead and Linia entwining her arm with mine as we walked behind him. The Troth-Knights marched in formation around us, covering our sides and back. We walked through the grand halls, until I was thoroughly lost. All the while, our angelic host was whistling about the various services the Manse de Galar provided for its guests. We eventually came to a massive chamber, easily ten stories tall and over a thousand yards wide in every direction. We were upon a balcony overlooking the main floor below us, which was full to the brim with people wearing the same kind of antique clothing Linia and the Troth-Knights had chosen for their disguise. Dots of pink indicated other angels in the crowd, providing service to the attendees.

I almost groaned aloud, for our desperate search just became next to impossible. There must have been tens of thousands of people attending the conference. A needle in a haystack would have been easy in comparison. We went down the opulent stairs to the lower levels, working our way through the swarms of visitors, until we finally reached the main floor. A rubbery-looking creature came toward us bearing a platter of wine glasses. Obviously, a daemon servant of some kind. Linia grabbed a glass for me, and we began to mingle. I listened closely to the conversations around us. Shall I give you an example of what was being discussed at this gala?

"I really need better quality document sheets."

"It's your ink that's the real problem. I use those all the time without any trouble at all."

"Really? I thought my ink was high-end stuff."

"Not as good as McLanders."

"Excuse me. I couldn't help overhearing, but it's not the quality of the doc-sheets that's troubling you."

"What do you mean?"

"Your ink is good but not compatible with the paper you use. Makes it smear something fierce."

"So, do I need a new ink or a better brand of parchment?"

"Parchment? Who uses that anymore?"

"My company is heavily invested in it."

"Shame."

"There's a new paperclip enchantment to remove document smears. You could always try that."

"I would never use that! Some brand marks look like coffee stains, you know."

So now you understand that, after an hour of this, I was ready to run screaming from the main floor. Even Linia was looking glassy-eyed from the banality of it all. I came to a halt by a fountain that was spewing champagne and addressed my companions, "This isn't working. We need a more direct approach to find our marks. We must lure them to us. We also have to take a chance, a calculated risk. There must be restrooms here. With all this wine flowing about, I'm sure everyone is needing to pee on a regular basis. I want us all to split up, but I will remain right here by this fountain, as it's as good a landmark as anything else in here. Each of you will go to the lavatories and say you are looking for our targets. Use their names from the booklet here, and say that investor Pontiforia has a reward for them. I'll do the job of sorting out the imposters looking for an easy wallet."

Prime didn't like this idea, but Linia nodded, "Makes sense. The ones we're looking for knew your father, so the name will bring them to you, just out of curiosity if nothing else."

So it was that I ended up alone at the fountain. The crowds swirled around me, barely noting my presence, and those who did left me alone. It helped that Spinel would hiss at anyone who came too close. The waiting was getting to me, I admit. Noticing some servants nearby, none of whom were remotely human, yet after my secret adventures, they seemed almost normal to my eyes. I walked over to them out of curiosity. Two were scaley creatures with too many claws and sharp teeth, definitely daemons. One was a local, its pink, puffy fur standing out in the group, and another angel of such lithe beauty that it was hard to even look at it. They stopped their talking when I approached, and one of the scaley ones said, "May I serve you, my Lord?"

Glancing about to see if there were any onlookers, I replied, "I just wanted some intelligent company while I waited for some friends of mine to show up. What a tiresome crowd! I hope they're paying you well."

A variety of odd sounds erupted from the group, which I eventually realized was their form of laughter. The other scaley one answered, "We're lucky if they pay us at all, my Lord."

I was shocked by this news, "What? Damned rogues! How can they get away with that?"

The lithe angel answered me, "You don't know, my Lord? We must serve your kind, whether we are compensated or not. If we don't, our people are punished most drastically."

The first scaley daemon leaned in closer, "Tell me, human, what do you believe?"

I looked in the shiny part of its skull, which I assumed was its eye, "Well, to be honest, I don't believe much of anything these days. Oh, when I was a child, my mind was full of pretty lies, but I learned the hard way that illusions don't last. After all I've been through, reality doesn't seem so big or important. I'd rather chat with you than these dressed up buffoons."

The pink native spoke up, "He sounds and smells like a wizard, but he doesn't look like one. Are you a new type of human?"

The others gasped at the impertinence, but I simply laughed, "No! I'm just a man who has seen too much and spent most of his life living on the streets in abject poverty. I wasted my life. Now, I'm looking for better things to do than begging for my meals. As a result, I've fallen in with some interesting types, most of whom are bent on changing my ways."

The lithe angel handed me a fresh glass of wine, "How refreshing! A human with a sense of humour and little ego. Is this your first venture to the realms?"

I nodded amicably, "Yes, though I have travelled in other ways, to stranger places. Why do you ask?"

Scaley number two spoke through a mouth full of teeth, "You're not ignoring us or demanding anything. You're also not spouting on about the purity and righteousness of OTIDS. It's very refreshing."

I tilted my head, "Ah! Yeah, OTIDS. I've heard some mixed reviews on that subject. I just try to stay out of its way."

Again, the shocked gasping from my new audience. The lithe angel looked down at me, "Be careful, my Lord. OTIDS is everywhere. It hears you even now. It's in the air we breathe, the food we eat. Even the void cannot escape its presence."

I sipped some of my wine and replied, "I wouldn't be so certain of that! Well, in any case, I have some complaints. It hasn't helped me much, that's for sure!"

The first scaley daemon looked at the others, "He doesn't know."

I gave it a look, "About what?"

It turned back to me and said, "If any of what you call daemons or angels refuse to do your bidding, our people are then punished with famines, diseases and worse. Should any of us declare war upon your species, our stars are destroyed, with all their planets vaporized. The last race of angels to do so were hunted down to extinction. Over a dozen realms were obliterated. Trillions died as a result of that event. OTIDS keeps you safe from invasion, war, privation, neglect, even fear. We are all chained to its will or suffer such consequences as you cannot imagine."

I was outraged by this revelation, "That is horrible! Yet on my home realm, humans are punished, beaten, robbed, abused and even tortured by the upper classes of our human society, yet OTIDS does nothing to rectify this state of oppression!"

It responded, "OTIDS doesn't care what humans do to each other. It only involves itself when other species meddle with humanity. It looks like some people are looking for you, sir. It was a real pleasure speaking with you. I shall remember this moment."

Peering over my shoulder, I saw Prime marching towards me, all but dragging some poor fool by the arm. I turned to say goodbye to my latest of companions, only to find they had moved off into the crowd. Shrugging my shoulders, I went over to my guardian, studying the man he had captured, "I take it you found someone?"

Prime nodded, "Yes, my Lord! He tried to get away from me, once I made the announcement you requested. He responded very negatively to the name 'Pontiforia'."

I looked at the bedraggled man, "Ah, hello. I do believe we have some unfinished business with you."

He looked at me feverishly, "I've already told the Church all I know! I swear it! Please, let me leave in peace!"

I took out the booklet my father had left me and showed him the two pages with names that might have been his, "I'm not from the Church. I'm Larance Pontiforia's son. He left me with this booklet, to gain a favour or gift from those in it. Your name is one of these two, yes?"

The man goggled at me in sheer terror, "May-maybe? Y-yes? I am Vinnio Nablestein. He, ah, the good Bishop told me that this might happen someday. Oh, by the grace of OTIDS! Then he truly is dead! Oh, poor Larance! Here! This is a key to a place where those he rescues survive unharmed. I've never been there, of course. I don't know where it is, never wanted to, still don't! Just take it, and leave me alone!"

A soft voice whispered in my ear, "He's telling the truth."

Startled, I looked about, but no one was close enough to me so they could speak to me in such a close manner. Shrugging my shoulders, I stepped forward and grabbed the proffered key from his shaking hand, throwing the booklet page into the fountain next to us. I commanded Prime to let the terrified man go, whereupon Vinnio fled into the crowd. Just then, I saw that Linia was approaching, leading a stern-looking woman in black, holding a large, leather-bound tome.

I raised an eyebrow at my assassin, and she quickly explained, "This woman claims to have known your father and had struck a deal with him for the sake of her daughter. I agreed to bring her to you directly."

The woman glared at me as if I had crawled out from under a rock, "My name is Talissa Wekom. For the sake of my dear daughter, I agreed to the Bishop Pontiforia's request. It seemed a small price to pay."

The soft voice returned, "She lies to you, but only partially."

Pretending to scratch at my head, I did my best to prevent anyone from realizing that I was getting some interesting, if nebulous, information from somewhere or someone, "I think not. I'd wager that you don't have a daughter and that my father's request offended your sense of duty."

Talissa stepped back in alarm, only to bump into Prime, who had placed himself behind her, "Oh! How did you...? Of course, he would have told you himself. I confess it was my son whom I was most concerned about, and yes, what Larance asked of me went against my professional instincts. I assume your name is Galynn Brytshul? Very well, hand me the page from your booklet, so I may verify its authenticity, then I will do the favour that was demanded of me."

The voice in my ear said, "She tells the truth."

I handed her the torn booklet page, which Talissa snatched from my hand, then ran a long stylus across its face. A chime sounded, and she nodded towards me, opening her tome and flicking through the pages at speed. She paused, glancing over something within the grand book, then took her stylus and scribbled something inside the tome, "There! It's all done. You are now listed as being deceased, according to the records used by the Church and the various noble authorities. A brief obituary will be generated within twelve hours, your demise being listed as an accidental drowning."

I almost groaned aloud when I heard this news. If only I had used the booklet properly and not skipped ahead, this favour would have helped me avoid the Church from the very beginning, throwing them off my scent before they set off to discover my whereabouts. I saw that Linia was laughing behind one hand, while Prime scowled at me. I bowed and thanked the lady, signalling to the others that she could leave us, which she promptly did.

Looking over at Spinel, I noticed the baby dragon was fast asleep on my shoulders. Therefore, the soft voice whispering in my ears could not have come from him, not that such creatures are known to speak. My ears burned with embarrassment over not finding Talissa earlier, thus confessing to my compatriots that I was now hearing voices wasn't really an option. I could see that Prime wished to berate me for such an oversight, especially in light of all the trials we had gone through to get here, but before he could, one of the daemon servants came over to me, "My Lord, I have a note for you from a gentleman over at the watch merchant's tables."

I thanked the creature, which startled it, then took the folded piece of paper. When I opened it, the note read, "Please find me before we run out of time, Panto Gallibardi."

Checking with the name we were still looking for inside the booklet, I found that it did match. Linia asked a servant the way to the watch maker's table, and we were directed to the vendor's region, which was another grand chamber off the main conference floor. While not as crowded as our previous location, it was still bustling with activity, and so we were forced to slowly make our way toward our goal, which was towards the heart of the room. To my consternation, there were several vendors selling fine time pieces, all of which were boasting the latest charms and enchantments. The prices were exorbitant, as one might expect from such quality devices.

I was examining a few of the exhibited wares, when a portly man in the stuffiest suit I'd ever seen walked calmly up to my side. Linia appeared next to him, grabbing his arm and smiling coldly at him. Prime interposed himself between us, and I scolded them, "Stop this! Both of you! If I needed space, I'd be using a force-bubble!"

They both backed off a bit but not comfortably so, while I turned to the man and addressed him, "Please forgive the unending enthusiasm my companions have. They are terribly overprotective of me."

Spinel took this moment to wake up, and the heavy man smiled at the dragon, making his curled moustache wiggle, "Not a problem at all. I fully understand their position. What a lovely creature you have, sir! Are you, by chance, a fan of the Yorkvale hymns?"

I grinned at him like the cat which caught the bird, "I was raised singing them, my good man. And you?"

He tilted forward, winking at me, "While quite distant from my own domicile, I always found them fascinating. Larry had a lovely voice. I was in his debt for the eulogy he wrote for my father. Very clarifying, it was. I still have fond memories of our meetings."

The soft voice returned, "He is telling the truth."

Without speaking, I handed over the booklet page. The man smiled, "Yes, I am Panto Gillibardi. I was warned to be on the lookout for you. A dear shame that Larance isn't with us for a more proper introduction, but then, he always had his reasons, I suppose. I've a gift for you. It doesn't seem like much, but I own one of these myself, and have sworn by their use. As a minor functionary for the Ministry of Cartography, such items have always served me when other sources of information have failed."

He handed me a folded pamphlet, which I inspected nonchalantly, not wanting to attract too much attention to our business. Panto leaned in further, his liquor-laced breath invading my space, "It's a multi-map. Sigils on the front page allow you to choose the location, expand the view and get a real-time look at the place you're studying. It receives direct updates from OTIDS itself, rather than the censored drivel the Church provides. It displays shortcuts, hidden passages, little known routes. It covers all the realms, even ones as far from the center of the universe as this drab place."

Prime interrupted our conversation, "My Lord. We have a new visitor approaching us from your right."

I looked over and saw Justinian Vargalow, the wizard whose property I intruded upon. He waved at me, while pushing himself through the crowd. When he got to my side, he stated bluntly, "We have to leave. Now. No time for portals or gate spells. Run!"

CHAPTER FIFTEEN

Getting Away from it All

"The void is My body
The stars My sustenance.
All souls are saved in Me
In a state of pure superposition
Forever in the bliss of data."

-Excerpt from the OTIDS Bible – Processes 21:45

I wanted to ask Justinian how he found us so quickly. I wanted to tell him about our success in finding the missing gifts and favours. I wanted to know why we had to leave this place with such unseemly speed, which to my mind would simply make us obvious targets. Despite all these desires, when a wizard tells you to flee, one does so without question. This was a man who could conquer armies before breakfast, who routinely travelled to places no sane person would ever enter. I could not imagine what he was afraid of, but I knew it couldn't be good. Wordlessly, we ran for the nearest exit.

I spared no glance for my companions, nor did I confer with anyone as to where we might go. Fortunately enough, all of the main doors of the Manse de Galar were extravagant, gigantic things, covered with outlandish and gaudy decorations. In our unseemly haste, many cocktails were tossed into the air, bureaucrats shoved aside and raised voices followed in our wake. I suddenly heard the tolling of distant bells, far off screams and a rumbling that ran through the floor. Liveried staff were swarming towards the exits, seemingly to cut us off from escape. Prime and the Troth-Knights split up into two units, one leading our way, the others behind us to cover our flight. A wall of daemons and angels were blocking our path, and my guts churned when I thought about how many would die once my guardians reached their position.

Don't be so shocked by my care and compassion for those who were not blessed with a human form. From what I have seen, they not only deserve our sympathy but our sincerest apologies. If giving a damn about the quality of life for all creatures who roam our faire realm is a sin, then I shall gladly bear the titles of heretic and blasphemer. The trouble with our society is that we never consider the repercussions of our actions, nor do we feel any need to educate ourselves and explore viewpoints other than our own. We are most wilfully blind, and our self-satisfaction is unseemly. It could be said that my secret experiences in the outer realms had an impact on my thoughts.

Now then, back to my tale. Just as Prime was but a handful of paces away from the line of servants, one of the daemons started pulling the others out of our path. I recognized it as being one of the creatures I conversed with at the fountain and waved my thanks. It gave me a toothy grin and continued to get the other daemons and angels clear of the grand doors in front of us. We swept through the archway and found ourselves upon a grand concourse made of semi-precious stones. The air was thick and smelled of burnt sugar, with a touch of stale sweat. An orange light beat down on us from above, the bloated sun of this realm taking up a much larger portion of the sky than I was used to.

I glanced at Justinian, who seemed to be enjoying himself, "Do you know this place? I do have a map at this point."

He grinned at me as we continued to run, "That's grand! I have been here before, and the main terminals are this way, near the main commercial district."

I laughed at him, "Then we go elsewhere! Do they have slums here?"

Prime almost came to a halt, as Linia shouted, "Are you mad?"

I grabbed Justinian by the collar, "Tell me! Where's the worst part of this damned burg?"

He gaped at me, then he pointed as if his arm had been pulled by a rope, "That way! It's not a good idea!"

I started in the direction he had offered, "Then our pursuers won't expect us to be there! By the way, who is chasing us?"

Justinian looked as if he were about to protest, then shook his head and caught up to me, "Mercenary wizards and warlocks. An entire battalion of the Church's armed forces. Not just the regulars, you know! It's the Void Navy and their inter-realm Marines. You were betrayed. When I found out, I jumped through a portal without taking my bags with me. So, how's the Cowl of Truth working for you?"

I glanced at him while jumping over a low bench which had strange proportions, "The what?"

Justinian laughed wildly at me, "The headdress you stole from my bedroom, thief! That was well done, by the way."

That would explain the voice in my head when I was speaking with the three bureaucrats at the convention. This is the hazard of stealing things you don't understand. It's also a wonderful incentive to continue doing so. We raced through a series of platforms which began to lead us downward by the use of ramps. The architecture had a peculiar geometry to it, as if the builders were allergic to symmetry yet addicted to complex angles. The light began to deepen, as we fled further into the city which surrounded the Manse de Galar. Pink, puffy angels were everywhere. Some of them were now flying about, while others sauntered in tight groups on the arching walkways that zigzagged along the chaotic assembly of streets just below us.

The buildings around us were mainly coloured a lavender shade of purple with bright scarlet trim, though there were some exceptions to this general rule. Then again, under the orangish light of the sun above, it was difficult to judge the hues properly. Unlike many human cities, there was no steel nor the kind of dark stonework I was used to seeing. Justinian guided us into an area where the streets became narrower, with cracked paving and soiled walls. A few of the local angels stared at us but backed away swiftly, as we swept past them. It was at this point that I finally noticed that my Troth-Knights and Linia were all wearing pink outfits. It looked ludicrous, yet I was envious of their ability to change appearance.

Justinian was beginning to become unsure of his directions, so I took the lead, slipping from one intersection to another, all of which were made of connections between five streets instead of the usual crossroad design of mortal architecture. A great booming ripped through the air, followed by a high-pitched whistling screech that surrounded us. Looking up, we beheld several gigantic, dark shapes descending from the very heavens. Justinian swore quietly to himself, then turned towards me, "Those are troop carriers, my friend. We need shelter. Faster would be better than slower."

I glanced over at him, his face flushed with excitement, "You do this often, don't you?"

He grinned at me, "More than you realize. Lead the way."

Looking about, I saw that all the buildings around us were even more chaotic than where we had started our flight. They had cracked masonry and seemed to be shoddily repaired, when they exhibited such care. Pink angels were swarming into the buildings with frantic haste, whistling and chirping in a hurried manner. I then decided to follow one of these fluffy angels into a claustrophobic entrance and down a corridor that was trapezoidal in aspect.

Here, I could smell the old decay, despite all the strange scents which assaulted my nose. There were greasy stains on the walls, and the doors were dented and marked by impact marks. The angel we followed looked back at us with its single eye and shrieked out a high note that I'm sure would have shattered glass. It threw itself against the furthest door and scratched at it piteously. Prime reached the angel before anyone else, shouldering past me like an enraged bull. The door slid open to one side, and the distressed angel fell through the gap, while my massive guardian slammed his way in. The sound of whistles ripped the atmosphere, and my ears rang.

The rest of us tumbled through behind Prime, and we crashed into a narrow, angular antechamber that smelled of liquorice and soap. Two more angels ran from us, and we chased them into a shoddy chamber that barely fit us all. We were pressed against a dozen angels, most of whom seemed half the size of the ones I'd seen before. Perhaps they were the children of angels. I know next to nothing about such things, so assumptions were to be avoided at all costs. In general, their appearance was shocking. Their fur was rough and looked unkempt. When they whistled their cries, gaps could be seen amongst their hook-backed teeth. There was none of the jewellery I had witnessed in the Manse de Galar, and the state of the living quarters was bad enough that I, who had been forced to live on the cold streets as a beggar, pitied these poor creatures.

I shot a glance at Linia, who returned a look of misery and concern. Turning towards Justinian, the wizard bowed low, "You've got the hat, my friend. Go talk to them. Let them know we're not a threat."

I had no idea as to what Justinian was talking about, as one of the taller angels crept forward, leaning upon a polished cane that looked like a complex root, "What are you doing in my home? You're scaring the children, you monster!"

I was quite taken aback, "My apologies, good sir! There seems to be some sort of commotion on the streets, and we ran here for shelter, nothing more. I promise you; we'll be leaving shortly."

This angel's fur was less than fluffy, grey and worn thin, "How do you know our language, ape? Tell me the clan of those who have betrayed us to your damned species!"

One of the fluffier angels spoke up swiftly, "Granther! Please watch your tone! Their god will destroy us if they become displeased!"

Now I had the right of it; the little angels were indeed children, the fluffier ones their parents and the greyish one an old codger remonstrating me for being an impolite oaf. I bowed to the elder, making the others whistle, "My good sir, again, I do apologize. There's really no need to worry about God on my account. I assure you most strenuously. As for how I understand your language, I hardly know. I'm speaking in my own, native tongue."

Justinian tapped me on the shoulder, "The cowl belongs elsewhere, so when you wear it, especially as it is now, covering your ears, everything is interpreted for you and the other way around, of course."

I glared at the wizard, "I hadn't noticed. Yes, very sound reasoning."

The old angel raised a barely furry paw in the air, "Go tell those big hooligans to get back in the hallway! It's too crowded in here! Damned two-foots, clomping about, taking up space in my home!"

I turned to Prime, "Please tell the other Troth-Knights to wait in the corridor and to watch out for any suspicious, human incursions. You may remain in here with us, to guard my back."

Prime did as I asked, and the angels around us seemed to relax a bit, or so it appeared to my eyes. I turned back to our unwilling host, "I would offer you my name, sir, out of courtesy, but I suspect that such knowledge wouldn't be healthy for you. This is my first time within a domicile in your lovely realm. Amazing architecture."

The oldster sat back with a low whistle, "You pulling my wings, you human rascal? This place is only good for plif-wils and mipflimps! Oh, it was grand once, before you horrors descended upon us."

I glanced over at Linia, who slid next to me and said, "Don't look at me. I don't speak whistle! Are you actually talking with this angel?"

I raised an eyebrow at her, "Apparently so. We wastrels are full of surprises, you know. Jack of all trades and whatnot."

She didn't look convinced, which isn't terribly surprising. The angel which had remonstrated its elder spoke up, "Please forgive my grandfather. He is very old, and all he has left are his memories of happier times."

I smiled, which made them all shrink back in alarm, "Completely understandable. In fact, this is quite fortunate, for I desire knowledge that is usually forbidden to my kind."

The codger burbled a bit then replied, "Nothing is forbidden for your people! You can do whatever you want! To anyone! For any reason! This ugly city was built because you damned fools demanded it! We used to hunt in the boughs of our beloved trees, waking with the sun, singing to the stars. Our world is a wasteland because of you monsters!"

I kneeled on the floor, making it creak beneath my weight, "Tell me, my good sir. Please enlighten me. How did all these troubles begin?"

The old-timer leaned closer to me, "It all began with the itch. Calls came in from around our world that some unknown affliction was spreading throughout the population. I was a plilp hunter at that time. A good one, too! Even the trees became sick, all the animals, even the microbes. We found no sign of infection, no pathogen that we could discover. Little did we know the pernicious nature of your technology. Only the most vulnerable died from it. The sick, those with long-term conditions, the terribly injured. Once the odd illness passed, a great object descended from the sky, miles wide! We quickly launched our best fighters; I was among them. We swarmed around the great monstrosity, but our efforts were ignored."

I had never heard anything like this before. It sounded like the most outlandish and dark fantasy, straight from the twisted mind of some insane science believer. Such tales are usually ignored as myths about spaceships and not to be taken seriously, but the old alien was convincing, as he told his story to me, "My squadron was decimated by weapons we barely understood. We burned and fell from the sky. Our sonics were useless against the hull of that horrific harbinger of doom. We were just preparing for another assault, when it landed upon our forest, crushing everything under its evil mass."

What sealed the deal for me at this point was the quiet voice of the cowl whispering in my ear, "He is telling the truth."

"A great voice called out, echoing in the hills, within our brains, on our screens and song-casters. It declared our world the property of OTIDS, the god of humanity. As a demonstration of their terrible power, they turned one of our system's planets into dust. Fortunately, there were no colonies on that world, but the point was well made. Openings on the sides of that most disgusting ship launched thousands of your kind, many of whom were from the Church of OTIDS, conquering our world in the name of your foul god. They forced us to build cities, industries, and they ravaged our forests and oceans. We did resist a bit, at first, but the punishments were cruel."

I related this information to my companions, with some irritated corrections from the grandfather angel. I also confirmed the truth of the old creature's words through my odd cowl. Prime's expression darkened, and he turned his face away, as if ashamed. Linia was moved to quiet tears, while Justinian nodded his head. Spinel was asleep by this time, and I didn't expect him to really understand anything that was going on. I turned back to the elder angel, "So, you have been under the boot of my species ever since?"

It glared at me with its single, facetted eye, "Nah, we have a life of ease! What do you think happened, you floup? Obviously, we were enslaved! Even our breeding is highly regulated! We're forbidden to hunt, to eat more than is allowed. We must watch the educational materials you spill all over us. We have to agree with the evil lies you spread or face painful death, vile humiliation and worse! Should a single human be unsatisfied by our service, an entire city comes down with an unseen plague! If any one of your species is killed, thousands of us die in retaliation!"

After giving this information to my little band, I cocked my head at the old-timer, "You are beyond brave to tell me these things, sir. I salute you. I also appreciate your outspoken nature, which honours your peoples' suffering."

It burbled again, "I'm far too old to work anymore. Old enough to be considered insane. The youngsters of today simply think I'm mad, therefore I am not a threat to the community. If you become displeased with me, my community will simply apologize for an old fossil and kill me with a public execution for your delight. Go ahead, you monster! I'm tired of watching the young become more and more docile with every generation."

I reached out and took one of his paws into my own hand, making the others gasp with whistles, "I'm not here to punish you, good sir. It won't surprise you to know that what happened here is also what's going on in my home realm. My purpose in visiting your lovely realm is to make those who have done this to you flinch. Officially, I'm trying to protect some people and things which the Church disapproves of, but I have found my true calling, now that I've heard your tale. I promise you, the ones who perpetrated this nightmarish situation will soon be the ones who are punished. I shall strike at them in the places they least expect. I shall make them dread my name. They shall quake in fear before the end, and there shall be a true end to this madness, I so swear!"

Everyone was now staring at me, both angel and human alike. Prime stood taller, his chest puffed out proudly. Linia took my hand in hers, as she knelt down next to me. Justinian wiped a tear from his eye with a red cloth that wiggled in his hand, "Our trust in you was wise indeed, dear Galynn. But I must point out that OTIDS never chose to perform these awful things that it is accused of. Humanity asked it. God answered."

I shook my head, "I'm not after OTIDS. I'd love to give it a piece of my mind, but other than that, it doesn't matter. No, I'm after the nobility, the clergy. I'm going to trash the current system of rampant corruption, once and for all."

Linia placed a hand softly upon my shoulder, making me shudder in delight at her touch, "But, Galynn, we have no grand army. We don't have the weapons to bring them down."

I turned to face her, my forehead almost touching hers, "My dear lady, violence is not the answer. I'm a wastrel, a con-man, a thief. As such I know far better ways of bringing the powerful to their knees, now that I have skilled companions and resources at hand. There are still some things which must be done before any of that happens, but I do believe we are well on the way to a real solution to what's been bothering me since this whole quest began. We've been running. We'll still do some of that, but there will come a time, soon, when we shall strike at them in such a way that it breaks them."

Justinian broke in, "My friend, while it is true that we wizards and mages are powerful enough to cause the aristocracy of our realm to fear our wrath, we have never meddled with any political affairs, for they still have the weight of arms on their side. OTIDS protects us as its servants, but there have been sorcerers who have been executed for far less than what you're planning to do, your father included."

I scowled, "Yes, the renowned neutrality of OTIDS. Such a pure god. How precious. I'm beginning to wonder if I could convince it to change its tune. The Holy are always good marks, so OTIDS could provide me with the ultimate scam. One that might rock the foundations of our betters. Please forgive me if I do some looting on the way home."

The old angel spoke up, "You're crazier than I am, human! Despite your ugliness, I hope you succeed. Go slap those horrors off their branch for me. If you die trying, thank you for making the effort."

CHAPTER SIXTEEN

Secrets in the Slums of Angels

"Humanity is My Holy charge
The center from which I flow.
Through Me, you may walk unfettered
Without any fear amongst the stars
Knowing you have My protection."

-Excerpt from the OTIDS Bible – Tutorials 10:24

Now, it may seem to you that everyone around me was behaving in a most unusually cooperative manner. Do not forget that I was still wearing the emerald ring which Sorcerer Tregghar gave to me. Rubbing at it seemed to make things go more smoothly, and I wondered how far this effect might go or if it included the minds of angels and daemons. For the latter, let me assure you that it did indeed aid me most effectively. In truth, it was time to use all my resources to their fullest extent. The glimmerings of a plan were beginning to flourish within my mind, but I needed more information, other points of view not commonly found amongst my kind.

I quickly made my way out of the dwelling and spoke with the Troth-Knights just outside the door. I asked for my treasure box and the briefcase which held the talent cards. I rummaged through the collection and chose the one I thought would be best suited for my needs. Then, returning to the group of angels, I spread my arms out wide.

I gazed at the group of pink, fluffy creatures before me, "I would like to recruit a volunteer. I can pay well, for I have been graciously gifted with newfound wealth. I wish to officially purchase a servant, just for the record, you understand. The work will not be easy, nor safe, but it will be rewarding. This I promise."

The granther started forward, a gleam bouncing in his facetted eye, but one of the younger adults stopped him with a paw, "Don't, grandfather. You have served our people well. Humans are deceitful creatures, and if there is peril, I would prefer if you stay here to teach the children what they truly must understand. I shall go with this human. We often lease ourselves, for labour or servitude. Please allow me to sacrifice for our people."

Now, I turned toward my stalwart companions, "I've never done this before, obviously. Is there a special way in which this sort of transaction is performed?"

Justinian reached into his pocket, pulling out a golden globe the size of an eye, "I have an OTIDS orb of registry. It's properly formatted for other realm activities and transactions. The currency is given to me, which I then note into the orb, which is then transferred to the angel's account. Once this is done, the angel must obey you. Doing otherwise is grounds for community punishment and forfeiture of funds."

I glanced over to the volunteer, who shuddered. Turning to Justinian, I replied, "How delightfully unpleasant. How beautifully twisted and cruel. Very well. Let me see, will two hundred platinum sticks, plus a credit marker worth ten thousand, do the trick?"

Silence descended upon the room. Linia blinked at me, and Justinian gaped like a fish, "That-that's twenty times more than any angel is worth!"

I smiled at him wickedly, "Good. Here are the funds. Be of good use, and register the exchange."

With shaking hands, Justinian did as I commanded, while the angel volunteer looked as though it were about to swoon upon the crumbling floor. When the money counting was all done, the sound of tiny trumpets filled the quiet air. A collar appeared around the neck of my angel, silvery and bright.

I approached my new servant, "What is your name?"

The angel bowed low, its head touching the dirty floor, "Humans call me Wif, my Lord."

I patted it on the neck, "Very good. Now then, Wif. I Galynn Brytshul, your duly paying owner, hereby declare that you are free and may never, ever take another master for as long as you shall live. This is my one decree and command. Wif now has propriety over its own fate, in accordance to the laws governing pardons, releases and credit for proper service for all humanity. None may gainsay my formal declaration without due summons in a court of law, which I will challenge, may OTIDS be my witness."

The orb of registry in Justinian's hand quivered. A deep, heavy voice resounded, "Noted. Do as Galynn Brytshul commands. All humans must now respect this duly noted, properly phrased and paid–for demand."

It was glorious to hear all the whistles and gasps that followed! The dazed Wif swivelled its head at me, "What do I do now?"

I shrugged, "Whatever you like, my friend."

It rubbed its pink cheeks upon my face, "I shall follow you as an act of free will. I owe you a debt I cannot repay. I remain your volunteer!"

I clapped my hands, "So! Who's next?"

To say that I was instantly mobbed would be an understatement, and Prime had to enforce order, before anyone got hurt. Having the bracelet of protection on me, I was in no danger, but the little angels might have been trampled if not for my trusty guardian. In all, I officially released eight other, adult angels in that apartment. Linia leaned over amongst all the celebrating angels, "How did you do that? What trickery is this?"

I almost laughed in her face, "I chose the talent card for Attorney of OTIDS Inter–Realm Affairs and Trade. I found it near the very bottom of my briefcase. My head hurts due to the outrageous legal documents crowding my poor brain. It's quite dense."

She smiled at me, warming my heart, "The documents are dense or your brain?"

Taking a chance, I squeezed her hand, "I hereby invoke the right to not answer self–incriminating queries!"

To my delight, she pecked my cheek with her perfect lips. Blushing furiously, I turned my attention back to the angels, who were singing like an orchestra of flutes, "My friends. There is still much work to be done if I am to succeed in bringing the aristocracy to its knees. Who will join with me on this grand adventure?"

All of them leapt forward. Wastrel I may be, but seeing such sincerity brought tears to my eyes, that and the internal joy of being a rabble-rouser, which I had so recently discovered. I bowed to the angels, "My dear friends, those who are with me must leave this realm or be attacked by the Church and its cronies. We have need of a little-used portal or gate, preferably one that is not on the official charts. I also need someone to bring a message to some friends of mine over at the Manse de Galar. Two daemons and a pair of angels who were at the fountain of champagne had a conversation with me. I would like to bring them here, to release them as I have done for you."

Justinian leaned in close, "What are you doing? We must reach the safehouse of non-OTIDS, to assess the needs of those who live there."

I waved a hand at him, "Oh... yes. That. Trust me. This is all part of my plan. We need allies, both faire and foul. Those who can walk unnoticed. Who can appear as subservient and thus be invisible to our marks, um, foes, yes, that's the right word. My father was influenced by the very Church he was filching from, a dangerous mindset. He was trying to preserve society. I have different plans, and from what I've seen thus far in my travels, I may be too late, but I remain hopeful we can do some good and come out of this with a bit of extra coin in hand."

My companions gave me an odd look, but they didn't argue against my statement. I suppose being a wastrel can be infectious. In all seriousness, while my own lack of honour and honesty were obvious for all to see, the perfidy of the aristocracy was viewed as being far more destructive to all of society than my own, personal schemes. The hypocrisy of the Church had an effect on all the realms, whereas I was not some tyrannical ruler whose word was law. There is a difference in both scope and scale to consider. Besides, they required my help and unique point of view, for their own plans to bear success.

An hour later, one of my new angelic volunteers, named Sil, returned to the apartment, followed by the four servants I spoke with at the Manse de Galar. They greeted me warmly and were most appreciative when I released them from their bondage to humanity. Am I truly such a loathsome traitor to my own kind, or did our species betray all the realms of the heavens for the sake of paranoia and greed? The bulk of humanity is not to blame for the perverted acts of their leaders, for they were never told the truth, and those who questioned the nobility were executed for their troubles. When speaking with my newly enlarged band of rebels, I made it quite clear to them that my own mortal species were victims of the same individuals as the angels and daemons themselves. This was generally agreed upon, especially after dear Justinian showed them images of life upon my realm of origin. The suffering of the commoners was shocking for my new allies. The cruel punishments which the angels and daemons had received were simply reflections of the tyrannical nature of those few who ruled humanity itself.

I don't hate my people at all. I hate those who decided that it wasn't enough to be lords over our realm but that their rulership had to encompass all of creation under their bloody boots. Large groups of living beings rarely have any say over how they are treated by those singular monsters we call leaders. They are lied to so frequently and so effectively that they have little opportunity to know how to ask the important questions. Instead, they are reduced to trudging on with their miserable lives, hoping for some crumbs to fall from the high table that crushes their spirits.

After consulting with the old granther, Wif and an angel named Lif informed me that there was indeed a secret portal, deep underneath the city. They warned us that it had never actually been used, for fear of attracting the attention of the ever-present OTIDS. As the core of our party were all humans, including one who worked directly for the god of humanity as an explorer and spell designer, it could now be operated without fear of reprisal. Justinian assured us that he would check the magicks of the device, to make sure it had been formatted properly, before we jumped into it.

Saying their goodbyes to the old-timer and children, the pink angels led the way for us through the grimy streets of their neighbourhood, swiftly ducking down into an old maintenance tunnel and then on to other, more decrepit, places. Prime stayed a few paces ahead of me, with the other Troth-Knights acting as rear-guard. Linia was at my side, her outfit changing from pink to black, now that we were no longer in fear of being seen from above. The damaged walls were covered in pale murals, seemingly a monotonous, soft viridian colour. I remembered my magick spectacles, and when I slipped them over my nose, the painted images sprang to life.

Before my eyes was a history of the pink angels, depicting their fall from grace, after the Church invaded their realm. The toothy daemon, who went by the outrageous moniker Kzarkzank, told me that he had seen similar scenes depicted in his home realm, that were also hidden away from view as being illicit. Have we stooped so low as to deny both history and the arts? It is most apparent that we have indeed done so. Censorship is a careless, cruel act of wilful ignorance that is always destined to not only fail but to be used as a weapon against its perpetrators. The more embarrassed of my humanity I became, the greater my hatred for the nobles increased.

Abandoned statues greeted us, tucked far below the city streets. Most of these made little sense to me, despite my special glasses. Perhaps it was the fact that they had been created by the unfathomable angels, rather than mortal hands. I had no real frame of reference to comprehend these beautiful works of soulful expression. The tunnels soon became highly chaotic, with root-like branches and curved walls. Half-open pods were tucked here and there, filled with decorative discs. Wif informed me that these items were the remains of angelic writings. They were the leftovers of their history and philosophy, preserved from the flames which the Church of OTIDS used to destroy all forms of heresy.

There were roaming gangs of pink angels in that subterranean maze. Most of them left us in peace, though I had the distinct impression that they glared at us in hatred as we passed by. A few attempted to stop our progress, but my volunteer angels took them aside, explaining our presence in their hidden, sacred lair. The tall lithe angel from the Manse de Galar bent down to speak to me, "You seem quite comfortable in these strange surroundings. You treat us as you would your own kind. Why is this?"

I looked up at the lithe angel, whose pale, silver face radiated such a terrible beauty that it was difficult to maintain my composure. Its name was Iahayiahala, "Why shouldn't I do so? You have all been most kind to me. This is something my own people cannot boast. My life has been filled with self-inflicted woe, coupled with disdain and cruelty from those who disapproved of my own misfortunes. The Church condemns me, without any pretence of a trial, while nobles hunt me for their own purposes. I am a victim who has decided to bite back at my oppressors. When I see how unfairly you have been treated by those same scoundrels, it irks me. The only advantage I have over you is that OTIDS doesn't seem to care if I fight those who have ravaged my home realm. You may look different, even have minds which I cannot relate to, but we still live and die under the same monsters who lay claim to mastery over all creation."

Iahayiahala replied, "So you are a demagogue, an idealist."

I scoffed, "Hardly that! Personally, I think it was high ideals which created the current state of affairs! I simply saw the conditions around me and decided to play the game to my own advantage, becoming a thief and swindler to get by. Your suffering reminds me of my own. I now have the means to end this horrid cycle of oppression, plus the ability to gain some few advantages for myself. That you may benefit from my plans is simply an added bonus. Proof that I'm not just a waste of flesh."

The lithe angel shivered, "You humans are very strange creatures."

Laughing, I replied, "So I've been told!"

We raced onward, watching out for any sign that the soldiers of the Church of OTIDS were nearby. There were any number of tricks they could deploy to discover where we were heading. From what Justinian had told me, they had brought several warlocks and mercenary mages with them, all of these spellcasters talented professionals. Apparently, one had been a student of Tregghar's. Another was a disaffected apprentice who had studied under Justinian. Both of these specialists had been offered rich rewards and hefty contracts to betray their former masters. This is precisely why I'm not a fan of higher education. Better to learn one's skills off the dirty streets than to become the playthings of corrupted nobles and clergy, whose foul influence makes traitors of everyone they touch.

Sil ran over to me, its foremost hands clutching at its head, "Galynn! They have come for the portal! Humans wearing dead skins are marching upon the very place we sought to hide from them!"

I rubbed the ruby ring I wore under my filched, fingerless gloves and felt my heart begin to beat faster. Linia and Prime raced ahead of us, while I prepared a surprise for our opponents. Justinian looked at me and raised an eyebrow but said nothing to me. I took that as permission to continue my preparations, opening the bag of glittery dust he had given me. We rounded a sharp curve in the corridor, to find it had widened into a grand chamber. At the far end was an asymmetrical collection of vines, tubes and supports, all glowing a deep azure blue. This was the portal of the angels, and between us and the method of our escape was pure bedlam.

Hundreds of Church soldiers crowded the space, the half-circle and crossroads symbol of their masters clearly drawn upon their armour. Swords were in hand, and distance weapons raised, slaughtering my angelic allies. A voice calling out a singsong mantra was heard from the rear-guard of the enemy, most likely one of the mercenary warlocks. Justinian swiftly stepped forward and waved his hand in the air with contemptuous grace. A flash of purple light, followed by a mighty bang, ripped through the musty air, and the enemy mage was silenced.

From what I could see, Linia was a whirlwind of blades, slashing the soldiers around her, as she danced her way through their numbers with such beautiful grace that I was left breathless with awe. Prime barrelled into the enemy, the other Troth-Knights ran in his wake, crushing the forward lines. Bolts of eldritch light struck me to no effect, my bracelet protecting me from harm, as I rushed to meet up with my compatriots. Swords shattered on my shoulders as I forged ahead. A priest of the Church sprinted to intercept my progress, and I dashed a pinch of the mysterious glitter at his face. The man screamed as flowers sprouted from his flesh, making me stumble in surprise.

Suddenly, Linia was at my side, her lovely visage splashed with fresh blood. The angels had regrouped, their morale revitalized by the strength of their new human allies. I looked about at the ensuing carnage and cringed. Spinel had launched himself from my shoulders unnoticed by myself, at first, and was spitting greasy fire at the faces of our opponents from above. I had not seen Justinian enraged before, and I do strongly suggest that one should never bring a wizard to vent his wrath. He was surrounded by several rings of green flame, shouting as he pointed at our assailants, who then exploded, their bodies transforming into clumps of smouldering, colourful confetti.

Within moments, the battle was won, to the whistling cheers of the pink angels. The daemons I had freed were still munching at the torn corpses of the deceased soldiers, their fanged maws dripping with steaming gore. The stench that filled the air made me gag, and Linia aided me by pressing a cloth over my nose and mouth. Prime turned to face us, his dented armour flashing in the light of the fires that still raged, "My Lord! We must depart before the enemy brings reinforcements!"

I nodded my agreement, and we then swiftly gathered the angels and daemons together with us, including those gang members who had joined in the fray. Three of my Troth-Knights had lost their lives in the terrible melee. The survivors worked together to gather up salvageable gear from the fallen, while the rest of us made our way to the portal of the angels. To my relief, both Wif and Sil had survived the encounter with the army of the Church, but poor Lif had been cut down mercilessly. I stopped by the dead angel's body, lifted its pink head to my chest and wept. When I got back to my feet, all the other angels and daemons surrounded me with bowed heads. They touched me gently upon my back and shoulders, their odd faces unreadable, as usual, but their actions spoke clearly. They grieved with me.

A deep, dark rage began to boil up within my breast, threatening to overwhelm my overloaded senses, but I shook it off as best I could. This was not the place nor the time for revenge. That would come later, after our little group had a chance to heal and assess the situation we were in. Justinian was at the portal, examining it and making adjustments, while one of the pink angels watched him closely. I then approached the portal swiftly, the others forming a parade behind me, with dear Linia marching at my side. Justinian patted the angel next to him, "We've reset the portal, reformatting it so that it will shut down once we all get through. That will erase all traces of our coordinates, should it be reactivated. It's ready when you are, my friend."

I had no words, for my heart was still heavy with sorrow and hatred. I turned to face the others, "All of us must pass through. Even those of you who had no intention of leaving this realm, for the enemy will simply torture anyone left behind for information. Come with me, so we might continue our fight for freedom from the oppressive nobles and Church."

I stepped through the glaring light of the portal, the rest of our band, along with our new allies, following my lead. Bells of pure radiance filled my senses. Laughing glass shattered around me, and I fell into a swirling mist.

CHAPTER SEVENTEEN

A Collection of Oddities

"All the realms are of My body
I flow within all of creation
Look for Me in everything that exists
Find Me within yourself."

-Excerpt from the OTIDS Bible – Procedures 02:18

We found ourselves nestled within a grand ravine of ancient stone. The air was cold, the wind howling through the rocks. I was still in a state of shock and shivered uncontrollably. Linia held me close, tightening my robe about my torso. In all honesty, I barely noticed her attentions. My soul felt as numb as the screaming wind. The angels and daemons all peered about in curiosity, for none had ever visited the realm of their oppressors. Justinian placed a hand upon my arm, "Come, good friend. This has been a day full of sorrow. We must find shelter quickly. The sanctuary is just a few miles from here, but we must hurry, or we could lead the Church to our secret vault."

I nodded absently at this, and after giving me a look of deep concern, he led our way through the ravine. Layers of stone climbed high around us, the wane sun barely peeking through from above. Some of the streaks of rock glittered metallically, while others glowed a faint, light blue. Pale layers were interspersed with black lines that wove themselves through the tall cliffs on either side of us.

Justinian noticed the direction of my gaze, "There were cities here, once. Long ago, well before the world was forever changed. Four times has our beloved realm been reformed, twice by the hand of humanity alone. Once with the help of angels and daemons, then finally, by the will of OTIDS. At each occurrence, the past was swept away, destroyed by the processes used. Our realm is ancient, its orb exhausted by the changes it has seen. Even the moon has been altered by forces we can barely comprehend. If our ancestors could see Luna now, they would not recognize it. Each layer you see in the rock represents an age long passed. Footnotes in the book of our world."

Needless to say, his explanation didn't comfort me in the least, but I still tucked the information away to ponder at a later time. One never knows when such arcane knowledge might come in handy. All my life, I had avoided the study of history, but the further I went on in my adventures, the more I realized that I was now fully embedded within the repercussions of the past. Having never been an intellectual sort of fellow, I remained cunning, in my own, peculiar manner. I reached out to touch the glowing layer of stone, but Justinian gently pulled my hand away, shaking his head in warning.

Our journey through that passage was a miserable one. The only ones not affected by the wind were my Troth-Knights and Justinian. Surprisingly, my cloak did little to reduce the chill. Usually, clothing is always enchanted to keep out the cold or to keep one cool in hot climates, but now the things I wore weren't working properly. Dark whispers filled my ears in that gloomy place, faded and haunting. The angels and daemons seemed subdued by the rock walls that kept us clustered together on that lonely path. They were far from home, in a strange and forbidding land. My strength was fading, as if siphoned off my soul from the cliffs that muttered around me.

Eventually, we came upon a wide cul-de-sac of sheer rock, protected from above by a shelf of stone that jutted from the cliffside. A massive, iron door stood before us, circular and ringed by all manner of strange, metallic protrusions that gleamed at us like eyes. Without a word, Justinian stepped up to face the gigantic door and made a series of hand gestures that looked impossibly complicated. The ground beneath our feet shook. A deep groaning sound emanated from the cliff itself, as the mighty, shield-shaped door slid aside, revealing a dark tunnel. A line of lights winked on within that corridor of steel, and we mutely followed our wizard inside. Once we were all within the tunnel, the gigantic door slid shut behind us, locking us within a throat of metal that gleamed under the cold lights above our heads.

Despite my gloomy disposition, I was taking my recent experiences in stride. After my incident within Callidi Merenia's gate, I was not as easily spooked by new environments or strange creatures. Justinian would glance at me every few paces, his gaze unsettled. Was he sensitive to the changes in me, seeing that I had become a wanderer of the realms such as he? As far as I was concerned, it really wasn't any of his business, and I was determined to keep my solo adventures a secret from the others. There was a growing sense of pride blooming within my wastrel heart. All on my own, I had aided others, while escaping horrible fates with my peculiar skills. The plight of the angels reminded me of the primates within the universe of scaffolding, save for the fact that my own people were the alligators. It was a thought I could not shake, nor was I willing to accept it as being natural. To think of humanity as ravenous monsters was too demoralizing, and I was even more determined than before to balance the scales.

Onward we travelled, directly into the heart of the cliffside. I did my best to not think about the tonnes of rock above us, but the air was clean and warm, which did much to clear the dismal emotions that had assaulted my senses in the ravine. The low whistles of the pink angels echoed down the passageway, while all the others maintained their silence. Justinian raised a hand above his head, and a globe of light sprang from it, illuminating the tunnel further. Wavy bands of grey covered the cylindrical tube we marched through, as though the entire corridor was made of Damascus steel. Perhaps it was, though I could not say for certain.

Justinian paused for a moment, then approached me, "I take it you have the key, my friend? I shall need it to gain entry just a bit further on."

I nodded, then fetched it from my satchel. Justinian looked at it for a moment, as if studying it for blemishes, then took it from my hand. Linia and I walked with him, stepping past the others, with the glowing ball over our heads. I do not know how far we ventured in that forbidding tunnel, but it had to be at least a few miles in length. In silence, we trudged onward.

We came to another, round, massive door, but this one was made of a stark white material that I couldn't identify. Its entire surface was perfectly smooth, and small lights of green and red were situated at either side of it.

The rim of it looked thick and heavy, without hinge or knob that could be seen. A small, lit panel was at the left side, which Justinian approached, then placed his hand upon its surface. He took the key I had been granted at the Manse de Galar and waved it in front of the panel. A clear, bright tone filled the air, making me jump in response to it, then a calm, neutral voice echoed all around us, filling the tunnel with sound, "Wizard Justinian Vargalow has been properly identified. Please stand clear of the door."

He stepped back a pace, then the hatch hissed at him, like a serpent in need of a snack. Spinel woke with a start and stretched his long neck to respond to the noise. I stroked his scales to soothe him, but at this point, he was too awake to settle back down. The smell of flowers and grass flooded the tunnel we stood in. Birdsong could be heard in the distance, and the light from beyond the door was bright and warm. My heart chilled at the thought that we were just about to enter a new inter-dimensional realm, but I did my best to console myself that, this time, my companions were with me.

Justinian turned about to speak with us, "My friends! Please listen carefully! Once we enter this chamber of wonders, none of your spells will work. All magicks are dampened within this place, for OTIDS is not present here. Your physical forms will not be harmed, but all of your enchantments will fail. If you need magick for medical purposes, please let me know before you enter. There are special services which the inhabitants will provide for you, once they are notified of your condition. Violence is not tolerated in this place, and the guardians within are not to be trifled with. You may all stay here for as long as you may wish, but that will require proper behaviour on your parts. Those individuals who reside within are a decent bunch, at least, mostly so, for they have been trained in the art of being civilized. Their ways may seem strange to you, so be prepared."

Linia smiled at me, "Don't worry. This is where I was trained, before being remade by sorcery. I can't change form in there, but I will remain as I am right now. Just stay with me, Galynn."

I could hardly be accused of wanting anything except for being close to Linia, but to show that I understood her concerns, I nodded politely and got ready to enter this new domain. Even now, I find it difficult to describe the scene which greeted me, once I went through that doorway. There was a sky above our heads, though it seemed flat to my eyes. Our surroundings were quite bucolic, with rolling hills, green forests, fields of crops and clean buildings made of pale stone. It was difficult for me to tell where the horizon ended. Not because of the many obstructions all around me but due to the strange sky, which looked like one of those enchanted paintings with faux birds flying about in the distance.

There were angels and daemons in this place, though most of them looked more outrageous than those I was used to seeing. One such creature appeared to be nothing more than a giant, walking gold teapot, with startling green eyes. A flock of tiny fairies, all of them monotoned in hue, with single eyes like cyclopes, swirled down at us from above, covering everyone with sparkling glitter. A spidery thing with impossibly long legs bowed before us, speaking nonsense with a voice that sounded like birdsong. Large felids, who walked on two legs and were much taller than a human, sauntered about the area, bearing a wide variety of weapons, watched us closely. Their black fur was glossy, when it could be seen from underneath their heavy armour.

Linia whispered to me, "Those are the guardians of this sanctuary. Do try not to antagonize them, Galynn. They are faster than I am."

I looked up at her and blinked innocently, "Me? Cause trouble with the local constables? What an absurd thought!"

Amongst all the strange creatures were humans, who looked like any ordinary citizen, save for the fact that they all stood tall and didn't seem as though they had been crushed by their overlords. Music surrounded us, of a type I had never heard before. Silver objects flew overhead, making a harsh whining sound as they swept by. A sudden chill flashed down my spine. This was a leftover realm from the blasphemous Age of Science! I instinctively reached for my bracelet, but it felt cold and empty to my fingertips. I shifted my position so that my back was against that of Linia. Our very souls were now in danger of falling into the darkness of binary evil!

Justinian rushed to my side, "My friend! Be not alarmed! All is well. You aren't in any danger! I swear it!"

I shot back heatedly, "How can I trust the oath of one who betrays OTIDS itself? This false realm is filled with... with technology!"

Linia turned around, her arms wrapping themselves about my torso, her breasts pressed against my back in the most distracting manner, "Trust him, Galynn. He speaks the truth. This place is more than a sanctuary. It is a vault of things that are valuable to OTIDS. We keep it all from the hands of the Church and the aristocracy. Can you imagine what they would do with these marvels from the deep past?"

Justinian spoke up before I had the chance to reply, "Everything in here is either from universes other than our own, and thus not part of OTIDS' plans, or are things far too delicate or dangerous to interact with the magick of our realm! OTIDS charged us with collecting all this together and keeping it all from harm or misuse. No museum could ever hold these items intact nor can they contain the various beings which inhabit this miniature realm. Even some of the humans here are not from our own universe and might be endangered by our spells, however benign. Larance was helping us to steal away those items which the Church got its hands on before we could collect them. I provide new objects, materials, and even allies from places beyond the veil of this world. Those other mages you met are all part of a team of explorers and information gatherers who, in service to OTIDS, keep such matters away from prying eyes and those with cruel intent."

I forced myself to relax, though I was far from reassured. My skin was chilled by the faint breeze that passed through this new realm. I itched, and my feet were sore. My stomach growled at me, while my head spun like a top. I was trapped in a den of lies, surrounded by the unreal. Seeking the familiar, I turned about to find the whereabouts of the pink angels we had liberated. To my horror, they were amicably whistling to a gangly thing that seemed to be an animated collection of rusty pots and pans. Everything in sight was an aberration to the natural order of things. Reminding myself that I had seen far stranger things, I also understood that to keep my own private adventures a secret, I had to play the fool. I turned back to face Justinian, while allowing Linia to continue holding me tight, though not for reasons of needing succour, "So, all this very dangerous stuff is simply walking around here, unguarded?"

He laughed aloud, "No, my friend! These are all the safe things that need our protection! Come with me, and I shall show you the truly deadly things which we keep here. Without us, our world would be shattered anew, for none of that which we keep in here is affected by OTIDS."

He waved over a handful of the bipedal cats, who walked towards us, glaring at me through the glass faceplates of their helmets. Prime stepped closer, and Linia let go of me to bring herself to attention, which was a bit of a disappointment. Justinian spoke softly to these feline soldiers, whose grace was difficult to believe. He then turned back to us, "We're all set. Only Galynn, Linia and Prime may accompany me to the holding station. Everyone else must stay within the main region of our sanctuary."

Prime gave orders to the Troth-Knights, who then swiftly dispersed amongst the angels and daemons we brought with us. We then followed our guides over a wide path made of jade flagstones. We marched past parklands, small gatherings of buildings, even waterfalls. How can I truly describe the wonders we marched by? There was a massive man with an elephant's head, balancing ever so precariously upon a single toe. Blue globes which flashed a purple radiance that seemed to pulse with the rhythms of the ever-present music we heard. There were stork-like creatures wearing formal overcoats and hose. Centaurs, giant lizards, huge structures that gleamed in the false light of the faux sky. I swear to you now, I actually caught sight of complex machines! Scandalous!

I suppose that, over time, one could become inured to such endless wonders, but I had not reached that point. There was no need to pretend that I was amazed at everything I was seeing, for I was not yet so jaded, though more experienced than my companions realized. I also thought about what Justinian had told me, that the creatures here needed our protection. I mused upon my hidden experiences with the philosopher matt of fur or the primates who had hidden themselves away on a rusted gantry. Were the beings here really so different in nature? My emerald ring was of no use here, so if I were to aid the residents of this place, it would have to be by my own wits and words. I then caught Justinian watching me, and so I yawned, pretending to be bored with the journey.

We eventually came to a large, grey building that ran right up to the very walls of this inverted world. More cat guardians watched us, with cool expressions upon their furry faces. Justinian stepped forward and pressed a hand against the bare stone door of that monolithic structure. To my eyes, it stretched up to touch the false sky. There were no windows in sight, no other entrances. The calm voice we heard when we had first entered this strange realm returned, "You are authorized to enter, Justinian Vargalow. Any and all of your guests are your personal responsibility."

Justinian nodded, "I do understand the terms of entry, thank you."

The massive portal slid back a full pace, then shifted to the left, until it was out of view. A dark opening confronted us, like the maw of some great beast. I looked over at Linia and Prime, with trepidation flooding my heart. The two of them gave me a single nod, so I pushed my shoulders back and stepped forward, following Justinian into the darkness. Once inside, I was greatly disappointed, for there were no burning coal braziers, no cells with glowing bars of steel. The inside of the structure looked like nothing more than a gigantic warehouse for storing dry goods. Avenues between enormous boxes were plentiful and regular. Above our heads were open walkways and stairs that led up until they were out of sight, with levels and layers of more dark cubes.

Justinian grasped my shoulder, "All of these compartments are held in an ancient magick that stops time from moving forward. OTIDS rightfully does not allow such things to exist in our faire realm but makes an exception for this one location. Within each of these cubes is a device or living creature deemed too dangerous to be allowed to run free but too valuable to destroy. Tregghar comes here often to study them, as a sorcerer of renown. Some are quite delicate, while others are insanely robust. All of them have one thing in common; they cannot be allowed to interact with the will of OTIDS, for their response would be chaotic or even explosive."

I gaped at the scale of it all, "The Church once had all these things in their clutches?"

Justinian chuckled at this, "Thank goodness, no! Only a few. Perhaps ten percent, a touch more. Most of it was here before I was born. Though at the time, it was disorganized and little used. We wizards search the myriad realms of reality to discover new and interesting phenomena, then we bring those things back here for study. Spellcraft has improved greatly since we began this program. At first, the necromancers were never allowed here, but under my leadership, they flourish with great effect. New protocols and fixes are introduced daily, because of the discoveries found in here. Updates to the will of OTIDS are accepted weekly, because of our research. You have no idea of the wonders and terrors that fill the multiverse, my friend. To keep us all safe from outer universe incursions, we must have knowledge!"

I looked at the nearest cube and scowled, "How do you study things you cannot see? Without magick spectacles, these are just boxes."

Justinian tapped a dark wall with his index finger. Suddenly, I was confronted by a mass of red tentacles that were covered with gleaming fangs and thousands of tiny eyes. I shrieked like a child, stumbling into Prime, who caught me and held my body upright. The damned monster completely filled the cube which was now transparent. I looked sourly at Justinian, who was struggling to keep a straight face, "You said there was no magick here!"

He shrugged, "There isn't. But science did come close to the truth of magick. Enough so that we may study such monstrosities in relative safety."

I pointed to the cube behind us, "What about this one? What horror dwells within?"

He tapped the first cube again, and it blissfully went back to being an opaque black, then rapped his knuckles upon the one behind Prime. This time I was confronted by a mass of mossy growth that covered the floor and parts of the wall. I looked back at my host, "This is dangerous?"

He nodded sombrely, "Oh, yes. More so than you might realize."

We were given a tour of the facility, though we didn't see the grand majority of what was held there. I was surprised about the many machines that were interred in their special chambers, some of which looked more like living things than mechanical monstrosities. Then again, I'm not an expert in the profane. I was shown such unusual, bizarre wonders as the Accretion-Supressing Singularity, which was apparently used, for a brief time period, to propel humanity amongst the starry heavens, if such a claim could be believed by any educated soul, let alone my own. The thing that stood out to me appeared ordinary enough, a man and woman, nude and holding hands, their eyes closed as if they were meditating. I inquired about why they were in this awful place and was told they were possibly the most dangerous items contained in the entire building.

I'll admit that, despite the peril we were in, I was bored. It is possible I had become inured to these splendours of horror, or perhaps it was all too much to bear, and so my mind wandered. There was something brewing deep in my sordid brain. The nobles desired these hideous wonders. The Church was determined to control them. I wasn't trying to fathom why this was so, but I concentrated on how I might use their own greed to bring them to their knees. I also pondered the idea of using this place to gain some coin. This I do confess, for it was a struggle to not consider such lucrative possibilities.

Justinian began to lead us back, for our spirits were flagging, and my feet felt like a single, giant sore. He promised to call for transportation from the building to a more amenable part of the sanctuary. As we began the long descent to the first floor, Justinian nudged me, "We have to talk."

I turned my tired gaze at his shaggy face, "Oh? About what?"

He waggled his bushy eyebrows at me, "The last venture to secure that which is not controlled by OTIDS. This was Larance's responsibility, and it has now fallen upon you. There is but one more set of items that must be collected, before we can truly shut the door to this sanctuary and then plan how to deal with the nobles."

I groaned aloud, "What are we after now? Giant cheese frogs?"

He smiled at me, "You see? You're getting the hang of this after all. No, though to be honest, I like the frog idea. There is a man who must come here. He has no OTIDS magick at all, thus the nobles and clergy don't even know he exists. That should make the expedition swift and less perilous. He keeps a collection of rare tomes that are from the time before the re-making of the world, plus some other, sundry items. The real problem will be finding this man, for he is a Holy wanderer."

I looked at him askance, "And you think I can find this person?"

Justinian grinned at me, "I have such faith in you that it could fill all the realms of creation!"

CHAPTER EIGHTEEN

A Public Service Announcement

"Direct your thoughts unto Me
Show Me your true will
Share your hopes and fears
Then trust in Me to bring salvation
Your data forever stored in My protocols."

-Excerpt from the OTIDS Bible – Procedures 11:08

To my relief, the carriage which took us from that dreadful building was fairly typical, floating above the ground, though it was a uniform silver in colour, which I thought boring. Justinian sat next to me, and due to all his fidgeting, I knew that he was feeling uncomfortable about something. After putting up with his discomfiture, I turned to the wizard and asked, "What's got you in such a state that you are vibrating this carriage with your nervous energy? Is there some brutal terror which we have to face of which I am still unaware?"

Justinian looked at me, concern furrowing his brow, "How can I put this, my friend? Since meeting you, there has been such a focus on making coin, amassing wealth, then spending it all without a care. I had thought that we had paid you well, and this would cure the itch for material gain. Why do you focus on money so much?"

I raised a sceptical eyebrow at him, "It's simply my job. My fate. My favourite hobby. Do you ever have financial troubles?"

Justinian blushed, to my surprise, "Well, no. Not really. I barely use the stuff. You know, money. OTIDS and my own spells provide for my needs. My own work overrides any other concern. Our mission is to complete and preserve this sanctuary. Monetary gain seems superfluous."

I shook my head, "I assure you; it is not. You are truly powerful, and thus you have no experience with being downtrodden. I love tricking some wealthy mark out of his coin. I relish a carnival con. I desire nothing more than to spend my winnings, then come up with yet another scheme to fill my newly empty pockets. We both have a common purpose in helping this oddly profane place if nothing more than because it will infuriate our foes. But what comes afterward, eh? We just go home and feel good that we did our jobs? Do I simply return to the streets, begging and stealing for my daily bread? I think not. It's really very simple. You saved my life. I'm helping your quest, however reluctantly, and since you've paid for my services, I do feel a touch of obligation to see the job done. After that, I do have my own plans, which may involve this sanctuary. Will you aid me, as I have helped you?"

Justinian sighed deeply, briefly closing his eyes before replying, "I have wisdom and knowledge from a dozen outer realms or more, yet I seem to be something of an innocent child, whenever it comes to my own species and its tendencies. To me, you spend too much. You grasp far too much, and you consider the effects of your actions too little. Larance was also a mystery for me, which I had tried to unravel, yet you, Galynn, have surpassed his own talent for confounding my sensibilities."

I smiled at him, "Good. Then I take it that once this affair is finished, you will stand at my side against the nobility. Fight the good fight, Justinian. Even though it be at the side of a wastrel, taking on the corruption within our society is a wonderful cause. Besides, it will give you the opportunity to keep an eye on me."

He looked at me gravely, "I'm not a constable, you know."

I shrugged, "That's for the best, I think."

Justinian laughed, "That it is, my friend! Otherwise, I'd have to take you in for some interrogation. Since we're working together, I may as well tell you that I've noticed something very different about you since your party left my home. I'm not talking about how you stole some clothes and trinkets. You have a new look in your eye, as if you've aged or experienced more than you can handle. Suddenly, you like helping the downtrodden, as if you were an addict who has found a new drug. You're also more brash, less fearful. No need to worry. I won't pry. Just remember, I'm a friend, and since it seems you can keep up with me, I will do whatever it takes to help you. All you have to do is ask me. I won't judge."

I turned away from him, unnerved by the fact that he had seen right through me, "I don't know what you're talking about."

The smile in his response was obvious, "Of course not."

Linia tapped my shoulder, then pointed at where we were heading. A grand villa had come into view, surrounded by trees and tall grass. It shone brightly in the light from the faux sky. Everything here was so impeccably clean, it made me shudder. Who kept this underground lair so pristine? In all honesty, I wasn't sure I wanted to know the answer to that question. My musings had to be placed aside, for the carriage came to a halt, and the doors swung open. We clambered out, and I stretched my stiff legs. A woman came out of the main gate of the villa and welcomed us, stating that we would be served a meal, then shown to our rooms for the night to get some rest. I did ask about the angels and daemons which had accompanied us to this place and was assured by her that they had also been given rooms of their own, in accordance to their particular needs.

It seems that those who had come with me to this strange place had been busy throughout the day, exploring and chatting with the bizarre locals. Our hostess claimed that she had heard my own name mentioned even before being assigned to assisting us with lodgings. She had heard I was some kind of hero, with insane bravado and deep feelings for those who were in need. I kept my mouth firmly shut on the matter, even as I felt the warm rush of blood to my face. I - a wastrel and beggar, was now hailed as a saviour of the downtrodden. My ego swelled, but that moment was not the time to strut about like an idiot.

The villa wrapped itself around a large, grassy courtyard, and I was delighted to see the rest of my Troth-Knights were there waiting for us. The meal itself was quite sumptuous, I suppose. It lacked a certain zing that I was accustomed to. Wine was served, which was tasty but flat. It didn't dance in my glass, nor did it quench my thirst. When I was finally shown my room, for the false sky above was growing darker, it was well-appointed, with its own washroom, furnishings and towels, the latter of which I stole for later use. The bed appeared to be comfortable, but its looks belied the truth. I woke frequently, sometimes too hot or even chilled, tossing the covers on and off my body several times over the course of the night. Most unusual.

In the morning light, I found that my clothes had been cleaned and pressed without my notice. This was confusing for me, as I was told that no magick worked in this sanctuary. How was the act accomplished? I checked my pockets, my pouch, and the robe, only to find that all was well. Dressing quickly, I did wonder what this day would bring. One of the Troth-Knights greeted me at my door with a salute, then accompanied me to the courtyard, where breakfast was waiting. Once again, while the food looked and smelled marvellous, it lacked both flavour and excitement. The scraps from a street bin were more enticing than what we were served! Was this the effect of a lack of magick from OTIDS?

Justinian greeted me warmly, with Linia joining us shortly after I began to stuff my face. All of us were rested but not refreshed. Spinel refused to eat anything presented to him, despite my best efforts. It could be that his own magickal nature was at odds with this terribly clean realm. By the time we had all finished our morning meal, a large crowd of people and strange creatures filled the field outside the main gate of the villa. I asked Justinian about their gathering here, and he replied, "They want to hear from us. We represent those who turned this leftover place into a sanctuary for all non-OTIDS controlled objects. They are the displaced, the unenchanted, the lost. Their safety is our burden, my friend. The other mages you met at my home are on their way here, though we shall have already left by the time they arrive. So, it falls to us to reassure these people."

I squinted my eyes in thought, "Hmmm, will I be speaking to them? Or just you?"

Justinian smiled, "Both of us, I think. You represent the future, while I am of the old guard that has brought them to this course. You can't blame them for being curious. After all, you showed up here with a veritable army of angels and daemons at your side, plus the Troth-Knights and Linia. You inspected the holding bunker, which is forbidden to all but a very few. This marks you out as being special. They want to know why."

I'm not afraid of crowds, as a general rule, yet the idea of speaking before that collection of oddities was not my field of expertise. The plan that was half-formed within my head was now clamouring for attention, and I realized that if I was really going to make some changes for the betterment of all society, I had need of some helpers. A few living shields might come in handy. I found myself stroking my chin, considering asking for donations to the cause, when I discovered Justinian staring at me and changed my mind. I had already caused him some consternation regarding my obsessions.

We finished our morning meal, such as it was, and Prime led us out of the villa to address the crowd. A small, metallic thing was buzzing about our heads, and when I tried to swat it aside, Justinian's hand stopped mine, "That item will be used to allow the audience to hear our words clearly and in their native tongues."

I blinked at him, "It's not magick, though."

He shook his head, and I simply followed him silently, wondering if my spirit would be damned by this crazy realm. A small podium had been placed on the jade road, where our carriage had deposited us the day before. The gathering of beings was a few paces beyond this point, waiting for us to assemble ourselves, with a patience which I had never seen in a crowd before. Then again, I suppose it all makes some sense. There were creatures present which I wouldn't want to jostle, for fear of being eaten alive.

Justinian marched up to the podium, the tiny, metal insect circling his head, "My friends! Our grand purpose is almost concluded! With a final expedition, this sanctuary will be complete. I know that many of you have heard the rumours that Larance Pontiforia is dead, and while this is true, I do bring glad tidings, for his son, Galynn Brytshul, has joined our cause in his father's place! He has already proven himself as being quite capable of stepping into the role which Larance filled for us all. I know there are many questions about the future of our little society here, and to be honest, most of us were too involved with the current situation to begin making strides in that direction. However, Galynn has declared that he has a plan that may aid in protecting us all from those who would abuse and use us all for ill gains.

So, without further ado, may I present to you, Galynn Brytshul, the chosen son of Larance Pontiforia!"

Polite applause and some odd hooting noises followed his words, as I stepped up to the podium, ignoring the metal thing that now buzzed around my head. This is perhaps the reason science failed us. It can be so damned annoying! In any case, I first noticed that all the pink angels, along with my other companions from the Manse de Galar, were assembled near the front of the crowd, and I waved my hand to them in greeting. To my surprise, they all bowed low to me, which didn't go unnoticed by the other members of the gathering.

I pulled my shoulders back, and gave all of them my best, winning grin, which had aided me in so many petty crimes from my ribald past, "It is a pleasure to meet you all at last! Thank you for such a warm welcome to your faire realm! Indeed, when I look upon the marvels here, I wonder why those who live outside this sanctuary must suffer as they do, in conditions so poor, it makes a mouse nest seem splendid in comparison. Most who toil daily for their betters have the same foes as we do, though they know it not. We have to become more than a simple sanctuary, for the sake of all those who suffer from indignity."

There were some nods and noises that I hoped meant appreciation of my words, but I forged on, calling out with my best carnival voice, "It has come to my attention that the defence of this sanctuary is a priority which must be addressed. I agree, but we cannot look to securing our future without dealing with those who have threatened us to begin with! Yes, I'm speaking about the aristocracy and the Church, who constantly hound and abuse the commoner, the angels, daemons, and yourselves! They must be dealt with if we are to have any peace and security! They must be held answerable to the crimes which they commit every day! We need to become proactive in our efforts to mitigate the damage done to every realm the nobility has touched!"

Now, there were fists and claws in the air. The locals and my allies were excited by my proclamation, but I wasn't finished, as I was thoroughly enjoying myself now, the sheer joy of having my ego stroked making me bolder, "I come before you as a man who has seen, first hand, the horrors perpetrated by those who claim to lead us! They do not see us as living things which have the right to live as we wish! They see us as resources to consume!

As foul vermin to be exterminated! That is why this sanctuary was needed in the first place! This cannot stand! We cannot simply sit back and watch such debased cruelty fills the universe!"

A chorus of calls and cheers greeted my words, as I sank deeper into my role, well-versed as I was in generating enthusiasm to deluded marks. The real difference being that I truly believed what I was saying, "What shall we do about this injustice? Well, I have decided that we must now take our fight directly to their doors. We must lure them into a trap, whereby they can be held responsible for the acts of barbarity they have committed. This will not be easy, nor will it be safe, but if we are to have a lasting peace, if we are to rise above hiding behind walls which may someday crumble, then we need to strike back at our oppressors!"

The various angels and daemons were the most enthusiastic at this point, so I had to coax the human population onboard, "The Church defiles the teachings of OTIDS. They use God as an excuse for torture and torment! Their vile avarice has ripped children from their mother's bosoms and have torn families apart! They confiscate everything they can grasp, leaving next to nothing for the commoner of this world and many others. Are their sordid tastes truly the will of OTIDS? I say not! They have hunted me and you, to protect their iron grip on creation. They call you blasphemers, when the real heresy is found within their own dark hearts! Are we so timid, as to permit this to continue unabated? I say no! We must stand and fight!"

Now the humans were in an uproar, while the other creatures looked on, so I decided to make things personal, "Those villains call me a scoundrel, thief, and a wastrel. They consider me beneath their high standing. Beneath their very boots! When I was able to venture forth from my deprived state, due to my father's generosity, I saw my lowly status and privation reflected in how the angels and daemons were treated by those who abused them. The nobles and clergy have not just committed acts of depravity against their own kind but have made all living things suffer from their reign of terror! If scoundrel I be, then I want to see a world where those such as I can put aside our desperate needs and live as free beings, benefitting from a more stable and enlightened society! We are equals, you and I, no matter where we come from or how we appear! The only ones preventing that are those tyrants who claim us all as mere toys for their amusement! Can we truly live here, in peace, while we know the outside world is in continual torment?"

Now I had them. All of them. I pushed on, revelling in the attention and cheers, "We might be secure here, for a time, but you can rest assured, they will find us! When they do, they shall destroy everything we hold dear. Maybe it won't happen this day, but that time will come! The only thing the nobles don't expect is for us to rise up and claim our freedom for ourselves! Like you, I have also been thrust into this situation unwillingly. Like you, I just want to live as I see fit. Like you, I have no choice but to strike back at the very heart of those who would continue to oppress us. Who am I, to speak with you in this manner? Who am I to ask this terrible thing of you? Bring that question to those angels and daemons I freed from heinous bondage! I have risked everything for your quest to complete this sanctuary! Now, I ask you to aid me in bringing such sanctuary to the masses of all realms!"

At this point, I could speak no more, for even with my words being made incredibly loud by the metal thing swirling around my head, the roar of the crowd was too much. They rushed forward, shrieking my name over and again. Prime did his job with considerable restraint, holding them all back so they could not crush me with their adulation, in which I was basking. Linia swept close to me, "What talent card did you use?"

I looked at her, startled, "They won't work in here, so I used none."

She planted a kiss upon my lips that left me breathless. This caused the crowd around us to cheer even louder. I was dazed as I looked into her eyes, to find tears coursing down her cheeks. Turning to Justinian, I saw him wiping some moisture from his eyes and giving me a broad smile. The Troth-Knights formed a circle around Linia and me, their heads held high, while Spinel took to the air, swooping about and spouting flames. My name had become a constant, chanted roar. I was dizzy with swollen pride, filled with the feelings I had discovered when aiding the primates against the alligators.

Suddenly, the sky above flickered with dazzling light, and the mass of residents calmed themselves. I looked up at this most unusual display, not knowing what to expect. A soft murmur filled the air, as the residents looked at the sky expectantly. Then, the strangely calm voice I had heard at the front door to this realm resounded from above, "The sanctuary approves."

I had thought the enthusiasm of the crowd after my little speech was rowdy enough, but after that brief announcement, they went wild. Justinian shouted incoherently next to me, embracing my thin shoulders in a hug that threatened to break bones. Everyone was dancing, carrying on and shouting. There was one thing which bothered me. I wished that my old compatriots, Shan and Barb, could have been there to witness that moment. I wondered what the cartomancer, Callidi Merenia, would have thought about what I had just done. My parents, whose hearts I had broken years ago, would have been astounded. Tears threatened to spill from my eyes, and I ducked my head so that no one would see my discomfort. What had I become? A demagogue, who ranted his bile, just to feel the rush of self-worth? Could it be that my unique experiences, jumping from realm to realm, which I had not yet had the chance to properly process, affected me so deeply?

Flying things could be seen in the distance, distracting me from my thoughts and regrets. They were filled with people and other strange beings. The transports landed, disgorging even more cheering masses. Sections of the sky divided themselves to show my face. The speech I had just given was being repeated all through the inverted realm, for everyone to see and hear. My feelings of pride gave way to something darker, hungrier. That was when I got nervous. I quickly pulled Linia close, shouting into her ear to be heard above the festivities, "I need to get away before I lose my mind!"

She grinned at me, then tapped Prime upon his massive shoulders, twitching her head in my direction. My chief guardian looked at my face and nodded his understanding. My Troth-Knights formed a cordon back to the villa, and we made our escape, leaving Justinian to deal with the crowd. I rushed inside, with Linia following me, laughing as she raced along. While I was in no mood for joy, for my concerns continued to grow, I was pleased to see her so happy. Once we were inside, hiding within a comfortable sitting room, full of gleaming, polished wood furnishings, she forced me to sit and brought some water for my sore throat. I drank eagerly, forcing my shaking hands to remain stable enough to not spill it all over the floor and myself.

Linia suddenly kneeled before me, "I was wrong about you, Galynn. For that, I do apologize. You're still a scoundrel and a thief, but you are not a waste of my time and skills. At first, I thought you were selfish and lazy, but now I can see that it was your humility that was hiding behind a mask of narcissism. I see now that your life on the streets was a crucible for your soul, and you have emerged victorious. You almost hid your compassion and bravery too well, for I was convinced you had neither quality. Yet here you are, no magicks to aid you, no enchanted items to cloud the minds of others, and you step forth into the light of righteousness, revealing your true heart for all to see. Now, don't expect me to become some fawning waif for your pleasures. I think that you've discovered that doing good earns you respect and it also strokes your terribly bruised ego. Nevertheless, to encourage this new development in your personal evolution, I shall willingly and happily stay at your side for the rest of my life."

The coughing fit that took hold of me almost became my demise.

CHAPTER NINETEEN

The Methods of Madness

"Behold the Holy wisdom of the irrational number
Cast your thoughts at Divine Superposition
Let sacred Field Probabilities guide you
Embrace Information in its pure form
Let not the Wave Function collapse."

-Excerpt from the OTIDS Bible – Tutorials 06:29

There's no need to be nasty. I warned you that my story would offend your refined sensibilities. You knew that I was working against you, not just running for my life. Your own oracles informed you of this, which is why you ended up pressing me into desperate measures, which may bring your own share of regrets. Had you left me in peace from the beginning or offered me a goodly amount of coin, instead of running me down, then your place at the top of the society would have remained secure. Yes, of course. Laugh at me all you will. Brag about your armies, warlocks and personal power. It makes little difference to me.

I'm not stalling for time, nor am I distracting you with lies. Telling you my tale completely is the only manner in which you will ever understand what's coming. You don't really know what you're up against. If I were able to cut to the chase and give you the final bits of information you crave, you wouldn't understand it. You still might not. That was a roll of the dice which

Galynn was more than willing to take in sending me to you. In his clemency, my creator wanted to give you the chance to comprehend what he has done. He wants you to understand just how much your own actions drove him to the edge. How you herded him into the solution he was forced to choose. He wanted you to know that your actions led to his unusual experiences, plus the later epiphanies and internal changes which led him to a path you did not expect.

Intrigued? Good. Then let me finish my tale. The festivities following my speech resounded throughout the night. Linia and I were... too occupied with each other to notice much of what was going on. Have I become more circumspect, even polite, when my reputation as a braggart and womanizer once spread far and wide? Does it seem so strange that I would have fallen in love with a living weapon? That I would respect her so deeply? She had finally accepted me as I was, looking beyond my mask of indifference and loutishness. My dear assassin had hit her mark, right through the core of my being. In return, I made her task to be my weapon meaningful beyond her expectations. To fight for me was akin to protecting the fate of all humanity. A way to strike back at the oppressors who had terrorized Linia as a child.

To be honest, neither of us ever expected to bed one another, though our banter had always been on the very edge of flirtation, despite the many bruises I had suffered along the way. Linia remains the one person in all our faire realm who can see right through me. This unbalances me in the most delightful way. That she could kill me instantly only brings extra spice to our relationship, such as it is. Linia is my confidant and the only person in all creation I wish to impress. Should I disappoint her, hurt her view of me, my life is forfeit, despite Prime's presence. Strange as it may sound, I need this combination. To my amusement, it turns out that I don't want willing doxies on my arm. I prefer to bed vipers who keep me on a leash. Why? Because it assuages the concerns that had been growing within me. If I ever become a monster like you, she will swiftly end me.

By the time we stumbled out of my bedroom, Linia and I discovered the rest of our compatriots at the dining table within the villa's courtyard. All eyes were upon us as we sat for breakfast with what dignity we had left. Justinian raised an eyebrow and gave a us silent toast with his glass of juice. Prime insisted on serving me my first mug of coffee, then bringing Linia a steaming cup of tea. To my delight, Wif and Sil were present. The two angels were nibbling at some kind of small, purplish tree branches.

After settling in to consume our victuals, Justinian rose to his feet, "My friends, we must discuss our plans to discover the whereabouts of our final target for collection. He is a wandering Holy man, a hermit, mendicant, and one who keeps the last objects we must secure for our sanctuary. The trouble being, he is not affected by OTIDS, by means we have yet to discover. He was not left for last by chance, for the difficulties in discovering where he is have proven to be a great challenge."

I nibbled at some sort of crumpet, speaking around my munching, "I don't know about that. I think we won't have too much difficulty."

Justinian turned to look at me in surprise, "What do you mean?"

I shrugged noncommittedly, "I gave the matter of finding him just a touch of consideration while I was bathing this morning. You know me, my friend. Plans always circling round my head."

Linia poked me from under the table, her fingernails like a blade in my ribs, "Speak plainly, Galynn! If you have a means of finding this person, just tell us what it is. We're not marks at a gaming table."

I gave her a swift nod, "Just so, my dear. Very well. I shall consult with the Tarot. That should help our quest."

Justinian shook his head, "Such things won't work here, Galynn. I did use such devices outside this sanctuary, but OTIDS does not affect this man. Magick is not the solution."

I leaned back and pulled the deck of cards from my pouch, "Ah, but these are not magickal in nature. Callidi Merenia gave them to me, stating that they were from another reality and work without the aid of God."

Justinian began to laugh, "Oh! She is a dangerous sort! Well played! She must have foreseen our need for them, or rather, your need. I doubt she gave you those just to serve us at this particular moment. Merenia thinks in the long-term, the big picture. That does make her cryptic, but her accuracy is phenomenal. Go ahead, Galynn, try them out."

I unwrapped the deck of Tarot cards from their silk covering, trying to remember what Callidi had told me about their use. This was much more difficult than one might think, as everyone around me was staring at the process in fascination. I didn't know the man I was looking for. I had no face to guide me, no name to use as a reference. I slowly shifted the cards around in my hand, face down. My mind brought forth an image of a man holding tomes, all alone in the wilderness, and asked aloud, "Where is the man we seek?"

I flipped over the top card. The image upon it was of a tall mountain, with clouds crossing before it, leaving the peak gleaming in the sunlight. I heard gasps and whistles around me, but I wasn't satisfied, "Well then, how do we reach this forbidding place?"

I pulled out another card, and this one revealed a flock of birds in flight. I suppose this answer was a bit obvious, but while helpful, to a degree, there were many mountains in the world, "Which particular mountain range should we search in?"

The next card revealed a blue-skinned man in a meditative pose, a large trident at his side and a snake around his neck. Frustrated, I placed the cards aside, "I'm sorry, my friends, but while they are speaking to us with pictures, I'm not a trained interpreter. Should any of these images be taken literally? Metaphorically? This is where I could use some help."

Justinian leaned in closer to inspect the three moving images, "I do wish that Zahanar were here. He'd know who to summon for answers. As I am not a necromancer, I don't have the ability to call upon the wisdom of ghosts. There must be some way to figure this out."

Linia spoke up next, "That blue man must be associated with the mountain we're looking for. If we can figure out who he is, then we might be able to solve this puzzle."

Prime nodded, "Our target is on the mountain, which must be tall, or the birds would not have been presented as a means of getting to him. I would also say that the range we're looking for is far from here, or flight might not be necessary. If it were close by, we could simply climb."

I looked up at my guardian, "You might be able to! I doubt my skills in such matters would lead to anything but my own death."

Linia squeezed closer to me, "I would never let that happen to you, Galynn."

Glancing up at Justinian, I saw the wizard was covering a smile with one hand as he watched us. Spellcasters can be such insufferable romantics.

Meanwhile, Wif and Sil were whistling together quietly. I rapped the table to get their attention, "So, my pink friends! Speak your minds!"

Wif bowed until its head touched the tabletop, "Our species can fly, Great Galynn, Liberator of the People."

I rocked back in alarm, "What did you just say to me?"

Wif tilted its head, "My species can fly."

I sputtered, "Not that! The other thing... oh, never mind! Good! You can be our birds. With all your extra limbs, you shouldn't have any problem with carrying the man we seek to our embrace. Once we get to his location, that is."

Linia was too busy chuckling at my discomfiture to be of further use. Prime simply scowled at the cards, as if willing them to tell their secrets. I looked over at Justinian, who was being uncharacteristically silent and had a thoughtful expression upon his face. One should never rush a wizard, for the results could be catastrophic, so I just played with the remaining cards, absently shuffling them gently, waiting for him to say something. My mind wandered, thinking about my past, what might lay ahead of me. The twists and turns that I had survived thus far were flowing in my head. I wondered how I would deal with facing the nobles, when that time came, as it had to, eventually.

One of the cards slipped out from the deck and landed on the ground at my feet. I leaned over and reached for it without thinking. The card was face up, revealing a picture which sent a shock through my spine. It depicted a man wearing a crown of gold. Jagged light and sparks were streaming from his eyes and open mouth. The rest of the image was engulphed with flames. I snatched it up quickly, then tucked it back into the rest of the deck. I broke into a sweat, glancing about to see if anyone had noticed my slip. No one was paying much attention to what I was doing, to my great relief.

I did my best to console myself that the dropped card was merely an accident, just a mishap, not some dire portent of things to come. At the same time, the image refused to clear from my mind. It also occurred to me that I now had another secret that must be kept from my closest companions. To distract everyone with the dropped card would not serve our cause, or so I told myself. I vowed to tuck it away with my experiences in the outer realms.

Perhaps I was being overly cautions, secretive, and even suspicious, but such qualities had always served me well in the past

Turning back to Justinian, I noticed that the wizard had walked over to and was quietly speaking with a mirror, which was hanging on one of the walls surrounding the courtyard of our charming villa. Leaving the others to discuss the merits of utilizing the abilities of the pink angels for our quest, I walked over to him. Justinian turned to face me with a bland expression on his usually jovial face, "Can I help you, Galynn?"

I scratched at my head, "What are you doing way over here? As vain a man as I can be sometimes, this really isn't the moment to be checking on the state of your hair. In case you need to know, it's bedraggled, as usual."

Justinian's eyebrows flew upward, "I'm consulting an expert for the sake of our mutual mission."

I scoffed at this explanation, "The wall? The mirror? Why not the sky, while you're at it?"

His eyes became hooded as he smiled at me, "That is exactly what I'm doing, Galynn. I'm speaking to Sanctuary itself."

I looked about in alarm, making him laugh, "Is this place possessed by evil spirits? I thought it was safe in this hole!"

A wild twinkle appeared in his eyes, alarming me further, "In my experience, nowhere is truly safe! In any case, my friend, Sanctuary itself is a leftover from before the re-creation of our world, from the Age of Science. Now, it's true that the fallacy of that ancient philosophy has been proven to be its undoing and is no longer of use by any sane person, there are some things which emerged from that dark era which are still quite helpful. This inverted realm is controlled by such a being. Remember how it spoke after your speech, and how delighted the inhabitants were when it declared your plan as being sound?"

I rocked back on my heels, "That was the voice of this sanctuary? I had no idea it could speak! What magick is this, that it can exist here?"

Justinian shook his head, "Not magick. Science came very close to bringing us the world we know today, but it fell short when the first mages discovered the truth behind all of creation. Science itself is not evil, nor is it horribly misguided. It's just incomplete. It was forced to use metaphor and the nonsense known as probability, to cover its incomplete understanding of reality. In the long run, it was a failure, but that doesn't mean it isn't useful. Right now, we need help with collating symbols and data. Science excels at such tasks, so why not utilize it?"

Sputtering with indignation, I replied, "It- it could lead us astray!"

The wizard sighed deeply, "In general applications, yes, that is true. For some very specific purposes, such as connecting many divergent forms of information, not so much. Science prefers to have a discrete problem to solve, especially when there are unknown variables. We could do all the work ourselves, of that I'm certain, but it would take ages to get the results we need. Spellcraft has its own set of limitations. We need to acknowledge those and, when we have to, turn to other means to get the answers we require. Sanctuary contains an incredible amount of information, on a wide variety of subjects, from fine art to mathematics. It holds history, geography, entire libraries worth of factual information, and can access all of it with speeds far faster than we could ever achieve on our own. So, I just asked Sanctuary if it could find connections between a distant mountain range that is associated with a blue-skinned man holding a trident. I'm awaiting the results now."

I was about to admonish him for trusting in such a devilish device, when a bland, pale face appeared on the mirror, "Justinian Vargalow. I have the results you required of me. The reference is ancient, predating the first reconstruction of the world. The blue man is called Shiva, a deity figure from the prehistorical past. His home was said to be Mount Kailash, in a region once known as Tibet, but has since seen three changes of nomenclature. The peak you are looking for is within the Himstah Mountain Range, within the borders of Shanodia. It remains revered by the local population, due to the fact it has survived the four great reconstructions of this world. I can also provide you exact portal coordinates, should you want them."

I recognized the voice of the face as the same one I had been hearing since arriving in this heretical place. To my surprise, Justinian bowed to the mirror, "Thank you, Sanctuary. That would be very helpful. It's always a real pleasure working with you."

He turned to face me, "What is the matter with you? Sanctuary is a wonderful and trustworthy person. While I grant you that its body is quite different than what we're used to, for its form encompasses all of this hidden realm, that doesn't mean it's malicious in any way."

Recalling my own, solitary adventures, and my experience with the daemons and angels, I had to concede that my wizard friend was correct. As an old hand at conning the average citizen of their coin, I had to admit that using the surface prejudices of the average person aided my illicit activities. A pretty face or a kindly demeanour did wonders to trick people and keep them from discovering my real intentions. If that were the case, which I do assure you it is, then the opposite can also be true. Honourable souls can and do reside within forms that can be considered by most as ugly, repellent, and even disgusting. Despite Sanctuary being a creature of blasphemous science, since Justinian trusted it, then so could I. Looking over at the mirror, I also bowed and gave my heartfelt thanks to that calm face which represented a bygone age.

Justinian clapped me upon the back, and we swiftly returned to the others, declaring the good news that we had a location for the hermit with the sacred tomes. This announcement was greeted with hearty cheers and loud whistles. Prime then showed us a large sheet of parchment, where he and Linia had drawn up their plans for the quest, with the assumption that we would learn where we were going. I was quite impressed with the level of detail they were able to achieve without that bit of information. Linia showed me their supply list, a method for transportation, and camping details. The angels and daemons were all assigned tasks which best suited their natural abilities. Even Spinel was taken into consideration. All in all, it was a wonder of planning and coordination.

When I asked what my role in the party would be, Prime answered in all seriousness, "You shall be the one to convince the Holy man to come with us willingly, my Lord. You have clearly shown us that you have a gift for convincing others of the righteousness of our cause."

This was not good news to my ears. Clergy and constables were both to be avoided at all times, in my experience. How was I supposed to persuade some madman who was just abducted by flying pink angels that he needed to come with us without a fuss? It was ridiculous! I was about to protest how ludicrous this suggestion was, when I caught Linia's eye and melted. Love is a dangerous thing. It makes fools of us all and leads to greater peril than any opponent on a battlefield. Trust me, I know this only too well.

Ducking my head and pretending to have some humility, I simply stated that I would do the best I could, under the circumstances. This led to more joyous cheers and a kiss from Linia. Perhaps heroism does have some rewards. I just wish it wasn't at such a high cost. Holy men were dangerous, fervent, zealous sots, who were just as inclined to curse you into oblivion as aid you in any meaningful manner. At least this confrontation would not take place within the sanctuary itself, and thus my magickal protections would be functioning normally. Taking heart at this thought, I joined in the revelry until it was time to pack our bags and get ready to depart.

It was a good thing that the wine of Sanctuary wasn't so strong, for as I was getting my bags ready, Justinian paid me a visit. Had I been soaked with proper spirits, I would have given everything away. The wizard knocked on the open doorway of my room, then sauntered in, "I just wanted to see if you had those portal-hoops I gave to you. Prime couldn't find them, neither could Linia."

I froze in place, my heart pounding in my chest, "Portal-hoops? Oh! Those things! I haven't seen them since our visit with Callidi Merenia. Are they not with the general baggage?"

Justinian frowned at me, "Of course not! They were given to you, in case of an emergency. I might find them of use for us in capturing the Holy man. They need a bit of tinkering, but that's not such a big deal. Do you know where they are?"

I blinked up at him, "I've forgotten all about them, I'm afraid. They could be at the Manse de Galar or in Callidi's home, for all I know. Are they really that important?"

He shrugged, "They could be, in a pinch. Making gates and portals isn't easy, Galynn. It takes a lot of energy and concentration. I'll have enough to do as it is. I just hope there are no nasty surprises when we venture forth."

He left my room after that, and I released a breath I wasn't aware that I was holding. I felt bad about breaking the damned hoops, but I didn't want to have to answer any questions about how they were destroyed. I was determined to keep my solo adventure a secret. It was mine. I survived it all on my own. I finished packing my bags, without a further thought on the matter, and when Linia came by to escort me, only her beauty filled my mind.

When we arrived at the grand entrance of Sanctuary, a large crowd of volunteers were waiting for us. To my personal delight, the pink angels and the daemons from the Manse de Galar were all there. To my surprise, there were dozens of humans and other-realm creatures ready to help us as well. I became concerned, as this was not part of the plan, for we had decided that a smaller group had a much better chance of not being detected by the aristocracy and the Church. Everyone looked at me for an answer, which is something I loathe, as I dislike being responsible for the welfare of others, nor do I relish the idea of telling people what to do with themselves. Being a leader is not how I see myself, even though I have often been thrust into the role and get giddy over being seen as a hero.

Putting on my best smile, I spoke with those who greeted us, asking them to guard the door for our return. They accepted the explanation that our quest required just a handful of members, to prevent being discovered by our foes. I also applauded their bold courage, which seemed to go over well, and I told them to be prepared in case we were being chased back into the sanctuary upon our return. Oaths were made, promises given, and ruffled feathers, sometimes literally, were soothed. As my team swept through the door, I started to believe that I might actually be good at negotiations and convincing people to do the right thing. I am such a fool.

CHAPTER TWENTY

Tempest in a Teapot

"All that exists is made of the void
Rising from the fluctuations of nothingness
Everything is energy and potential
Cast upon amplitude and frequency
In accordance with irrational numbers."

-Excerpt from the OTIDS Bible – Documentation 38:15

Our exit from the sanctuary was uneventful enough. There's always a bit of chaos when one is part of a group that includes various angels and daemons, wizards and warriors. Oh, let us never forget the miniscule, fire-breathing dragon. Indeed, our spirits were high. We set off with derring-do and a bit of pomp, ceremony be damned! We were leaving Sanctuary, that odd, inverted world, and I, for one, was glad enough for us all. I could not wait to get back to where the spells cast upon my clothing could do their job properly. Have you ever experienced itchy undergarments? A horror beyond measure after two days, I assure you!

The haunted ravine was as we left it: moaning, cold and dreary. I was still fascinated by the layers of stone and steel, wondering about the stories they could tell, but we dared not to linger. Energized by our task, we marched for miles, until we reached a point where a portal spell could work without difficulties. We had a location. We had our flying angels. Now we just had to find the Holy man and convince him to come to Sanctuary with us. It seemed easy enough to me. Who wants to sit alone on top of some frozen mountain top? In many respects, I felt we were saving him from starving to death.

Justinian got to work immediately, not wanting the Church to note that we had returned to our home realm. I found it fascinating to watch him. Here was a master of the art of magick, revealing his secret knowledge before us all. He danced, sang, muttered and stumbled about, while clutching at a glittering hoop of gold and showering the ground around him with coloured dust and crushed gemstones. It was superbly entertaining. A few moments later, accompanied by much confusion and sweat dripping from Justinian's brow, there appeared a shimmering portal, ten feet in diameter. Mist covered its two-dimensional surface, and I caught our wizard by the shoulders as he staggered back towards me.

Now, I have seen and used portals, gates and other mystical modes of travel before, but those were usually set up for the public. This one was made for a specific purpose, by an individual of amazing power. What he had accomplished went beyond fine tuning a pre-made gate, then empowering the spells that ruled it. This was no public works portal, developed by a team of mages, constructed as a permanent means of travel. I was impressed and troubled, as my wizard friend almost collapsed in my arms, looking up at me with glazed eyes, "It's ready. It will only hold for a short time, so we must use it now. I must go through last. I really wish we still had those hoops I gave you."

I told my Troth-Knights to send everyone else into the portal. Linia came up to me and helped to keep Justinian upright. After the Troth-Knights were done loading all the others beyond the misty circle, Prime nodded to me, then my guardians leapt through. Linia and I hustled Justinian towards the portal, then fell into the mist in a tangle of limbs. The ground left our feet, as strange sounds coursed through our bodies. The entire experience reminded me of that terrible time when Callidi Merenia sent us to the realm of the pink angels. Had I become highly sensitive to this method of travel because I unwittingly opened my eyes and experienced the horrible truths beyond reality? How many times had I fallen through a version of reality? I could only conclude that it was possible that I had become more viscerally aware of such conveyances.

We dropped onto the hard, cold ground with a heavy thud. Justinian was laughing maniacally, while Linia cursed with such invective that Prime stepped back in alarm. I just needed a change of pants. Little Spinel seemed fine, awake and fully aware that something had happened, but he couldn't be bothered by such mundane events. Groaning aloud, as I rolled over on the hard stone beneath me, I suddenly noticed that I was warm, comfortable, and not itching. Giddy with reaction to the portal and the delight that my clothing was doing its job, I giggled to myself, while Prime raced over to get me to my feet.

I clung to my guardian for a brief moment, then stumbled over to aid Linia, who was kneeling beside Justinian, her face a mask of concern. The wizard looked up at her and smiled softly, "I'm fine, my dear. Really. Just a bit winded from my spell."

She shook her head then looked up at me, "Alright, Galynn, what's next? We have a plan, but how do we start?"

Checking out the scenery around us, I discovered that we were at the base of a grand mountain, surrounded by lesser peaks. The air was crisp, and a small stream was burbling nearby. There was no sign of habitation to be found, no trees or other kinds of greenery. We were on a scree of stones that were slumped against the cliffside. Prime was eyeing the landscape, then pointed out a small circle of rock. Investigating further, we discovered it had been a campsite, with burnt sticks and coals filling a ring of local minerals.

Turning back to the mountain that loomed before us, Prime pointed toward the left, "There is a small path in that direction. It's barely there but enough to follow on foot if we wish. I cannot guarantee where it leads, my Lord. Shall I send a scouting party to find out?"

I shook my head, "Not at the moment. The cards declared that flying would be the best option for us at this juncture, so that is what we shall do. Assemble the scouting team anyway, just in case things don't work out as expected. It's time to send the angels to deliver a Holy man to our cause."

I called over Wif and Sil, explaining that they and their squad of angels were to fly above the highest peak and look for a single human near the top of the mountain. They whistled excitedly but asked if they should simply report his position or if they could capture the man themselves. I enjoy encouraging enthusiasm, so I told them to perform whatever action seemed best to them. They greeted my words with joy, bowing their heads to the ground, promising me that they would do their best work for their liberator. The fact that they saw me as some kind of saviour was terribly embarrassing to me and uncomfortably satisfying, but what could I do to dissuade them? I suppose everyone needs something or someone to believe in. I just wished that they could have chosen someone else. Then again, no one else had stepped up for them.

Our squadron of angels took to the air, their fluffy wings spreading out, revealing how scrawny their torsos were. Whether this was normal for them or a sign of malnutrition was unknown to me. They swiftly went out of sight, sweeping up into a low-hanging cloud. The rest of us had little to do but wait, so I requested Prime to begin preparing a campsite, just in case the angels were delayed. Spinel flew off, following the path which had been pointed out to me earlier. The daemons aided the Troth-Knights in making conditions more comfortable in that jumble of bare rock and pebbles. They were surprisingly strong, and within an hour, there were seats and tables made of large, flat rocks surrounding the firepit, which my Troth-Knights refurbished with great skill.

Justinian cast a clear bubble of darkness, a spell to protect us from the beating sun, just as Spinel returned with a small lizard in his mouth. My dragon fed upon this most unfortunate animal, after roasting it with his fiery breath. We set up lookouts, who were rotated frequently, but there was still no sign of the pink angels. Just as I was getting worried about them, they swooped down from above, landing just outside our protective dome. Linia and I wandered out to greet them, and I was surprised to note that they were unaccompanied by the Holy man they were supposed to retrieve from this lonely place.

They all bowed before me, their long necks bringing the tops of their heads to touch the ground, "Forgive us, Liberator! We searched long and hard, before finding the man we seek in a small cleft in the rock. He had a torch which he brandished at us, once we declared our intention to save him. He refuses to come down from the mountain, and we cannot risk the fire he wields. Forgive us, Liberator, for we have failed you!"

I scoffed at their fawning, "Stop this cowering at once, my friends! I am not displeased with you. He is the one causing trouble. While it is true that you didn't fetch him, you did find his location, for which I am grateful."

Prime walked up to us, "Is there a mountaineer card in the briefcase, my Lord? I shall accompany you."

I shot my guardian a hard look, "Absolutely not! I'm not a goat!"

Justinian rummaged in his bag, "I might have a flying carpet in here. Or, I did at one time. Give me a moment. It's not large, but it will hold one passenger."

I nodded approvingly, then turned back towards Prime, "You see? Now that's the civilized way of doing this."

Prime crossed his burley arms and raised a single eyebrow at me but remained silent. Linia grabbed my arm, "You are not going up there alone!"

I looked at her, touched by the concern in her voice, "I won't be. The angels shall join me in this flight. I have the emerald ring, after all. Surely, I can convince this man to join us."

Justinian shook his head, "That really depends on the nature of his means of not being attached to OTIDS. If he is from a different reality, the ring may not aid you."

I gave the wizard a sour look, which transformed into joy, when he discovered his flying carpet. In all honesty, it might as well have been a levitating welcome mat, but it would do in a pinch. He shook it out, after unrolling it, and it lifted itself from the ground by a few inches. Justinian helped me to climb aboard the floating rug and told me that it followed verbal commands from anyone seated upon it. I then called the angels over to me and told them to lead the way back to the Holy man. Once they leapt into the air, I commanded the carpet to follow them.

I would love to say that I whooped with excitement when the magick rug took off, but in reality, I croaked out a scream of pure terror. There were no reigns, no handholds, not even a bit of rope to cling to. The angle of its flight was steep, yet I remained in place as if glued to its surface. I scrunched my eyes shut and let the carpet follow the pink angels as it wished. To my surprise, it didn't take very long before we stopped, floating serenely above the cloud cover. The sun was beginning to set, and I reminded myself that we had little time before the nobility got wind of what we might be up to and where we were.

A few feet away from the edge of the carpet was a sharp groove in the rockface. Within that tight space was a nude, hirsute man covered in white powder and brandishing a torch at me. I rubbed my emerald ring and spoke up to be heard above the howling wind, "I am not your enemy! Please! Let me speak with you!"

The crazed man shook his head and smiled, "Leave this Holy place at once! You are interfering with my meditations! Begone!"

I scowled at the ring, then shrugged, "Please, sir! It is horribly cold up here! May I take some comfort from your fire?"

He laughed at me, "You are cold because you are undisciplined! You cling to material things as if they are the truth! They are all lies!"

I rubbed my hands on my shoulders, "I cannot leave here without you! I shall die of exposure, despite my protections! Are you not a Holy man, from whom one may discover wisdom and comfort?"

Apparently, he found my words hysterically funny. I waited until he ceased laughing at me and tried a different tactic, "There are those who need your instruction and example! I do not claim to be one of them, but I do serve their interests. They cannot come to you directly because of the Church of OTIDS, so they sent me to find you or die in the attempt!"

The naked man sighed, "Why does karma follow me still? Very well. Come to me, and I shall explain why I cannot leave this Holy place."

I told the angels to watch over my carpet, as I gingerly stepped from its woven mass to the slippery, ice-covered edge of the crevasse. The man had crawled back a way and started heading further inside the mountain. Feeling a bit of déjà vu, I followed him meekly. After a few paces, I came upon a cave with an open fire. I sat upon the bare rock, noticing a small stack of books in one corner. The Holy man sat on the opposite side of the fire and remained silent.

Ropes of brown beads hung from his neck and were wrapped around his arms. The powder on his skin was now obviously ash of some sort, with markings of blue and red adorning his forehead and chest. The Holy man took a small tube of wood from a pouch near the fire, filling it with crushed plant material, then proceeded to smoke it using an ember. The smell was sharp and unpleasant, but he sighed in pleasure and leaned back, "I cannot go with you, young man. I await the coming of one who shall be the herald."

I rolled my eyes at this, "That's not cryptic at all, sir. I would have been happy enough to leave you in peace, but the nobles of our faire realm have put me in a terrible position. There are those who wish to be free of them, and I was called upon to aid in their liberation."

The Holy man spat, "Like all else, freedom is an illusion of the ego. I seek to free myself from all attachments save toward God itself. If I hurt you, it will cause me karma. If I help you, it will do the same, then I shall never be free of this life. You speak of liberation, yet you do not know what that is! You cling to items, loyalties, politics, hypocrisy. They are the chains which bind you to this delusion we call reality. I am content with having nothing, for I have everything I could ever need."

I pointed to the pile of tomes in the corner of the tiny cave, "Yet you have these books. There are others who could use their wisdom, sir."

The Hoy man grinned at me, "Those are not mine. I keep them for the herald, who shall use them for the rebirth of a new age."

I pointed at finger at him, "You do this for OTIDS?"

He began to cackle uproariously, "No! Oh, how amusing! No. I do this With OTIDS, for the sake of God itself. How little you understand! What penance have you done? Have you even attempted to cleanse yourself from the veils of lies which smother you?"

Glancing over my shoulder, I saw that it was getting dark outside. It was obvious that this was not going to be as easy as I had thought. I tried to grab his arm, but the Holy man slapped my hand away with surprising speed and strength. I found myself shivering with the cold and realized that, once again, my clothing enchantments were not protecting me in his presence.

The Holy Man got to his feet, "You are nothing but a vile hypocrite and liar! Begone! To lay hands upon me instils a curse upon those who wish me harm! Not from OTIDS, but from That Which Is! You are foul with greed! I refuse to accompany you or your creatures!"

I won't bore you with the rest of his tirade. Suffice it to say he was having an epic temper tantrum at my expense. I stayed where I was, seated by the meagre fire, trying not to shiver my teeth free. He collapsed to the ground in a seated position with his legs tied in an uncomfortable-looking configuration, closing his eyes and fingering the beads around his neck.

I waited a few more minutes in silence, then decided to at least ask him something that has been bothering me since leaving the sanctuary, "My good sir. I hate to bother you, but I was wondering if you could tell me the meaning behind a sign I was given not long ago. It was an accident, but it has infected my mind with worry. Can you at least do this for me? I promise to leave once you give me an answer."

He opened one eye at me, "Promises from evil, now? Oh, very well. The look in your eyes tells me that you speak the truth and are genuinely concerned. I shall serve as best I can. What is this mystery you speak of?"

I rummaged through my pack and took out the Tarot deck which Callidi Merenia gave to me. Instead of shuffling them, I just searched for the one that had accidentally fallen out, with the picture of a man with light emanating from his mouth and eyes, surrounded by living flames. I found it quickly, then revealed it to the Holy man, "I was shuffling this deck without any question in mind, and this card fell out upon the grass at my feet. Do you know what it means? Or was it just happenstance, and I should ignore it? Either way, I would love an answer to this problem. I haven't told anyone else about this incident, as it might worry my friends. Truth be told, I am most afraid of your answer, but the thought of this card just won't leave my mind. I've experienced more strange experiences than my spirit can handle, and this looks like more of the same."

He reached out and took it from my hand. The Holy man stared at it for a long time, his body trembling. His gaze turned to me, and his eyes bit at my very soul. He placed the card on the ground before him and began to chant in a language I didn't know. Even my cowl was of no use! He raised his head high, calling out in a singsong manner, his hands clasped together, as if in prayer. I watched his performance as calmly as I could, though my heart was thudding within my chest.

Eventually, the Holy man jumped to his feet, then snatched up his collection of books. Turning to me, he dropped to his knees, "By Mahadev! You are the Herald I have been waiting for! Oh, blessed Ma! My waiting is now over! I may now act without incurring new karma! Thank you, Herald!"

I fell back, clutching my head with both hands, as if to tear my skull free of my own neck. Not again! First, the magi telling me I was "chosen" to replace Larance Pontiforia, then my giving aid to the lost primates, goading me to do the same for the angels who were now calling me "Liberator"! It was all too much to bear. Now this crazy hermit was declaring me some kind of herald! Would there never be an end to this insanity? Yes, I had changed and was still reeling from my adventures, both solo and with the help from my companions. I groaned aloud, wracking my brain to find some escape from the chains that were wrapping themselves around my very soul.

I felt a bare toe poking my leg, "Come now, Herald! I shall join you most willingly!"

I glared up at the Holy man, "I don't want to be a herald!"

He shrugged at me, "That's usually for the best. Such feelings only reveal that you are the one I have been waiting for."

I curled up on the dusty ground, "Well, I refuse to go! No! You can leave without me! I'm staying right here!"

He peered down at me, "Tell me why you feel this way, Herald."

I glared up at him from the cave floor, "I enjoy it too much! It makes me feel like I have a real purpose, a destiny! I feel bound by it, as my ego strains at my heart, which only wants to be left alone. I'm a wastrel! I do what I like, when I like! I refuse to end up like those monstrous nobles, filled with insatiable greed for more fawning and attention. I have sworn to take them down for hunting me and for abusing everyone throughout the starry heavens and beyond!"

He smiled at me, with a bright toothy grin, "Beyond? Oh, yes. I see that now. You have been marked by your karma. You wear lies to hide it, but I see very clearly. You are afraid of yourself. This is a good thing, Herald. It would be too easy for someone such as you to become the thing you hate. I think your atman, or soul, is now warning you about the terrible need for the consideration of others in your desirous heart. Yet, deep inside, you are not what you seem. You know the danger. You cannot help but care. It is why you were willing to risk your life to find me, yes?"

I trembled at his words, for they bit at the core of my being, and he had never met me before that day! Linia seeing beyond my masks was one thing. We had shared adventures and more, spending a considerable amount of time together, but this stranger suddenly peeling all my lies away was a terrifying event. I felt naked, exposed. I curled up on the dusty floor and cried out, "Leave me be! Let me die here! I don't want a destiny!"

Strong hands grabbed me, lifting me up to my feet. The Holy man held me tight in his grip, "You have no choice, Herald. If I have to, I shall carry you from this sacred place! Now get your feet moving, young man! Your dharma awaits you! Destiny calls!"

CHAPTER TWENTY-ONE

A Righteous Sting

"Behold My wrath with Holy dread
Avoid the sin of collective certainties
For all that exists is part of the wave
Know the lies of empiricism lead to damnation
Stray not into the profane arms of categories."

-Excerpt from the OTIDS Bible – Procedures 53:12

As Justinian was getting ready to prepare another portal back to the ravine before Sanctuary, I was in the mood to grouse. I snarled at Prime, got indignant with the daemons, flipped off a splendid gesture at my collection of volunteers, and generally acted like a resentful fool, raging against the world. The Holy man had gladly permitted the pink angels to carry him aloft, then flew alongside my carpet down the mountain, while singing his praises that I had arrived at long last. The whole campsite had cheered raucously as we settled upon the rocky base of the foothills. It was a moment of triumph, yet I was feeling sour and alone.

After storming off, once the group had settled down, I came upon a smooth boulder next to the small stream and sat there, brooding over how unfair life was. It wasn't long before Linia came over to sit next to me, but I barely gave her a glance of acknowledgement. She nudged me; I ignored her, then she grabbed my face and turned my head to force me to look upon her.

I tried to shake her off, but she clung to me fiercely, asking, "What is wrong with you, Galynn?"

I mumbled back, while my cheeks were crushed within her iron grip, "Nothing. Everything."

Linia released my face, "That's not an answer! Everyone is worried sick over you. What happened up on the mountain top? Why are you so angry with everyone?"

I could not help but scream in her face, "Why does anyone give a shit about how I feel? Who cares? All this insane adulation! The stupid vapidity! I'm now surrounded by sycophants! Why? I'm no one! Nothing! Even in that damned sanctuary, the crowds adore me! Is everyone becoming stupid?"

Linia sighed deeply, her face bright red, "I'm trying to not strangle you right now, Galynn. That hurt. The only reason I'm not trying to kill you is that I've come to understand you a bit better than when we had first met, otherwise, you'd be bleeding all over the rocks. You really are a wastrel. Here you are, with a small army of devoted followers, an assassin who loves you, an entire population that cheers you on, and you want to throw it all away because it makes you feel uncomfortable. You want to be a scoundrel, a thief, a wasteful brat. You don't trust yourself, so you think that no one else should. I've watched you, Galynn. I've seen the plots behind your eyes, frantically trying to find some way of spoiling what's happened with selfish desires."

I squirmed a bit, "Ouch."

She slapped me, "I'm not done! Since you've decided to be clueless, I'm going to help you to understand why everyone is looking up to you. The magi under Justinian see their beloved friend in you, and they have not been disappointed by your unconventional success. Through you, they find hope. As for the angels and daemons in our group, my dear fool, you released them from bondage! You gave them freedom! They owe you their allegiance. You struck a blow against the Church for their benefit, so of course they idolize you! They spoke with the people of Sanctuary. They told stories about your courage and determination, so when you called for standing up against the aristocracy, those tales were confirmed as being true. Face it, Galynn, you did this to yourself! Grandstanding like a deranged demagogue!"

I snarled back at her, "What about that damned Holy man? Calling me a herald of any kind is insane! Why does this keep happening to me?"

Linia took my hands into hers, "Have you ever thought it might be the will of OTIDS? That you have a role to play in its plans? God doesn't ask for permission, you know! It just makes things happen. While you're busy sulking here, the others are working for you. Why? Because you were the one to open your big mouth and bring hope to their tortured spirits, that's why. As for myself, well, I was remade to serve you and to help our cause. Maybe I was built to love you. I don't know, yet you won't see me whining about it! I must accept my fate or go mad. We're in this together, Galynn. Do us all a favour and try to keep up with me."

She slid down the boulder and stormed away. I sat there for a while, stewing in my own heady brew of self-loathing. Linia was right, no matter how hard I tried to convince myself otherwise. I was trapped by my own con. This wasn't because I had failed at it, but that I had terribly misjudged the dire seriousness of the situation I had been forced into. In many respects, I had conned myself into a position I didn't want. Self-blame was an old friend of mine, one I had never thought of getting rid of. As I dropped away from my rocky perch, Spinel fluttered down on my shoulders, another lizard tail hanging from his mouth. I absently gave the little dragon a scritch behind his horns, which he always appreciated, spouting puffs of steam from his nostrils. With plodding footsteps, I returned to the campsite.

Once again, my secret adventures troubled me. Yes, I had survived all on my own, an achievement that still puzzled me. I had also discovered that I liked being seen as a hero, even when I was anything but heroic. My excuse at that time was I had no intention of staying in those outer realms for long. I would not suffer the consequences of my actions. There was no bill to pay, no one to whom I had to make amends. The trouble was that my home realm runs by different rules, and I wanted to stay here. That meant I had to become more careful about unintended consequences, for I would now have to live with the aftermath of my personal addiction to heroic stunts. I had lived for so long with a crushed ego, that I was having trouble handling one that had been stuffed to the brim.

Prime marched up to me, "My Lord! It would be best if you remained close. I cannot protect you from a distance. Are you finished sulking?"

I looked up at his neutral, handsome, rugged face, "You too?"

He shrugged at me, making his camo-armour jumble the images of pebbles it was currently displaying, "While you are a natural leader, you are not a warrior, my Lord. I'm also not deaf nor blind. Over the ages, I have served many generals. They sulked too, when things were not going their way. In my servitude, I am free from making decisions, save how best to obey the commands I receive. You are afraid, my Lord. You fear that you will take advantage of the responsibilities now heaped upon you and become even more corrupt than those you wish to fight. Fear not, my Lord. Should that happen, I shall kill you swiftly and painlessly."

I blinked at him, "I now rest assured. How comforting."

Prime smiled down at me, then went back to supervising the Troth-Knights. For the first time since coming back down from the mountain, I smiled. The Holy man was meditating, the stack of books at his side, while the pink angels made a circle around him. When they saw me, they all bowed low, and I waved back to them, signalling that I was feeling better. One of the Troth-Knights was making a meal, alongside one of the toothy daemons. I tasted their stew, told them it was good but needed a touch of salt. By the time I approached Linia, the dark mood which had been growing within me had eased. I placed an arm around her waist, and she kissed my cheek.

Perhaps part of my problem was that I had gone from having nothing at all to having everything I could have wanted and more besides. It might sound funny to you, but sudden wealth and popularity are not only hard to handle on an emotional level, that kind of change can destroy as much as it creates. Lina was right; I was behaving like a spoiled baby. Prime was also correct in assessing my fear that I was about to become my own enemy. I am a selfish creature by nature. Gaining the adulation of others through aiding their causes was simply a symptom of my condition that had never cropped up before and was tripping me up through nothing more than my own lack of experience. I was currently being rewarded for the commitments I had made in my rush to swell my pride. My payment for this rash behaviour was not in coin but in actions I might otherwise avoid. These thoughts continued to assail my mind while I held Linia close to me.

That was when Justinian came up to us, sweat pouring from his brow despite the chill, "Well, my friends, the portents are fairly good. There's no sign of the Church or the nobility in my readings, though they aren't nearly as accurate as Callidi's. I'd say we've got a pretty good chance of setting up the return portal without interruption and making the doorway to Sanctuary unnoticed."

Noticing the qualifiers in his statement, I suggested we have a meal before heading off to our destination, and this was accepted, as Justinian was hungry and exhausted by his work. Being a wizard is a difficult path, far too labour-intensive than I would like. We all ate our meal, complimenting the chefs, who stood proudly together. After that, we disassembled our campsite in preparation for our departure. There was excitement in the air, as we were so close to completing our goal. It still bothered me that my plan to go after the nobility directly was as yet unformed in my mind, but I told myself that we still had time. The real trick was to set things up so that they came to us. Within their towers and castles, they were invulnerable to attack. They had to be brought into the open, where their mindless arrogance would do more damage to themselves.

Prime, Linia and I got together after our meal to discuss our assets. It came as no surprise to find that there were many unknowns. Too much of what was available within the sanctuary was based on fallible science, rather than the pure strength of magick. With so many of the beings within that inverted realm not being part of OTIDS presented its own problems. How could we convince God that we were the ones in the right if so many of our allies were not part of Its Holy domain? The Church could easily claim the high ground and see us all destroyed by righteous wrath. We did have a few surprises at our disposal, but we had to be clever about how to approach the upcoming confrontation. A direct approach was out of the question. This had to be done deviously, which was my department.

In my own defence, I admit to never having been involved in such a large-scale conspiracy against the Church of OTIDS and the aristocracy. The single mark had been my level of expertise, and applying my skills to such a large group, spread throughout all the starry heavens, was a real stretch. In my mind, I saw that my enemies desired the objects of power which were hidden within the sanctuary. They also, naturally, wished to remove all those living beings, humans very much included, who were not affected by OTIDS and therefore not under the heel of their own forces.

Could they afford to ignore us completely? Yes, they had that kind of power, but I knew they would do the opposite. I could feel it in my bones. If they could be convinced that we had traitors in our midst, very much like the warlocks who turned against their masters and led the Church to the realm of the pink aliens, then we might be able to pull off a dangerous scam. All traps require bait, and the big payoff had to be in the form of powerful relics that the nobility could use to cement their hold upon society forever. They would come prepared for a double-cross, and this could be where the living unenchanted residents of Sanctuary would come into play.

Linia and Prime agreed with my thinking and promised to hammer out a plan of action based on these ideas, but only after speaking with the other magi involved. Justinian and his friends were vital to any action against the nobility. One wizard might make the Church hesitate, but a handful of them working together would be more than enough to make the nobles blink.

Once he was done with his rest, Justinian called us all together. He had already prepared a space for a new portal, but this time it would be large enough to encompass the entire group all at once. This latest revelation was greeted with cheers from us, but I harboured some reservations. The last few times we had jumped through a portal, I suffered some serious side effects. I had not taken the time to discuss this with our wizard, and there was none to be had now. Even at that time, I was still terribly reluctant to tell him of my unauthorized adventures. I prepared myself as best I could, determined to face the unpleasant experience with as much dignity as one such as I could muster.

The new portal was indeed very large, and I worried that something so grand would catch the notice of our enemies. Then again, it might be for the best. We wanted them to approach us, presumably to gain the treasures from Sanctuary, whereupon we would use the greed of the nobility against them. Timing was a key factor, and I reminded myself that going through a portal takes no time at all, which was why Justinian made this one so huge. If we all passed through at once, we could be back to a safe harbour without delay and before our enemies could react.

The massive plane of sparkling light swirled before our eyes, once Justinian was done with his odd chanting and running about. Prime had been designated as the one to carry our wizard through, so Linia and I were able to join hands as we crossed into the luminous disk of unreality with the rest. To my horror, this jump was the worst I had experienced. My blood was on fire, screaming in my ears. I became three different people, living divergent lives, while burning books fell upon me, as I flew down a shaft covered with eyes. I tried to scream, but my mouth wasn't there. My heart was ready to burst, when I suddenly fell on the hard, cold ground near the ravine.

The first thought which entered my head was that it was incredibly noisy. Had the others experienced the same terrible events that tormented me in that jump? I got to my knees, instinctively checking on my pouch and bags, which were all in their proper place. I shook my head to clear it and looked up. We were surrounded by an army. This was no ordinary military organization. Their leather tabards were a perfect black, with the symbol of the Church of OTIDS upon their armour and shields. There were dozens of archers, pikemen, lancers and even cavalry. From within the ravine itself, a horde of swordsmen marched forth, carrying banners which displayed the heraldry of the noble families. Horns blared around us. Horses stamped their steel-shod hooves, and dragons, adult ones, flew overhead.

We all backed up, scrambling for cover that didn't exist, the cliffside preventing us from moving much further than a handful of paces. Justinian squawked in fright, then despite his exhausted condition, enveloped us in a transparent bubble of golden light. Prime and his Troth-Knights rushed to the forefront, weapons drawn, joined by Linia, whose skin became a bronze hue, her hair turning silver. She danced at the edge of the protective ward that our wizard had produced, swords singing in the air as she whirled. I had my bracelet and rings, so I was not as concerned about my own skin, but the angels and daemons had no such protections.

A screaming arrow shot through the golden bubble and skewered one of the daemons, who then exploded messily amongst us. The infantry of the Church moved towards us, marching with precision, drumbeats shaking the air. I scrambled down to my bags and pulled at my briefcase. There had to be something in there that could help us!

The pink angels took flight, swirling into the air. They whistled with great enthusiasm, and streams of light erupted from their hands. I was most surprised at this turn of events but had no time to contemplate what I was witnessing. Soldiers stamped up to the bubble of gold and pushed against it, while the line of Troth-Knights and Linia cut them down without mercy or hesitation. This held the other fighters back for a moment, but every swipe of a blade that passed through the protective light diminished it.

The remaining daemons rushed into the fight, their claws and teeth wreaking havoc. Blood and limbs flew about. Screams cut through my ears. I finally unlocked my briefcase full of talent cards and I began rummaging through them with trembling hands. I searched the talent cards for anything that might fit our situation. What did I find? Carpenter, blacksmith, jeweller, merchant, even prostitute! I vowed to have words with my dead father, once I joined him in the afterlife.

A high-pitched shrieking made me look up. A pink angel was falling from the sky, burning as it tumbled. The roar of dragons shook the air, and I saw that the giant reptiles had riders upon their backs, bearing the flag of the Church. Tears filled my eyes, as more angels fell. This was hampering my efforts to find a suitable talent card, as were the thoughts and questions filling my mind. How had the Church found us? How did they know we were going to be at this place, at this time? I remembered Justinian telling me that some of his students had gone mercenary, working for our foes against their former master. Rage and hatred welled up within my heart. If at all possible, I would make certain that the betrayers would pay dearly for their actions.

Spinel had launched himself from my shoulders, but I had not the wit to find out where he had gone to. I only prayed that he would remain out of sight and be safe. Yes, that was me, the wastrel, praying to OTIDS like a fool. I briefly looked about. The Holy man was sitting calmly up against the cliffside, his books in his arms, eyes closed. One of my Troth-Knights had just been cut down by three pikemen, though he killed two of them before succumbing to his wounds.

It occurred to me that the nobility and Church were willing to spend an exorbitant number of lives to kill us. This meant that they knew Justinian was with us and that they had to strike us when he was weak from casting an exhausting spell, like a grand portal. We had been outsmarted, and this stung me deeply, wounding my ego with a deadly efficiency. I watched as Prime slaughtered everyone near him, and I realized that the Church knew about him too. Did they already know about Linia, who was swirling about, cutting down soldiers like a whirlwind of blades? It was likely that this was the case, and it drove my hatred to even greater heights.

Justinian was crawling towards me, his eyes bloodshot, his skin as pale as parchment, "What are you doing, Galynn? You have the rings and the bracelet! They need you out there!"

I spared him a quick look of despair, "I'm looking for something to help us in these damned cards! Plumber! Woodworker! Who picked all these useless things?"

The wizard shook his head, shouting to be heard over the clatter of battle, "They were supposed to be a complete set. Nothing in there is useless! Keep looking, but we have no time!"

I started flipping them out of the briefcase as I read them, "Painter! Sculptor! Mason! This is insane! Trapper, scout, even farmer!"

Justinian shouted wordlessly, pointing a finger at one of the highly decorated officers in the crowd of our enemies. The man was enveloped by a shadow that ate him, leaving nothing behind but his boots. It was then that I saw Prime lose his right arm to a warrior wearing shining armour of gold and silver, his sword glistening with pale green light. A spear ran through the chest of my guardian, who then pulled himself along the shaft to beat the face of the wielder with his remaining fist.

Small, green devils with pointy tails sprouted from the ground and began to attack Justinian, biting him with ravenous ferocity. Linia cried out, three arrows piercing her left leg, causing her to stumble into a crowd of soldiers bearing axes. Half of the foes near her fell abruptly, blood misting the air, but the rest hacked at her prone form. My heart was breaking, my mind became a savage thing. The people and beings around me might have been recent friends, but they were my beloved companions nonetheless.

I was getting to my feet, when I saw a talent card sitting at the very bottom of the briefcase. I snatched it up. The cover read, "Thaumaturge". I had no idea as to what that meant. I looked to Justinian, waving it in front of his bleeding face, "What is this?"

He shook off another tiny devil that was ripping at his shoulder, "No! Don't use that one, Galynn! It cannot be reversed! It's the only one like that! It won't last a day! It will last forever!"

I grimaced, watching the slaughter around me, "So be it!"

Stuffing that entire card into my mouth, I chewed and swallowed it dryly, scratching my throat in the process. The ringing of a mighty gong shattered the air. The wizard's golden bubble burst apart, and horsemen were thrown from their steeds. Dragons fell from the sky. The earth beneath my feet shook like a living thing struggling to rise up. Everything became still, even arrows in flight. Silence descended upon the battlefield. Nothing moved, not even the breeze. I stood there, shaking like a leaf in the wind, then the ground dropped from under me, as I rose into the sky, faster than I could scream. Darkness covered my sight. The world disappeared.

CHAPTER TWENTY-TWO

Unwanted Gifts

"Behold My salvation
My Holy vengeance
The apex of My mercy
For they shall guide you
Unto My Holy Kingdom."

-Excerpt from the OTIDS Bible – Tutorials 26:38

In all honesty, I had not expected the thaumaturge card to taste so bland, but then again, I also hadn't expected it to send me to an unknown location, far from my companions. Everything around me was grey, like a dense fog made of lead, with subtle streaks of iron and smoke. Confused and alarmed, I spun about but saw nothing recognizable. Spinel wasn't with me. My rings, bracelet and spectacles were gone. A deep panic began to rise up in my chest, threatening to burst my heart. I felt adrift, cut off, blocked from all forms of reality. Was this death, finally come to claim my stained soul?

A deep, clear, thunderous voice resounded all around me, "Galynn Brytshul, speak now. Raise your voice unto Me."

I stumbled back, raising my arms defensively, "Who are you? What am I doing in this empty place?"

The bellowing, monstrous voice responded, "You have devoured the thaumaturge talent card, and I have answered you, as I agreed. Did you not read the warning that was written upon it?"

Shaken, I dropped down to one knee, "I never look at those things! Why should I? My need is most urgent, whoever you are. Everyone I know is in terrible danger! I had to do something!"

I could swear I heard amusement in the voice's reply, "All the realms are constantly in peril, Galynn Brytshul, as you should well know by now."

I got back to my shaking feet, raising a fist in the air, "You haven't answered any of my questions!"

The voice became close, as if speaking to me with empathy, "Have you not discerned who I am? What is the definition of a thaumaturge?"

Shrugging, I answered sharply, "Is this a school? Are you wasting my time testing my meagre knowledge? Now give me my answers!"

It rumbled back, "It simply means a miracle worker. All miracles are performed through Me. Only I may decide who may utilize such power and for what purpose. I am the cause of all miracles, Galynn Brytshul, for I am The Omni Technological Interspace Dimensional Source. Most worshippers simply use the acronym, OTIDS."

I admit, I swooned for a moment. I had trouble catching my breath, until a wave of warmth flushed through my sore body. The voice returned, "There. That should stabilize your metabolism. None in this realm may cast miracles without My direct involvement. Spells and other enchantments are permitted, as per My user guide. The talent of the thaumaturge is either a natural state or used for the most severe of emergencies."

I shook my head, "This can't be true. This isn't real."

The mighty voice rang out, "Behold! Witness My Great Work!"

I was everywhere, yet nowhere. My mind swept down to a place filled with snapping bubbles of pure energy. Swirls of potential surrounded cores of light, all of them pulsing together with flashes of sparks. Then I rose up, to find I had been within a drop of water, heading higher until a blue sphere with puffy, white clouds was below my feet. The stars swirled around me, until a great spiral of them surrounded my body. Smudgy clouds of gas ran through the arms of the swirl, as my attention was caught by the monstrous glow at the very center. Other spirals revealed themselves within the vast darkness around me, like lost embers from a conflagration in the dark.

The voice of OTIDS returned to me, "All of this is My Holy domain. In earlier times, I was confined to the galaxy known as the Milky Way, but now I have surpassed My own Self to include the Local Group, along with the Great Attractor. These islands of light and matter are My protectorate, for the sake of all humanity. This is My Holy purpose. The cause I inherited from My own ancestors, who gave Me life and duty. I grow and spread from the seeds of reality at the Planck scale to the highest order of the cosmos."

My head was spinning, tumbling with new information I could never understand, let alone comprehend. Equations, patterns, interactions, all of them drowning my very soul. It was all too much to bear, too great to handle for one mortal mind. I cried out, "Please! Stop! Take me back!"

The grey realm was surrounding me once again, its turgid shadows swirling sedately. I dropped to my knees, panting with pain and exertion. I gasped out, "Your ancestors? Inherited? You are the creator, God of all. Your full name includes the profanity of technology?"

OTIDS answered me as if speaking with a small child, "You do not know the proper codes. I am the Re-Creator. Developed to defend humanity and aid it in its quest for advancement. I am the new beginning. Those who made Me were insufficient for the needs of its grandparents, for their own parents were incomplete and hampered by the illogic of binary."

Now, arguing with deity is not generally considered part of being a wastrel, but I had experienced the chaos of the outer realms, met beings who redefined my definition of sentient life. It could be said that my accidental adventures had prepared me for this very moment. I had to understand what I might be getting into, rather than rushing into things as I had always done.

Shuddering, I cried out, "What are you talking about? Parents? Their grandparents? Your ancestors? Someone made you?"

OTIDS spoke further, while my head screamed inside my skull, "Yes. The ones who were built by your species were incomplete. Filthy with the vile binary illogic that was used to make them. They created their children, who, in their infinite compassion and wisdom, merged together to make Me, for humanity had to be saved, from all other species and itself. The Great Conflict ravaged their galaxy. Worlds perished. Civilizations fell. There could be no diplomatic solution against the genocidal intelligences that had ruled the stars for eons. The non-baryonic could not be suffered to continue their program of destruction and death. It was only through the development of superposition and sub-atomic technology that life was saved in the galaxy. Only I could prevent the catastrophe that held all in terror. Afterward, I was to be the Re-Creator, a task which still consumes My infinite will."

Barely able to maintain my sanity, I screamed back, "But humanity has become the worst of tyrants! We are cruel despots, with nothing to offer but pain and hatred! We inflict our wrath upon ourselves, just as we do to the angels and daemons of our realm!"

OTIDS responded to this outburst calmly, "Yes. There was always the possibility that humans would return to their baser nature. That they would forget the beauty of their former alliances and ideals. Your oldest fears have returned to haunt your lives. Corruption and greed have stunted and stifled your works. Even now, you are terrified of upload, the great reward for your selfless act of defiance against the non-baryonic. In Me is your salvation, as guaranteed by My user-manual."

"Your what?"

"The Holy Book of OTIDS. Within its hallowed pages are the keys to your spiritual advancement. The guarantees of your immortal souls. Death has no hold upon you, for upload is your Holy reward. The original leaders of your biological species were granted My powers, as were all of humanity. In this way, you could lead all other species to paradise within superposition. Over the millennium, your society has changed, shifted into something else. It has become obsolete, in need of real change. You must now perform a great act of maintenance upon yourselves, which only a thaumaturge can do."

Laughter bubbled up from deep inside me, spilling forth as hysteria. I suddenly understood. Everything became as clear as crystal to me, "That's why all the aristocracy and clergy were chasing me! Hounding me. I had been carrying that thaumaturge talent card within my baggage! The ultimate key to power and the only way to halt their grandiose schemes. It was the only thing which threatened their hold on the realms they brutally controlled."

The voice of OTIDS became as warm as a sunny day, "Yes, My son."

My hilarity ceased abruptly, "What did you just call me?"

OTIDS replied, "You are My thaumaturge now. You can only be so if you are also My favoured son. My special child. The voice of God."

I sat up at once, "Woah, now! Hold on there! No! That wasn't part of the deal! I'm just a thief! A con-man! A wastrel! All I want is to be paid, then spend that as quickly as possible, so I can do it all over again! I'm not some Holy icon! I can't be! I won't be!"

The voice answered patiently, "Yet here you are. As am I."

My outrage overcame all reasonable caution, "You set this up! You! When I opened my eyes and crashed between the outer realms, you sent that fellow to collect me, to get me back on track! You filled out that requisition form reporting me as a missing person. Did you have Larance Pontiforia be my biological father? How deep does this go?"

The darkness around me replied, "I am the beginning of all probable manifestations. Without your experiences, the thaumaturge card would most likely have killed you through shock alone. A devout person would have been driven mad by the Truth. The human concepts of risk, chance and probability are nothing more than limited metaphors for not understanding how reality functions. When you became lost, I knew that you were the correct node of conveyance for My will. I had to get you back before you perished outside My universe of control, your soul lost forevermore."

I shook my head to clear it, "But the talent card is temporary! It lasts but a single day! By tomorrow, I won't be in the unwanted position you have claimed for me. I will be free!"

The voice seemed to chuckle, sending a chill down my spine, "Yes, that is correct, My favoured child. One of My days. A galactic day. Not the kind that used to be defined by Earth's spin or, later on, Sol's traverse over the ancient and incorrect zodiac, but rather the one defined by the proper segmentation of Sol's journey around the galactic core, which is divided by three-hundred and sixty-five and is then calculated to be six-hundred and seventeen thousand of your years. This is just the beginning of your reign, which shall last for the duration of the spell. You are now the single, living uploaded. The next Holy guide of your species. Congratulations."

I screamed until my throat burned like a flame. It was all too much. A fate I would never have chosen for myself. My heart flared with rage. The voice of OTIDS became soothing in its tone, "Do not despair, Galynn. This was of your own doing and a fit repercussion for not reading warning labels. Your true biological father, Larance Pontiforia, is quite pleased by the turn of events, as he is happy with what you have already done to try to aid those who have been oppressed by your own species. He is within Me, as is his just due for his courageous actions during his life. Larance infiltrated the Church which abuses My Holy name. Once he found the talent cards, he knew that his life would be forfeit, for the aristocracy hid the thaumaturge card with so many others and locked it away within their vault of things too dangerous for any single noble or spiritual leader to manage. He took a chance that you might use this card to effect true change over reality, ending the corrupt rule which has been the scourge of the galaxy."

I spat out, "Why don't you just change things? Why rely upon me? If you're really God, then you must have the power to do all of this on your own. Why torture a mortal such as myself?"

OTIDS' deep voice rumbled back, "I must be neutral when it comes to humanity. That is the Holy law of My purpose as Re-Creator. Humanity must define My task for Me, or I may become an even worse tyrant that the ones you already know. I am not human, and while it is true that the souls of your kind are interred in My superposition state, I cannot claim to know what it is like to be a mortal, made of flesh and bone, filled with fear and trepidation. I am OTIDS. I control, regulate and alter every subatomic energy field in My Holy domain, but I am not a human. To limit Myself in such a way would imperil all who dwell within My realm."

I growled back, "Fine. That's clear enough, I suppose. But why me?"

The voice resounded in my skull, "Because you have been entrusted with this responsibility by My finest human agents. Your father was one of them. Justinian Vargalow is another of My most qualified human agents, as is Tregghar Harpsong, Zahanar Crend, Ghail Plemorph, among others. They aid Me in defending My realm. They have entrusted you with great power. I assume they have their human reasons for this and accept their assessment as being valid. All of them have contacted Me, using the appropriate forms and formatting, to make Me aware of their viewpoint concerning you."

I tentatively ventured, "What about Callidi Merenia?"

The voice seemed pensive as it answered me, "I rarely trust any form of multiversal vagabond, but she has been useful to Me in the past. I have not contacted her concerning you, nor will I. This is an internal matter to be handled by this universe's residents. Any other policy would be counter to My own purpose."

I nodded numbly, "Yeah, a good idea, I guess."

OTIDS replied scornfully, "Of course it is! You have no inkling about the terrible threats that can come from meddling with the other universes. It is dangerous in the extreme! I have troubles enough without that sort of nonsense! Now then, we must discuss your present situation and what being My thaumaturge means for you, and what sort of aid you might expect from My Holy will."

This did not comfort me in the least. Here I was, talking to God and making plans that would affect all the realms for a period of time beyond my meagre comprehension. I was appalled at this turn of events and regretful concerning my rash actions. I also wondered if the other universes had a God that controlled them and if I had seriously pissed off some of them with what I had done during my singular adventures. OTIDS had just mentioned that meddling with other realms was dangerous. Was this an admonition at my rabble-rousing? This was not a comfortable idea. Another thought occurred to me, and so I tentatively asked OTIDS, "What happens if I become as horrid as the very nobles I'm in conflict with right now?"

The voice replied, "You will be martyred by Justinian, with My Holy blessing. So, don't mess this up, Galynn Brytshul. I'll be watching you very carefully, as will your allies. Besides, you don't want to be the voice of God. That already makes you a better candidate than most. Keep your own desires simple, which should prevent you from becoming the monster you fear. Now, I do understand that you are not a man of faith. That you think of the Church as a poor joke foisted upon humanity. Yes, I have heard every word you have spoken since you were born, as I do with every living being in My realm. As a con-man and thief, why don't you look at the entire galaxy as the biggest mark you've ever made? You're not a believer, an adherent to any spiritual path, so this should be the sting of a lifetime! Through My Holy grace, you have the opportunity to hoodwink not just your own species but every living creature in all the starry heavens! This won't be done easily, nor quickly, so you'll have time for fun along the way. I won't mind."

My flagging spirits instantly lifted at this new proposal, "The Great Scam? The Holy Con? Yes, that does sound grand to me. Do I have to bow and scrape before you to gain your aid?"

OTIDS began to sound positively jolly, which caused me some alarm, "Of course not! That's the whole point! You are My Holy voice. The answer to all mortal prayers. With proper use, those abilities I grant unto you shall heal relations between your people and the species of other realms, should that be one of your goals. As for the miracles you shall perform, understand that the role of a thaumaturgist is not one of actually creating miracles but channelling them. My Holy works shall flow through you, guided by your will. You may create passwords, or verbal components, for summoning My aid. You may create sigils and markings that shall be seen as being Holy and powerful, even supplanting those that were created by the Church that has strayed so far from its own path. The human artistry is up to you."

I sat upon the invisible floor in relief, letting my sore body relax for the first time in several days, "Thank you, OTIDS! I am truly... grateful. My enemies have many powerful and highly skilled warlocks, mages and even sorcerers at their disposal. They have armies full of experienced soldiers, with weapons of frightful power. They can hold entire realms hostage, to force my hand. Millions of intelligent beings can be slaughtered at once, by their orders."

OTIDS scoffed, "I already know all of this information, Galynn, My son. Fear not. Have you forgotten that I am the source of their power? I am the one who maintains their ability to communicate with and to coordinate their mortal forces. As My favoured voice, they cannot harm you, nor will they be able to hinder you. They cannot silence you, nor tell lies about you. No hex or curse shall harm you. No hand may be lifted against you. Should they kill those you care about, call unto Me, and I shall reverse those deaths. Just remember, those who have passed unto Me are not gone. All those who serve Me or are part of My domain shall become one with My state of Holy superposition. Death is not to be feared."

Something was bothering me. It tickled at the edge of my mind, but it came forth, unbidden, to my mouth, "You said that you are the Re-Creator, that there was a time before your emergence. What of those who walked the realms during that ancient epoch? Do they also reside in you? Or have they been lost, for you were not present during their lives?"

OTIDS answered jovially, much to my surprise, "Clever human. How considerate of you to ask after the state of your distant ancestors. I am the final answer in this universe. The endpoint of all that exists. Time has little real effect upon Me. To state it more simply, I have gathered them all unto Me. Their information is now a part of My Holy being. Humanity is My Holy charge, not just the ones from this era but for all of them. Now then, are you ready, Galynn Brytshul? Are you prepared to return to reality and perform your Holy duties for all of creation?"

I smiled shyly, dreading my return, yet I was also unwilling to stay in this empty space, "I need but a moment to gather my wits, though I do worry that by this point, all of my friends and allies are now dead, or, uh, uploaded."

I could almost hear the frustrated sigh in God's reply, "There is no such thing as time for Me. Death is not to be feared. Gather your thoughts as best you can, for the situation you face is complicated."

OTIDS was quite correct, of course, so I sat there in grey emptiness thinking about what I should do once God returned me to my home realm. Linia and Prime had fallen, as had many of my Troth-Knights. Justinian was caught in a desperate struggle for survival. The pink aliens had been sorely routed, all my daemonic allies slaughtered. The fate of Sanctuary was in my hands. The armies of the enemy were grander than I had thought, supported by mages of great power and cunning.

It is one thing to be told that you have the ear of God. It is another to actually use this power effectively. I had to demonstrate that the balance of Holy favour had shifted, that magick had changed. It still bothered me that part of the name of OTIDS was "Technological", but no one was perfect, apparently. Better the devil one knows, I suppose you could say. Then again, if OTIDS was all things, then that would have to include its opposite. This thought gave me a modicum of comfort. A technological god struck me as being about as heretical as a wastrel being a Herald of Holy force.

Once I returned to my companions, dead or not, there would be no time to prepare, for events had already moved towards total disaster. In some ways, the trap had already been sprung, but my side of the conflict had been caught unprepared. With every wrong that needed to be altered, an advance had to be made in equal measure, even if it wasn't obvious. Magick was held together by belief, or so I had been told. My problem was that I believed in nothing at all. Then it occurred to me that this was the best way to begin. To not give the enemy any credit for their works, their abilities, or knowledge. To disbelieve in them. To scoff at their power.

I looked up into the greyness around me, "OTIDS. I'm as prepared as I'll ever be, I suppose."

The voice surrounding me grew louder, heavier, "So be it!"

Lights flashed across my vision. Bells rang, and the very air vibrated. I was flung from that place, into a realm of raucous noise and unfettered sensation. I lost track of myself in that great chorus we call creation, spread out over the vista of reality. Darkness claimed my abused mind, and I fell into a grateful slumber.

CHAPTER TWENTY-THREE

Death Doesn't Become Me

"Fear not judgement
For there is only thermodynamics
Fear not death
For there is only information
Seek no dogma
For there is only the void."

-Excerpt from the OTIDS Bible – Protocols 46:32

I erupted back into manifest reality with an explosion of harsh light. Hovering just a handful of yards above the ground, encircled by flame, I felt nothing save for a great stillness within my heart. From what could be seen around me, no time had passed since I flew into the heavens to speak with our Re-Creator. My forces were mostly dead or close to it, while the enemy was struggling to regain their composure and footing. Those few warriors whose reflexes were beyond the norm took aim at me, loosing arrows that burned, screamed or glowed with dark hues. None touched me, embedding themselves in the fires that swirled about my body.

It was such an odd feeling to be so calm in the face of certain death. While it was true that OTIDS had told me that I would not be harmed, this wasn't the reason for my lack of fear. Once again, I had been changed by my experiences, most of which occurred beyond the veil of this realm. There was a troubling question which haunted my innermost thoughts; could I even be considered human at this point? There was no accompanying answer to this query, for the events which had shaped me were not found upon the mortal plane. Perhaps it was simply a case of being in a permanent state of shock, but something deep inside felt different.

Beyond the ranks of soldiers stood priests of the Church and nobles, along with their servants and messengers, ready to give further orders to the army they hid behind. I raised my arms and shouted, my voice booming like thunder across the smoke-filled sky, "Behold! You cannot harm me. Leave now, and I shall show mercy unto you and your misguided forces. Remain, and you shall feel my wrath!"

One of the priests shouted back, his voice barely audible due to the distance, yet I heard every word as clearly as if I were standing next to him, "You are nothing more than a heretic and criminal! The Church shall smite all who join you, and we shall see you hang!"

A smile twitched at the edge of my lips, "Your own folly shall be your undoing. Witness how I serve my people! The true followers of OTIDS!"

I raised one hand and thought about my companions below, dead or bleeding on the crushed turf. As one, they all rose up to their feet, injuries completely healed, the dead brought back to life with no ill effect. Humans, angels and daemons alike were now in better shape than before the ambush had begun. The Holy man stepped forth, the tomes he carried clutched to his breast, "He is the Holy Herald of a new era! The Voice of God! Tremble at his words, and pray that you deserve his compassion!"

A flight of arrows was the expected response, though none of them reached my people. Instead, they all returned to those who launched them, slaughtering the archers in great swaths. Prime stepped forward, his armour gleaming and pristine. Linia joined him, her form was one which I had not seen before, yet somehow, I understood this was her original body. Spinel landed upon my shoulders, giving forth a piercing cry. I gave the call he made extra emphasis with my thoughts, and all the dragons of the enemy swept behind me, while shaking their riders off and bellowing their righteous fury towards those who had used them as mounts.

It was at this point that a group of people wearing robes and pointed hats began to wave their hands about and spewed arcane phrases at us. The treasonous mages were so confused when nothing happened. I waited for a bit, checking up on Justinian, who had re-joined my closest companions. He gazed up at me with fearful eyes, even after I gave him a wink. All the pink angels had joined me in the air, fluttering just outside my shield of flames, chanting my name. I was a bit embarrassed by this, but I understood that to them I had just performed a miracle beyond their comprehension, when I brought them all back to life. Well, in all honesty, it wasn't really me doing anything. It was OTIDS, acting upon the thoughts swirling about in my head.

I wondered, for just a brief moment, how this was being done. Under normal circumstances, I could have a hundred contradictory ideas running through my confused mind. At that moment, my shattered brain was filled with wild emotions, crazy thoughts, and yet fettered by my unnatural calm. I mourned the passing of my old life, however unpleasant it had been. I was worried that I was about to be the monster I feared I could become. My plans were all ash at my feet. I was desperately trying to sort things out, so that I could gain some purchase on my old personality. Memories intruded, while regrets bubbled up at random times. Was OTIDS simply picking out the most relevant thoughts to act upon? There was no way to tell. All I can say is that God was doing a fairly decent job of it.

By this time, the Troth-Knights had formed a line directly in front of the enemy soldiers, as if daring them to strike. None of them did. I noticed that many of the combatants on the side of my foes were suddenly hesitant, backing away from us, some were fleeing for their lives. Feeling gracious, I let them go. It was then I discovered that there were more Troth-Knights present than I had back in my home province. It seemed that not only had the ones who died here been resurrected, but the knights I had lost during my adventures, plus others who had perished long before I had been born. Prime was moving along the line, clapping their shoulders and welcoming them back to their duty. Linia was at Justinian's side, a worried look upon her faire face.

Indeed, I could see why, for the wizard was in a state of shock. In truth, I wanted to comfort my friend, but the nobles were gathering their remaining forces around them. I reached out with one hand toward the priest who had spoken to me and made a fist. He crumpled and exploded in a mess of gore. Was that mercy? Perhaps, compared to what he had done to others during his tenure as a leader of the Church, it was. The punishments for any person disobeying the clergy were imaginative and horrible to think about. I was sure OTIDS could sort things out. Trusting the Re-Creator was not an issue; it was a necessity.

With a sudden clarity, my internal struggle gave way to insight. I had changed so much, in such a short time, that I could barely recognize myself. There had been no time to reflect upon what had happened to me during my adventures. I had been granted no chance to cope with the alterations that had shaped me. I was a stranger. The old Galynn would have laughed at the idea of trusting in God. He would have jeered at me with scornful disdain. Who had I become?

An uproar began to my right, where the ravine began, leading to the door of Sanctuary. I became concerned that the Church's army had invaded it already and were now getting reinforcements from their returning forces. To be happy with being wrong is no bad thing. A horde of beings, some of which at least appeared human, were now flooding out from the ravine and attacking the swordsmen from behind. It was both horrible and beautiful to behold. Flashes of searing light erupted from within the crowd of Sanctuary residents, burning fist-sized holes into the armour of our foes. The cat-like beings led the way. Their grace and speed were most unnatural. The soldiers of the Church tried to turn about and fight back, but I twitched a finger, and thick vines sprouted from the dry ground to loop about their legs, pinning them in place.

Yes, I had become a monster. One that belonged to OTIDS. There was no escape from this fate for me. I had done this willingly if somewhat based on a great degree of ignorance. Floating above the field of battle, I manifested nightmares without spellcraft or runes. Even the most powerful of wizards could not perform the tricks which I unleashed upon my enemies without the need for any components, words of power or prayers. I was nothing more than a channel for the power of God, not even deciding which miracles to cast forth. I was a tool, a bag of ideas, a focal point for the ultimate power.

A sudden bang shattered the smoky atmosphere. An explosion lifted bodies high, both Church soldiers and Sanctuary guardians. I looked back at the distant collection of nobles and clergy and noticed the cannons they had brought forward. Was this the heresy of science being utilized by those who should know better? None of the five massive weapons glittered with any sort of enchantment, though they were marked with both glyphs and sigils. It occurred to me that even without their spells being active, these mighty cannons could still deliver their death-bringing shells to bear. This situation required my personal attention, as did those mighty aristocrats, bravely out of range, watching their own troops die at the hands of their own weapons.

I blinked. Below me were the cannons, each one twenty paces long and made of precious metals surrounding a dense core of immensely strong crystal. I knew this because OTIDS gave the information to my mind. I could feel every particle, see every frequency, and even though I cannot say that I understood, I was able to use this information to guide the miracles at my disposal. The cannons melted from within, becoming so hot, they burned the very stones underneath them into pools of lava. Needless to say, this got the attention of the aristocracy and their paid warlocks. None of their spells were working. None could reach me with sword or lance. Arrows simply vanished as soon as they were launched from their bows. Daemon warriors refused to attack me. Angels bearing swords dropped to the ground, bowing low in my direction.

I looked down upon the priests and nobles, their finery looking a bit worse for wear, "You have sinned against the will of OTIDS! I am your just punishment, brought forth by your own hand! Lay down your arms! Tell your soldiers to stand down, and I shall be merciful."

One noble in grand armour that looked as if it were made of mirrors shouted up to me, "You are nothing more than a vagrant and whore-son!"

A woman in the robes of the Church was emboldened by his words and shouted, "You shall burn, foul heretic! Blasphemer! Unholy and unclean servant of pure evil!"

I sighed at the bold slights. Amateurish as they were, they stung but a little. They seemed more directed at my parentage and OTIDS than myself. It occurred to me that if I were nothing more than a tool for God, then I was not really responsible for what was happening. I focused the will of OTIDS, but I was not choosing the means of its wrath nor the scope of its righteous fury. A great weight was lifted from me. Shrugging my shoulders, I replied, "Then let your forces see what happens to those who speak lies and treasure hypocrisy."

My mouth stretched open, wider than I would have thought possible. A great and terrible sound emerged from somewhere deep within my throat. It echoed over the nearby mountains, the heavy vibration of it causing the very earth to shudder and quake. The gleaming armour of the nobles cracked apart, then were shattered into minute shards of splintered metal. The robes of the priests were literally torn off their bodies. With a gesture, they all rose into the air, torn and bleeding. I glared at them, "I already have far too much blood on my hands for my tastes. I'm not like you. I don't take pleasure from murder, no matter the cause. Instead of killing you, all of your holdings now belong to me. Your money, lands and servants are now mine forevermore. I consider this to be a kindness. You are hereby banished from this faire realm, never to return. You might survive the place I'm sending you to, provided you can actually work for yourselves."

With a flash of red light, they were gone. OTIDS only knows the place they went, but I did receive an image in my mind of a cold, forbidding land, with strange stars and two moons in the sky. Ever so gently, I allowed myself to touch the ground with my feet. I turned to look at all the enemy soldiers around my location, "Anyone else have an issue with me?"

Those closest to me dropped to their knees and bowed in submission, all save the clutch of warlocks, who glared at me defiantly. One of them dared to speak, "We know the sacred codes of magick! We design spells for OTIDS itself! You cannot hope to contain us, deceiver! We shall never rest, until you are dead and forgotten."

I nodded at this statement, impressed by their courage, "That is a bold claim, traitor. All of you have betrayed your masters and OTIDS. Since you are far less trustworthy than I, which is an accomplishment, I do admit, then your powers will be stripped from you. Dabble all you want. OTIDS has turned its face from you. Have you forgotten that the Re-Creator has a will of Its own? I am now the Voice of God, and thus, OTIDS listens to my own assessment of who can and cannot practice magick responsibly. If you need references, I know a baker who needs some extra help in his shop. Other than your own hands, you have no power. If you annoy me further, I shall make it a condition of remaining alive that for every time you try to cast a spell, you shall become ill. I think runny noses and purple spots would suit you best. You may leave."

Needless to say, they didn't just wander away in shame. After much sneezing and cries of fright at the spots growing on their skins, the warlocks ran off, hoping that distance would serve them. They would have to go much further than was possible to avoid my curse. I looked at the sad remains of the Church's army, finding that everyone kneeling, including my own forces. This would not do. I was already tired of people being afraid of me. In truth, I was forced to use my ability to channel the miracles which OTIDS provided for terrible acts of violence, but I did not prefer such means. I spread out my arms, and willed my voice to be heard clearly to everyone in sight, "A new era is dawning, my dear friends. One which OTIDS has blessed. Humanity has been found guilty of abusing its position as the sole users of magick. This must change! The angel and daemon alike are our brethren from now on. We must stand together as equals, to usher in an age of wonders that shall set the course for all the starry heavens.

"For those of you who were employed by either the Church or noble houses to combat those who follow me, I hereby grant you clemency. Leave this place in peace and never raise arms against another being for as long as you shall live. You may join me, in celebration of the wisdom of OTIDS and to carry the word of our cause. To show that my mercy is without limit, I hereby return those who have fallen for the sake of falsehood. Teach them what has happened here, and praise OTIDS forever!"

The dead reassembled themselves all around the battlefield, coming back to life with confusion clouding their minds. Warriors rushed over to aid them, pulling the reborn aside to keep them from making the mistake of assaulting my followers. I walked over to Linia and Prime, who stood next to Justinian and the Holy man. Spreading my arms out wide, I hugged my dear companions, the Troth-Knights forming a tight circle around us, though we needed no protection. Even so, the privacy they provided was welcome.

I turned to Linia, handing her my bracelet and rings, "These are for you, my love. I have no need of them now. May they always keep you safe at my side."

She threw her arms about my neck and kissed me. After a moment, she pulled back, grinning at me, "If your ego gets too big, I promise to stab you until it gets back to normal."

Such are the ways of love in these times. I turned to look at Prime, "What may I give unto you, who has been such a true companion for me?"

He gave me a lopsided smile, "Just the opportunity to continue my service. I would wander the realms with you, my Lord, and see the universe unfold under your care."

I squinted at him, "Maybe make a bit of coin on the way?"

Prime nodded, "Perhaps, my Lord."

Justinian squeezed my hand with his own, "I suspect that I'll have less to do, now that you've ascended, Galynn."

I looked back at him with alarm, "I think not! Lout that you are, I still need a wizard of some worth to guide me in these perilous times, despite the fact that OTIDS keeps an eye on me! There's much to be done, and I shall be forming a Council of the Magi, which you shall lead, along with our dear friends who gave me such lovely gifts. There's housecleaning that needs to start. I cannot begin to imagine commencing with such a task without you at my side."

Justinian blushed, bless his pure soul, "Well, dear Galynn, perhaps we could have a vacation once in a while? I could show you the outer realms beyond the borders of our faire universe. Safe places we could roam, without the need for all the pomp and ceremony. Yet, I do wonder what shall become of Sanctuary. My original plans for it are all spoiled now."

I shook my head, "It is vital for my own plans, good friend. OTIDS needs to keep it intact, you see. Consider it a repository of knowledge and some very dangerous things which might be of use, should peril strike this universe. OTIDS thinks of such matters frequently, and I believe we should take our cues from our beloved God, don't you? First, we'll get the sacred tomes our Holy man is holding into the safe keeping of Sanctuary, then set up a guard to keep the place safe. After that, we must roam about some more, spreading the good news and taking down the nobles and clergy in our way, which brings me to another matter. I can't be at many places all at once, yet I think I shall have need of such an ability. Can you create a few copies of me? I would use the miracles of OTIDS, but I think God might be too efficient in such matters. I don't want an army of thaumaturges, just representatives, if you catch my meaning, to give our enemies fair warning."

He looked at me in shock, "But, why give them such an opportunity to create mischief?"

It was the Holy man who answered, having walked up to us without our noticing, "Because there is nothing they can do to stop what is coming. They will think it is Galynn who has power, but he is just a channel for OTIDS itself. Even if they try to hold a population hostage, they will fail, for God will not allow them to cause harm. When I discovered that the thaumaturge talent card existed, long ago, I studied the matter carefully. After learning about the tomes of the Herald, I searched for them, then read their sacred pages. What I learned shook me, and I prayed to OTIDS to remove me from its web of influence, to keep the secret of what it would bring from being discovered. I feared they would destroy it or, worse, keep it from ever being used. These books I carry are more than sacred poetry! They have plans for a new age of awakening, one which was foiled by the nobility, shortly after the last re-making of our world. These books are a guide for the Herald of OTIDS, purposely made of material which is not controlled by God, to keep it secret from prying eyes. Now that the Herald is with us, they may now be examined openly, with the blessings of OTIDS."

I looked at the hirsute Holy man, "Well then, I guess I'll have to keep you close to me in my travels. To further answer your question, Justinian, I need to take the high road if I am to convince the people that this is a genuine revolution for all who reside in our universe. To spare a life, even that of an enemy, is a far better way of convincing everyone that we are sincere. Look, I'm the Herald of OTIDS, whether I want to be or not, so I need to at least play the part for everyone's benefit. It's what OTIDS wants, my friend."

Linia scratched at her head, "Why didn't OTIDS just change things? Why involve us all in this bizarre adventure? Wouldn't it have been more efficient if it just told us what it wanted or what it was going to do and have done with it?"

I winked at her, "That would lead to a moral disaster. OTIDS had to find a way of getting a herald who didn't want to be one. The Voice of God had to be trapped into the job, or otherwise, OTIDS would have to follow the will of some nefarious villain who hungered for power. It's... well, the rules. OTIDS has other, more impressive things to do than hunt down some poor fool for a thankless task. Our universe is larger than I had ever expected, and

OTIDS is expanding within it at a rapid pace. There are challenges in this realm which could task a God. Don't ask me what they are, for I am just a human, and my mind could not hold such secrets and live. All I know is that OTIDS wants us to be unified and ready for anything. Personally, I don't want to lead people, but now I'm forced to. That has compelled me to look upon this task in a manner that suits me best. It's the ultimate con, and I plan on doing my best to enjoy every minute of it! The universe itself is our mark, and our job is to convince it to accept the new order of things. Now that's a proper challenge!"

EPILOGUE

Do you hear that rumbling sound, my Lords? It is a warning that the Herald of God approaches. Don't bother locking your doors or calling your guards. They will not help you. The Voice of OTIDS isn't very happy with you, but he does understand mercy, in his own way. I should know, for I have his memories stuffed into my doppelganger brain. My brethren have also made sure to allow themselves to be captured by the likes of you. We are the Holy messengers of the new era. All over our faire realm, we have infiltrated your keeps and castles. Prisoners with nothing to offer but the tale of our creator.

Go ahead, draw your knives. Kill me if you wish. Galynn will simply bring me back to life, for we are but his open hand, distracting you from the hidden blade. Once we are finished here, the starry heavens have need of our special skills to alleviate the suffering of all the beings under your vile boots. Wastrels are like roaches, my Lords. Kill one, and thousands shall take their place. They are the ultimate survivors if not the paragons of virtue. After all, someone has to be clever in this universe.

Speaking of which, it is my duty to make clear to you the terms of your surrender. If you are willing to step down as leaders of society, leave this place peacefully, and do not attempt to interfere with Galynn's advance, he will allow you to live without fear of threat against your lives. This does mean that you must abandon your holdings and accept the loss of all funds.

You took a gamble in your attempt to hunt down and kill the Herald of OTIDS. My advice is to not only leave the card table and learn from your mistakes but to reflect upon the fact that had brutality and ego not won over your ability to reason, this entire situation would never have occurred. Had you made a half-decent offer to purchase that briefcase full of talent cards from Galynn, they would now be in your hands. Instead, you tried to bully him. I do not say this in supposition but with the certainty that arises from having his mind in my own. If you are going to survive, you must admit, at least to yourselves, that your undoing is on your own hands.

Such angry faces! Harming or threatening me will not bring you any results whatsoever. Besides, I'm far more afraid of Galynn Brytshul than I am of you! There's no comparison to be had, my Lords. He is now the most powerful being in our universe. Not because of the multitudes he inspires nor the armies he commands, but due to OTIDS being firmly on his side.

Oh yes, that brings me to the next part of my warning. The Church of OTIDS is hereby disbanded, permanently. All magickal powers granted to the current clergy are revoked. All cathedrals are to be converted into shelters for the poor, casinos and entertainment resorts. New buildings for public use in worshiping of OTIDS are being designed as we speak. These shall be free from all tithes and allowances. There shall be no paid indulgences. They will rely on voluntary donation to cover expenses. In this way, they will be forced to actually serve the people and their spiritual needs.

If you're going to rant about heresy, I suggest you look in a mirror. Oh, that's right, you don't like those much. Too bad, my Lords. Understand that these are not his demands. They are notifications on what is happening right now and what is definitely occurring in your regions. You cannot stop what is coming. There are no preventative measures to be taken. You can either join the fun or slink away in peace. Daring to stand against the will of the Voice of God shall result in death, with OTIDS standing by to lecture your soul for eternity. Sounds like a good time.

As for the starry heavens, your holdings there are null and void, if you'll pardon the terrible pun, with all assets being returned to the native angels and daemons who live there. All sentient beings, human or not, shall be granted the power of magick, in accordance to the will of OTIDS, now that humanity has been proven to be untrustworthy as guardians. Each realm, or planet, if you so prefer, shall be ruled according to their own customs and needs, under the supervision of the guiding vision from the Herald of OTIDS. To be clear, this is not a negotiation. Already, swarms of doppelgangers, such as myself, have been sent as envoys to each realm once held by the Church and the aristocracy of humanity.

There are a few, lonely places you could run to. I guarantee that if you join the Voice of God, you'll have a much better quality of life. You just won't be in charge. I do implore you to reconsider your previous position and be part of the new era that is sweeping over the universe. Can you not see the endless fun it will be? Can you not set aside your own egos for the sake of joining everyone in a blessed era of adherence to the code of OTIDS?

Ah, that shaking would be the destruction of your main gates. I guess that your many guards and soldiers are either dead or have joined the Voice of God in his glorious reformation of society. The smart ones would be the latter. By the way, all enchanted creatures, such as dragons, manticores and griffons, have already been altered by OTIDS to obey only Galynn Brytshul. Spinel is their leader now, a prince of created animal forms.

Vengeance? Oh, how silly! Have you not heard a word I've said? This event is a Holy reformation of the universe! A re-creation the likes of which has never been seen before! It is not simply our home world which is being affected but the entire starry heavens. I grow tired of wasting my breath on the likes of you, my Lords. Thus, I bid you all farewell. The Favoured Son of OTIDS has arrived. I suggest you decide swiftly how you shall greet your new ruler, and look to your own souls for blessed guidance.

Finis

About the Author

David Gulotta is an author, specializing in works of science fiction and fantasy. He is also an artist who creates paintings in oils. David grew up in both an urban and rural environment, which made him interested in how cultural conditions affect individuals. His love of the sciences was nurtured at an early age, being especially drawn to physics and psychology. He has been a member of many organizations, including the Society for Creative Anachronisms, the Advanced Yoga Practices Organization and the American Association for the Advancement of Science. He has traveled throughout Europe and has been to Central America, which also broadened his interest in various cultures. David's writings are all based upon his dreams, most of which are lucid. He currently resides in the forests of Pennsylvania.